I looked closely at the [illegible] thin to the point of bo[illegible] in a sweat-shirt, jeans, and white sneakers. Her hair was pulled back in a tight ponytail, and she held herself rigidly, one arm across her midsection, as she nervously smoked a ciga-rette. When she inhaled her cheeks collapsed over missing teeth. She stared at me with a fixed intensity as she exhaled a long blue stream of smoke, and said nothing. At first I thought she was Danny Ray's mother, and then it dawned on me who she actually was.

"Mrs. Causey?" I asked as Danny Ray stepped forward.

She took another drag on her cigarette before remov-ing it from her mouth and announcing, "Yeah, I am," in a smoke-and-whiskey voice.

"I'm very sorry for your loss, Mrs. Causey," I said to the sad woman before me. "I wish there was some way I could help."

"Danny Ray, here, tells me that maybe you can, Mr. Tanner. My daughter didn't commit suicide," she said as tears came to her eyes. "She was kilt. I know it, but won't nobody listen to me. Not the law. Not nobody. I need your help, Mr. Tanner."

I took a deep breath and then stepped forward. As the woman dissolved into tears, I put an arm around her thin shoulders and guided her toward my boat. "Come with me, Mrs. Causey, and you can tell me all about it."

LOW COUNTRY

ERIC L. HANEY

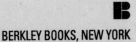

BERKLEY BOOKS, NEW YORK

THE BERKLEY PUBLISHING GROUP
Published by the Penguin Group
Penguin Group (USA) Inc.
375 Hudson Street, New York, New York 10014, USA
Penguin Group (Canada), 90 Eglinton Avenue East, Suite 700, Toronto, Ontario M4P 2Y3, Canada
(a division of Pearson Penguin Canada Inc.)
Penguin Books Ltd., 80 Strand, London WC2R 0RL, England
Penguin Group Ireland, 25 St. Stephen's Green, Dublin 2, Ireland (a division of Penguin Books Ltd.)
Penguin Group (Australia), 250 Camberwell Road, Camberwell, Victoria 3124, Australia
(a division of Pearson Australia Group Pty. Ltd.)
Penguin Books India Pvt. Ltd., 11 Community Centre, Panchsheel Park, New Delhi—110 017, India
Penguin Group (NZ), 67 Apollo Drive, Rosedale, North Shore 0632, New Zealand
(a division of Pearson New Zealand Ltd.)
Penguin Books (South Africa) (Pty.) Ltd., 24 Sturdee Avenue, Rosebank, Johannesburg 2196,
South Africa

Penguin Books Ltd., Registered Offices: 80 Strand, London WC2R 0RL, England

This is a work of fiction. Names, characters, places, and incidents either are the product of the author's imagination or are used fictitiously, and any resemblance to actual persons, living or dead, business establishments, events, or locales is entirely coincidental. The publisher does not have any control over and does not assume any responsibility for author or third-party websites or their content.

LOW COUNTRY

A Berkley Book / published by arrangement with the author

PRINTING HISTORY
Berkley mass-market edition / December 2010

ISBN: 978-0-425-23814-1

BERKLEY®
Berkley Books are published by The Berkley Publishing Group,
a division of Penguin Group (USA) Inc.,
375 Hudson Street, New York, New York 10014.
BERKLEY® is a registered trademark of Penguin Group (USA) Inc.
The "B" design is a trademark of Penguin Group (USA) Inc.

PRINTED IN THE UNITED STATES OF AMERICA

10 9 8 7 6 5 4 3 2 1

CHAPTER 1

THE DEAD HAVE A MYSTERIOUS WAY of returning. Three weeks ago I was working on the deck of my boat, the *Miss Rosalie*, when my friend Danny Ray Pledger came roaring up in his skiff, trembling and stuttering, unable to talk, and clearly in distress. He needed help, and he needed it badly.

While fishing, Danny Ray had found the badly decomposed body of a girl cast up by the tide in the remote wilderness of the great salt marsh of coastal Georgia. Not knowing what to do, he had come to me. We jumped in my sea skiff, and I returned with Danny Ray to the site of his grisly find. After calling the Coast Guard and having them alert the Chatham County Police, I sent Danny Ray back to my dock to guide the authorities while I stayed with the body.

Why had Danny Ray come to me first instead of going directly to the police himself? Well, the answer is a pretty simple one. Danny is a constituent part of society that always gets the short end of the stick. Poor as a church mouse, badly educated, slight of build, and with a bad stutter, no real job, and no connections, Danny is the quintessential Coastal Cracker.

Had he gone to the police with his discovery, it's a sure bet he would have been locked up as a suspect, and there's a strong likelihood he would have been charged with the girl's death. The law is applied in accordance with a man's standing in society, and the police and the court system are always quick to pick the low-hanging fruit. It ain't fair, but that's the way it is.

So I took the responsibility of being the official discoverer of the body. I had to answer a few questions about myself concerning my own standing in the community. But when the officer handling the case, Detective Patricia Latham, ran a background check on me, I no longer fit the potential-suspect category.

I thought that was the end of it, and a couple of days later Detective Latham stopped by to tell me the girl had been identified as Tonya Causey, from up in Effingham County, and that the cause of death was suicide by drowning. Turns out that four days before the body was found two witnesses had called in to report a slightly built girl with red hair jumping from the Talmadge Bridge in downtown Savannah. So the case, as far as the police were concerned, was closed.

But I was a little puzzled myself. It seemed to me the body should have been washed directly out to sea rather than lodging in the tidal marsh; but then again, the currents and the wind have strange patterns. Then I had taken an urgent job out of the country, and the matter had slipped to the recesses of my mind. Until tonight.

I had just returned home and was walking across the darkened parking lot to the boardwalk leading down to the dock when Danny Ray drove up with a visitor in tow, a woman. They got out of the car, and both stood hesitantly.

I looked closely at the woman. She was slightly built and thin to the point of boniness. She was dressed in a sweatshirt, jeans, and white sneakers. Her hair was pulled back in a tight ponytail, and she held herself rigidly, one arm across her midsection, as she nervously smoked a cigarette. When she inhaled her cheeks collapsed over missing teeth. She stared at me with a fixed intensity as she exhaled a long blue stream of smoke, and said nothing. At first I thought she was Danny Ray's mother, and then it dawned on me who she actually was.

"Mrs. Causey?" I asked as Danny Ray stepped forward.

She took another drag on her cigarette before removing it from her mouth and announcing, "Yeah, I am," in a smoke-and-whiskey voice.

"I'm very sorry for your loss, Mrs. Causey," I said to the sad woman before me. "I wish there was some way I could help."

"Danny Ray, here, tells me that maybe you can, Mr. Tanner. My daughter didn't commit suicide," she said as tears came to her eyes. "She was kilt. I know it, but won't nobody listen to me. Not the law. Not nobody. I need your help, Mr. Tanner."

I took a deep breath and then stepped forward. As the woman dissolved into tears, I put an arm around her thin shoulders and guided her toward my boat. "Come with me, Mrs. Causey, and you can tell me all about it."

I cast a glance over my shoulder to where Danny Ray stood waiting. "And you, too, Danny Ray. You're a part of this thing, too."

We sat on the aft deck and talked until well after midnight, or to be more accurate about it, Joree (as she bade me call her) talked and smoked, while I listened. I demonstrated my interest in her tale with frequent nods of the head and "uh-huhs," but that was all I had to do by way of encouragement. Joree gushed words with the physical force of water blasting forth from an uncapped fire hydrant. Most of it was only casually related to her daughter's death.

It seemed she talked about every other topic that came to her: about the sorry no-count men who had drifted in and out of her life; about the difficulty of making ends meet; about caring for her own mother and watching her die for lack of decent medical treatment; and on to a dozen other trials and tribulations she had ever suffered. Taken in total, it was a depressing tale of life at the bottom of the social scale. The only time she smiled and spoke in a positive manner was when she talked of her daughter, Tonya, as a child. Those seemed to be the few moments of joy and happiness in the sad litany of Joree Causey's life.

I let her talk until she ran out of steam. And as I listened I realized that more than anything else, she just wanted someone to pay attention to her. Someone to treat her with courtesy and respect. Someone to listen sympathetically, and not tell her how she should or shouldn't act, or feel, or speak. Someone to treat her as a fellow human being of worth and substance. This is a thing most of us take for granted, but something exceedingly rare and in short supply in the lives of the very poor.

And then, sending a last cigarette butt hissing overboard in a glowing red arc to the silent black waters we floated upon, she suddenly ran out of words and sat quietly, rocking back and forth in rhythm with the subtle movements of the boat, staring out across the darkened expanse of the great salt marsh.

While she talked I had held her with my eyes, never taking my gaze from her face as she poured forth her tale of hardship and sorrow. And I held her with my eyes still, as she quietly retreated into herself, her face softening as it relaxed, and becoming younger-looking, while her eyes took on the vacant emptiness of a thousand-yard stare. It seemed to me that she had gone someplace else, somewhere completely private, reflecting on memories old and new, and possibly seeing things that could have been but never were, and now, would never have the chance to be.

I left her alone in that place and we sat silently for many minutes, the quiet broken only now and then by the splash of a feeding fish out on the dark water or the lonesome cry of a passing nighthawk in unseen flight. At length, I saw her body shiver slightly beneath the wool blanket I had wrapped about her shoulders, and she came back to the here and now. Her face reassumed its hardened defensive set as she turned her eyes to me once again.

"You've been mighty kind, Mr. Tanner, to sit here and listen to my story. I 'magine you must think I'm about the sorriest piece a white trash you ever did come across."

"Joree, my name is Kennesaw, and that's what I want you to call me. My granddaddy is Mr. Tanner, and if I ever become half the man he is, then I'll be about as pleased with myself as a man can be."

She looked at me quizzically for a moment and then smiled for the first time tonight. It was slow in coming at first, as though it were an unaccustomed act. Her mouth relaxed just slightly, turned upward at the corners, and then a full smile blossomed across her face. She put a hand over her mouth to cover it and averted her face in shyness. I reached across the space between us and, gently putting a finger on her hand, pulled it away from her mouth and guided it to her lap. She looked up then, the smile still on her face, but also a look of wonder in her eyes.

"You have a pretty smile, Joree. I hope you get to wear it more often; it looks good on you," I said as I held her eyes.

She leaned forward, put a hand on mine, and gave it a squeeze as tears welled in her eyes and rolled down her cheeks.

"Thank ye," she whispered. "Thank ye for listening to a heartbroke old woman. If nothing more comes of it than that, it's been a blessing to me."

She gave my hand a final squeeze, and then, squaring her shoulders and sitting up straight, she shrugged off the blanket and stood up. She looked over at Danny Ray, asleep in a deck chair, and then glanced at her wristwatch.

"Lordy, Mr. Ta . . . Kennesaw," she said with a start, "it's long past midnight and I'm a-keeping you up." She nudged Danny Ray with a foot. "Come on, Danny, I got to git home, it's late."

Danny Ray sat up, instantly awake.

"Joree, why don't you stay here tonight? I have two spare cabins; there's room here on the boat for you and Danny Ray both."

"I 'preciate the thought, but no, I got to git home," she said with determination. "I have people depending on me. 'Sides it ain't all that far from here, only 'bout forty-five minutes this time a night. And don't you worry 'bout Danny Ray having to drive me up there. My car's parked over at his place."

She stepped close and extended her hand as she looked up and swept my face with her eyes. I took her hand, and then as I put an arm around her shoulders, she leaned her face against my chest and gave me a firm hug. As she stepped back and looked up again I saw that her eyes were wet once more, but the smile was back on her face.

"I'll do what I can, Joree. I don't know what that will amount to, but I'll do my best," I said.

"You done plenty already," she said in a soft voice as Danny led the way to the gangplank.

I stood at the rail and watched as Danny and Joree made their way up the ramp to the parking lot. I lifted a hand as the car pulled away and saw, through the mist that had begun to settle over the land, a fleeting view of Joree's face, and the palm and fingers of the hand she had placed on the passenger window as a parting salute. Then the red tail-lights turned on to the street above and were rapidly swallowed by the quiet folds of the night.

I stood in thought for several seconds, looking at the empty street and listening for—I don't know what. I turned to go below to my waiting bunk, but hesitated for a second at the companionway as my nose detected a shift in the breeze. *A front's coming through,* I thought. *I wonder what change it will bring.* Then I descended the six steps to below, closed and locked the hatch behind me, and turned in for the night.

CHAPTER 2

SOME PEOPLE SAY THAT THE TRUTH is a fixed quantity, unchangeable and permanent, but I don't think that is so. I think of it as something entirely mysterious and fragile. In my experience it is like the wind and the ocean currents, ever moving, swirling and dancing, now here and then somewhere else again. Try as we might to pin it down, it eludes us, floating and shifting shape, changing according to the viewpoint and position of the beholder. What is true to me may not be the same for you. And what you believe to be fact may be something else entirely to me, or another person.

Perceptions are filtered through the sieve of the experience of our conscious and unconscious lives. Even when a person is doing their utmost to relay the facts of a situation, it is never complete and never absolutely correct. That doesn't make it right or wrong, it just makes it the way it is. What Joree Causey had given me was a starting point, a place to begin.

And what Joree had told me was the truth of certain matters as they appeared to her, and nothing more. Again, what I had heard was a place to start, and for that I was grateful. I had heard the first notes of a song, but there was more to come, and I needed to listen to the music for a bit. In my mind the tune was still off-key and had not yet found its rhythm, and I was not quite ready to dance.

In all that Joree had said she had never once spoken of Tonya in the last year. Where she lived, what she did, how she supported herself was never mentioned. Either Joree had no idea concerning the missing portion of her daughter's life—that critical year prior to her death—or it was something that she just couldn't bring herself to speak of. Maybe it was a mixture of the two, a compound of willful ignorance and reticence. Perhaps she knew a bit but found it too painful or embarrassing to think about, much less tell to a stranger.

I intended to sleep in that next morning but awoke at dawn with a restless energy kicking me out of my bunk. I put on a pot of Mexican coffee, and then, as I shaved and readied myself for the day, I played Joree Causey's story to myself one more time. After that, I purposely put it away in a corner of my mind, where my subconscious could chew it over until I was ready to bring it to the light once again, and examine it with a new and critical eye.

Joree's belief that her daughter was killed by an unknown *someone* could be correct—but it could also be the case that the girl had indeed decided to end her life by taking a plunge from the Talmadge Bridge into the all-embracing and uncaring waters of the Savannah River. Only one thing was certain at this point: Tonya Causey was dead, and she wasn't about to become undead anytime soon.

In the galley, I opened a can of Spam, the staple food of refugees everywhere. I love the stuff. I fried a couple of pieces until it had a dark crust, and sliced some hoop cheese. Putting that delicious twosome between a couple of pieces of bread, I poured a fresh cup of coffee and went up on deck to enjoy my breakfast al fresco.

The morning air had a pleasant crispness to it that had cleared the atmosphere of all haze and made for a startling clarity of vision. The wind was dead calm, and as I looked across the unmoving immensity of the salt marsh, it appeared as though it were a still life, a painting done by a master's hand. Then the sun, rising from its watery bed of night, lifted its face above the treetops of Tybee Island, and cast a wave of golden light in a westward arc, enhancing and illuminating the sublime beauty of the natural scene until it was almost too much for mortal man to bear.

I stood mesmerized by the sight and thought, *If it all came to an end today, if life has run its course and I were to breathe no more, the gift of being here, right now, would have paid for the trip in full.*

Then the full body of old Sol heaved himself well above the green horizon, and the day was on. As I ate, the silence of the morning was broken only once by a boat full of sport fishermen. They waved in greeting as they passed by, and I returned the salutation. Soon they were out of sight, headed in the direction of Bull River and Wassaw Sound. I silently wished them good luck.

Finishing the last bite of sandwich and washing it down with a final slurp of coffee, I went below to the galley to wash and put away the pan and other utensils. While taking care of that chore I remembered that it was a Saturday and then determined what I would do with the day. *Miss Rosalie* had been tied to the dock for a while, and no self-respecting boat can stand that for very long. I would get her ready for action and treat us both to an excursion.

In the engine room I checked oil, transmission fluid, and engine coolant levels. A diesel engine will run almost forever if you give it clean air to breathe, clean fuel to burn, and clean oil to keep everything properly lubed. But diesel fuel loves water, so I drained several ounces from each of the three fuel filters to make sure there was no H_2O in the system.

Happy that no liquids were where they shouldn't be, I gave the engine and transmission the once-over, looking for leaks, drips, and loose hose fittings. The absence of any of those indicators of trouble made for a comforting feeling. The pre-ops check finished, I gave that magnificent Gardner engine a fond pat on top of the number three cylinder valve cover and went back above.

Up top, I hosed off the deck and pilothouse and then checked the rigging of the masts. Following that, I looked to the navigation lights, and then back at the helm, the radios, radar, and other electricals and electronics. If it seems I am obsessive about the condition of my boat—it's because I am. I learned many years ago that the things you fail to check are the things that tend to fail. And on a boat, they will always fail at the most critical time you could possibly imagine—or worse yet—not imagine.

The angle of the sun told me the hour was no longer considered as "too early." I picked up my phone, dialed a number, and got the answering message.

"It's Kennesaw Tanner on a bright Saturday morning," I said. "I'm calling in the rain check for that party of yours I missed, but this time, it's my treat. I'm making a trip to Daufuskie today and would be delighted if you could join me. If you can make it, meet me at the docks on Lazaretto

Island in ninety minutes. Just bring your excellent self, a camera, and a sense of adventure. Hope to see you then. Ciao."

I clicked off the phone, grabbed my wallet and keys, and headed to the local market to pick up supplies and restock the larder.

CHAPTER 3

I WATCHED THE OIL PRESSURE GAUGE as the indicator settled to its proper mark, then, giving a long blast of the horn to alert any nearby traffic, turned the wheel to starboard and gave the throttle a small push. *Miss Rosalie* quivered just slightly as the prop bit into the water, and then her bows came about and she slipped out into the stream. As we cleared the docks I gave her enough juice for seven hundred rpms and felt the engine settle into a contented throb that moved us at a stately pace, leaving barely a ripple on the surface of the water.

A couple of miles downstream was a narrow channel that would eventually lead to Lazaretto Creek. As I approached the entrance to the creek I saw that the oyster bar on the lower side was just about covered by the rising tide and felt sure there would be enough water under the keel to keep from scraping bottom.

I glanced at the depth finder as *Miss Rosalie* squeezed

through the narrow opening and saw that we'd made it with a good two feet to spare. I made a quick note of the amount of mud still exposed on the banks of the stream and, using that as a reference point for water depth, stored it away in my mind for future use. Then, within a hundred meters, the channel opened up, and *Miss Rosalie* and I were engulfed by the wilderness of the marsh.

The great prairie of sea grass and tidal water stretched away to the horizon, south and north, and out toward Tybee Island some four or five miles to the east. Small islands, known locally as hammocks, were dotted in haphazard fashion across the face of the marsh. I had explored several of the hammocks and on each of them had found the ancient shell mounds left by the original native inhabitants of this coast—a people who disappeared soon after the Spanish set foot in the region.

I always love being out here. It is a wild place, little changed in thousands of years. And even with the depredations of uncaring man, this is still one of the principal cradles of life. The great rivers of Georgia: The Savannah, Ogeechee, Altamaha, St. Marys, and others drain the interior of the land and pour their mighty waters into this vast catch basin. The tides flush in and out twice a day, alternately covering and exposing the wetlands, mixing and distributing the life-giving nutrients into a nutritious primordial soup.

Tiny creatures are born and find sanctuary within this fertile oasis. Some are food for others, and some grow and feed off smaller organisms. The bigger ones, when ready, answer the call of their species and follow their innate chart of life back out to sea, the cycle of life continuing thus. I have read that the productivity—the biomass— created and nurtured by an acre of salt marsh is twenty times greater than that of an acre of prime Midwestern farmland planted in corn. We mistreat this nursery of life at the peril of our own species.

I kept a sharp eye on the surface as I navigated this piece of water. The powerful tides of the Georgia coast scour deep channels in the salt creeks and other streams, but they are always moving soil from one place and depositing it in others. The swirl of the water shows where it flows around an obstacle, and the rise of a bank at an inside bend indicates where the water is deepest.

The waters were still rather warm but would begin to cool off rapidly now that the season was getting late and the nights becoming longer and chillier. The tropical animals, like the tarpon and the manatees, would be pointing their noses back south again and making their way to the perpetually warm waters to the south of Florida's St. George River. And before long, the right whales would make their annual migration from the North Atlantic waters of New England to the Georgia Bight, where they would give birth to that year's generation of calves.

Rounding a sharp bend that pointed *Miss Rosalie*'s bows directly to the south, I saw, in the distance, the hammock that was my reference point for where Danny Ray had found the body of Tonya Causey, where it had been deposited on a bank of mud and oyster shells by the falling tide.

That's a very long way from Savannah, where she supposedly jumped from the Talmadge Bridge. More than twenty miles, I thought. The body would have had to float, undetected, through a confusing labyrinth of waterways to reach the place where it was eventually found. Maybe it had washed out to sea, and from there, back into the marsh again. Who knows, maybe only God. But I was going to do my best to find out.

The channel made a hard turn to the left, bringing us back to an easterly heading and then abruptly opened into the wide upper reaches of Lazaretto Creek. Ahead, jammed deep in the mud on the left side of the channel, I caught sight of the dead bodies of two new victims. As we came abreast of the spot, I brought *Miss Rosalie* to a halt and took a good long look. It was a sad sight to behold.

The hulls of two shrimp boats had been abandoned to the ministrations of the marsh. The commercial fishermen of this area had experienced another of their seemingly perpetual financial calamities. Overfishing, bad weather, and now, the low price of shrimp being imported from Southeast Asia and Latin America and dumped on the American market had combined to wreak havoc on the livelihoods of the fishermen of the coast. With nowhere to turn for help, and in the face of nothing but hardship, men, from Virginia to Florida, were abandoning their precious boats, but the Georgia coast appeared to be the epicenter of this sad spectacle.

Economies of the market, spout the business gurus. *It's good for the bottom line,* they blather on. But I ask myself, *Whose economy? And whose bottom line are they speaking of?* Certainly not the men who have lost the work they've followed all their lives.

Those derelict boats may represent enhanced profits to a handful of huge corporations, but to the men who had depended on those boats to wrest a living from the sea and provide for their families, those same rotting hulks now represented hardship, desperation, and destitution.

So go ahead, America, ship those jobs overseas as fast as you can. And when the bulk of the working people of this country can no longer afford to buy the foreign-made goods we import, and when they can no longer afford to purchase the homes, and cars, and other major items that have kept our economy humming and growing for the last three-quarters of a century, well, then, don't be surprised if we end up with an economy similar to that of Mexico: with a small handful of *Haves* and a great mass of *Have-Nots*. And then we'll see how well the Wall Street robber barons and their political enablers in Washington like the society they've created.

I think then and only then the people of this country will wake up to the realization of what's been done to them; all in the name of greed; all to benefit a very few. And perhaps then, the people of this country may not be as supine as they have always been in the past. I fear that day will soon be upon us. I wish I had an answer to it all—but sadly, I do not.

Turning my view back to the channel before me, I pushed the transmission lever into the Forward position and got under way once again. To my left was the low causeway of Highway 80, running on to its eastern terminus on Tybee Island. It seemed odd to watch cars running along as though cruising through the marsh. But odder still was the sight of a huge container ship coming up the unseen Savannah River, only a half mile away, on the other side of the highway. Then, a sharp northward turn of the channel brought sight of the wooden docks and the few scattered buildings of Lazaretto Island.

I throttled back, just making headway, and looked for a place to get to the dock. There, on the far end, I saw a spot where I could tie up. Then, as I glanced to the land above the docks, I saw Patricia Latham toss me a wave of recognition. I returned her wave and motioned her to the end of the dock. She nodded her understanding, shouldered a small bag, and hurried down the ramp.

I brought *Miss Rosalie* gently near the side of the wharf, and Patricia, without hesitation, nimbly leaped aboard.

I touched the controls lightly, and with the help of the incoming tide we pulled away from the dock pilings with room to spare. Patricia stood and watched the landing as it slid past and then behind us, and then, glancing about the deck as though she were making a mental note of where everything was, she made her way aft to the pilothouse.

"Welcome aboard the *Miss Rosalie*," I said as Patricia stepped inside.

"Thanks for the invitation," she returned as she came near and gave me a smile.

I was struck once again at how tall she was; at least six feet, and maybe even an inch or two more. She was dressed in old faded jeans and a man's cotton shirt, but the garments did little to conceal either the strength of her frame or her marvelous figure. With thick auburn hair, eyes the color of light jade, and a face that seemed carved in alabaster, Detective Patricia Latham was a decidedly striking woman.

"Just back in town?" she asked.

"Got in last evening," I replied. I gave her a glance that met her eye and then returned my gaze back to the channel ahead. "And you were the first person I called."

I could feel her studying the side of my face for a few seconds before she answered in a soft voice, "I take that as a compliment, Kennesaw."

"It was meant as one, Patricia. I'm glad to see you again," I said as I reached over and gave her forearm a squeeze.

We watched in silence for a bit as the water ahead of us broadened to meet the mouth of the mighty Savannah River. I lifted a hand and pointed as we came past the Cockspur Island Lighthouse and turned eastward.

"That's Daufuskie, out in the distance," I said. "Two ways to get there. We can swing out the mouth of the river, offshore a ways, and then come back up the channel just south of the island, or"—I jerked a thumb back over my left shoulder—"we can go upriver and take the Intracoastal Waterway. With the incoming tide, it's sixes and two threes—take your pick."

A pilot boat sped across our bow, heading out to the sea buoy to meet an inbound freighter. I gave the wheel a quarter turn so as to cut the pilot boat's wake at an angle. Patricia put a hand on the console as we rode over the waves.

"I see that place almost every day when I go for a walk on North Beach," she said as she nodded to the island in the distance. "But I've never been there. It's always been a mysterious place to me."

She stared at the low green line of treetops floating out on the horizon. "Let's come in from the ocean—like we were seeing it for the first time. Like we were the first people to ever see the place."

We each turned to the other and I saw a look of expectant wonder on her face, like the happy look of a child contemplating an imminent adventure.

"From seaward it is," I said with a smile of my own and gave the wheel a turn to starboard that pointed us out toward the seemingly limitless expanse of the great Atlantic Ocean.

"This is a beautiful boat, Kennesaw," she said, admiringly, as she looked around the pilothouse and out across the deck. "Does she have a story to tell?"

I kept my eye on a couple of small fishing boats a few hundred meters ahead of us as I replied, *"Miss Rosalie* has been my home for the last several years."

"I've gathered that much already. It was listed as your residence when I first met you. But where did it come from, and when did it . . . she become your home? This isn't an interrogation, Tanner. I'm just interested. You know—call it women's curiosity."

I glanced over and saw that she had a teasing smile on her face.

"I'll tell you what," I said. "In the interest of allaying curiosity, why don't you go below and look the interior over? Once you've had a good look around I'll tell you all about her."

"Now that's the way to a woman's heart," she quipped. "I've been dying to see the inside of this boat since I first saw it at the dock."

"Well, make the most of it, me lady," I said with a theatrical flourish of the hand. "You enter through the companionway there on deck. Watch your head as you go below, and keep a hand in contact with something solid as you move around. You never know when we might hit a wave."

Patricia gave me a grin of expectation. "Thanks," she said as she practically skipped out of the pilothouse and went forward to the passageway. She took two steps down the stairs, turned and gave me a wave, and then disappeared below.

I held us on course down the Savannah. As we left Tybee Island behind to starboard I felt the first long heave of the open Atlantic Ocean. Ahead for the next thirty-five hundred miles or so was nothing but salt water. If you could hold this course and maintain this exact latitude, you would eventually run into the continent of Africa, very near the town of Safi, on the coast of Morocco. It's a trip I'd like to make someday.

I picked up my binoculars and scanned to the north until I found the buoy marking the entrance to the channel for Daufuskie. I held course for another five minutes and then started to bring us on a heading that would carry us straight in over the bar at the channel entrance. It was high tide now, and there was plenty of depth, but I didn't want to chance finding a newly formed shoal.

I was just beginning to wonder about Patricia when I saw her emerge from the companionway. She had a mug in each hand and made her way delicately the few steps from the hatch to the pilothouse.

"Here you go," she said as she entered and handed me one of the mugs. "You have a stash of some really good tea in the galley. It was one of the many things that surprised me."

I blew across the top of the mug and took a sip. "Thanks," I said. "You must have read my mind." I took another sip. "And this *is* my good stuff. I almost never serve it to company—most Americans wouldn't appreciate it. I'm glad you know the difference."

Patricia's eyes smiled over the top of her mug. "Oh, that is good," she breathed appreciatively as she lowered the cup before taking another sip. "Where do you get it?"

I reached forward and clinked cups with her. "A Chinese friend of mine sends it now and again. In return I send wild ginseng from up in the mountains."

"That's where you grew up, isn't it? The Appalachians? You don't have a pronounced mountain accent, but I can hear the inflections in your voice."

"You've pegged me," I said. "I first saw the light of day on the back side of Lookout Mountain, in a little place called Rising Fawn, Georgia, up near the borders of Alabama and Tennessee. But I've been gone from there for quite a while." I gave her a look. "And by the sound of your voice, I'd say that you come from somewhere just inland from the coast down here. Someplace like Statesboro or Glennville."

She gave me a laugh. "Pretty close," she said. "Claxton."

"Fruitcake capital of the world," I responded.

"Both the eating kind and the two-legged kind," she

said with a throaty chuckle. "It's a good place to be from—far from."

"I take it you've renounced the family fortune and turned down the trust fund that came along with it," I returned.

"Now that *is* rich," she said with an ironic lilt in her voice. "The only thing my ancestors ever left behind was debt and poverty. So as soon as I graduated from high school, it was the big city for me. I packed up my little car, came to Savannah, and never looked back."

"Haven't always been a cop, have you?" I asked.

"Always. Got a job as a night dispatcher and worked my way through Savannah State with a degree in criminal science. Police work, it's what I've always wanted to do. I guess I've been lucky."

"Family?" I asked.

"Now who's the detective here, Tanner? You or me?" she replied with a furrowed brow.

"I prefer to think of this as a pleasant conversation, Patricia," I said in a friendly tone, "not a grilling. It's just that I'm always intrigued when I meet someone who left home in search of greener pastures. Most people never do, especially if they come from a small town. They stay where they were born, where they know and are known by all, and never budge." I gave her a look and a smile. "It takes courage to set out on your own and follow a dream—and I admire that in a person."

Patricia took another sip before replying. "Kennesaw, I was just playing with you, I don't mind the question—yeah, my mother still lives there, along with an older sister and brother. They all live on the same street where they've always been. Mom is becoming increasingly frail, and it's good that she has family close by. I get down there as often as I can."

I nodded my understanding. "Sort of a tug, isn't it, especially for a woman? You feel you should be nearby to help with an aging parent, but at the same time you know you can't go back."

Patricia spoke with a sigh, "That's it. The pull of family is always there. And you? What about your family?"

I turned us a few degrees to port and took a heading on a point of the island. "Parents are long gone. I have a bunch of brothers and sisters—seven of us all together; all of them still up in the mountains. I'm close to one of my sisters; the others—well, that's best left unsaid."

Patricia went up several notches in my estimation when all she said to that was, "Uh-huh." Then looking around again, she said, "Now the boat. What's the story of the *Miss Rosalie*?"

I contemplated for a moment which version to tell. Then decided on one that was pretty close to the truth.

"She was payment for a job I did several years ago," I replied. "The client was in a tight spot for cash, so I took the boat instead. It had been lying derelict and neglected in a small port in the Netherlands, but as soon as I saw her, it was love at first sight. The engine was in great shape. The hull was rusty, but okay. But the masts, the rigging, and the interior were a wreck. I got her in seaworthy condition and took her over to Ireland for a full refurbishing. She's been my home ever since."

Patricia listened and then said in an even voice, "I notice you didn't say what the job was you did for the client."

I turned to look at her. "I notice that you notice things pretty well," I said with a slight smile.

Patricia nodded slightly. "Pardon the observation—it was my instinct as a professional snoop. No offense intended," she said with a friendly look on her face.

"And none taken," I replied with sincerity.

Scanning ahead I saw that we were about a mile from the south end of Daufuskie. Just then, the water off to starboard rolled in a bulge, and then I saw a fin push above the surface and rapidly disappear. But the fin, before it went under again, had been headed directly toward the boat.

"Patricia," I quickly said. "Put your cup here on the console and go to the bow of the boat. When you get there, hold on to the rails and watch the water in front of the bow."

She gave me a quizzical look.

"Take off," I said. "Quick, you don't want to miss this."

Patricia took a final sip of tea, set down the cup, and hurried from the pilothouse, across the deck, and up to the bow. She had just arrived when the first dolphin flashed to the surface and began to prance in the wake of the bow. Within seconds he was joined by another, and out to port and starboard I saw three or four others turn to converge on the boat.

Soon, a whole tribe of those enthralling, beautiful creatures were using *Miss Rosalie* as a plaything—dashing back and forth across the bow, dancing, leaping, and splashing with what could only be described as the pure happiness of being alive.

Patricia threw her arms wide in excitement at the scene and then repeatedly clapped her hands in delight. She leaned out far over the prow, and her head and shoulders swiveled this way and that, trying to catch it all, as the dolphins raced back and forth, streaming away before dashing back in again at an amazing speed. Patricia turned to call something to me. I couldn't make out the words, but the look of joy that shone on her face said it all. I waved in reply, and she turned back again to watch the fascinating show.

The dolphins stayed with us until we met the Intracoastal

Waterway and turned northward, leaving the open water behind and running parallel with the western shore of the island. One of the animals leaped high into the air and, turning on its side, threw a mighty fountain of water blossoming high into the air as it crashed back to its natural element. And then, as quickly as they had appeared, the dolphins were gone.

Patricia stood watching the water for a while longer, hoping, I was sure, that the dolphins would return. But after a few minutes she came back to rejoin me in the pilothouse. I smiled and said nothing when she entered, and she, too, was quiet, standing beside me and staring out on to the water.

"That was the most beautiful thing I have ever seen," she said at last in a quiet and reverential tone of voice. Then turning to face me, she said, "Thank you for that. But how did you know they were coming? You sent me up there before they ever arrived."

"I thought they would come, and then I caught a glimpse of one. Dolphins love *Miss Rosalie*. I think it must be the sound she makes in the water. But whatever it is, when any are nearby, they come running to frolic around her. I've seen them stay with us for hours on end. And I'm convinced the local dolphins know her from all other boats."

"If we turned around right now," Patricia said, "this would be one of the best trips I've taken in a long while."

I gave her a smile that said, *You're welcome*. Patricia gave me a kiss on the cheek.

"But we have a lot of day left to us, so let's not get in any hurry to turn back. Besides . . ." I pointed ahead. "We're almost there; the dock is just ahead. And we're in luck; no other boats are here. We can tie up instead of anchoring out. The tide is almost slack now, so it isn't going to be too difficult to get to the floating dock. But if you will, go stand at the rail, and when I put us against the dock, take that line you see there and throw it around the cleat on the dock. I'll take care of it from there."

"Aye, aye, Captain," she said as she snapped me a salute and then left the pilothouse to stand by at the rail.

Up on the fixed portion of the dock, a lone figure, with two fishing rods at hand, sat on a folding stool. I saw him stand and stare, and when he recognized the boat he quickly reeled in his lines and rushed down to lend a hand. As we came slowly alongside, he motioned to Patricia to throw him the rope she held. I brought us to a halt and cut the engine as the man quickly indicated to Patricia which other lines to toss him. By the time I cleared the pilothouse we were securely snubbed down.

"Parker," I called as I stepped on deck and leaned over to shake hands, "how you doing, man?"

Parker returned my grip and said, "What it is, Kennesaw? You've been scarce for a while, good to see you again."

Patricia was eyeing the man with what could only be called a police officer's discernment, and it wasn't hard to guess why. Parker Wells is a self-described Zen Bum, and he completely looks the part. Tall and lanky, he stands leaning forward slightly, in a way that always reminds me of Boris Karloff.

On his head he wore an ancient, ragged canvas hat festooned with feathers, small bones, and the large scales of a tarpon he had caught years ago. His well-brushed beard, falling to the center of his chest, ended in an elaborately woven braid. The sleeves of his flannel shirt stopped midway between the elbows and the wrists, and his jeans looked like he'd owned them since the time of Woodstock. He was shod in a pair of deerskin moccasins that I knew he had made himself.

With no fixed home, no job, no mortgage, no car, no insurance, no bank account, Parker is the type of person instantly distrusted by the guardians of society, because intuitively they know they have no hold upon a person like him and never will. A totally independent man, Parker is the perfect example of a modern nomad. And for that very reason, he makes those of us laboring under the harness of modern life rather uncomfortable, and often (me, for example) envious, in his presence.

I quickly made the introduction. "Parker Wells, I'd like you to meet my friend Patricia Latham."

Parker took off his hat, extended a hand, and spoke in a cultured and educated voice. "Miss Patricia, it is a genuine pleasure to meet you, and a great honor indeed to extend to you a welcome to our island paradise."

Patricia shook hands, and as she looked into Parker's eyes and recognized the kind and gentle man that resided therein, her initial reticence and distance dissolved and faded away.

"Hello," she said with a smile. "Thank you for the welcome, and I'm glad to meet you, too."

"Kennesaw, can I help you with anything?" Parker asked as I opened a deck locker and took out a small cooler.

"No, thanks," I replied as I set the cooler on the deck. "I think we're all set and ready to go."

While Parker gave Patricia a hand to the dock, I closed the door to the pilothouse and then turned to make sure the dock lines were secure. By the time I picked up the cooler, set it on my shoulder, and stepped off the boat, Patricia and Parker were chatting away like old friends well met after a long absence. Parker led the way, and we walked to the top of the ramp.

"How's the fishing today, amigo? This isn't one of your regular spots. I was surprised to see you here," I queried.

Parker gave me a close look. "Some people watch birds, I like to watch boats. This is the time of the year when the first flocks of Northerners pass by on their way to Florida. When any of them stop here, I do my best to add to the local color, and sometimes, by way of charm and graciousness, I manage to pick up a few dollars impersonating a tour guide."

"How's business?" I asked as we reached the top of the landing.

"Spotty," Parker replied as he picked up one of his rods and inspected it closely. "But I have hopes of improvement before the day is out."

He lifted his hat to Patricia and gave me a nod, "Y'all have a great day—Kennesaw, I'll keep an eye on your boat until you return."

He then plucked a fresh shrimp from his bait bucket, threaded it on the hook, and let it drop to the water below.

Patricia and I walked from the dock and onto land. Ahead of us, a sandy track, lightly paved with old oyster shells, led inland through a wooded glen. Massive live oak trees flanked the road and shaded the curve of the small bay as the land edged its way around the shore of the island. Behind the open glen the land was a jungle of tangled vegetation.

A hundred meters ahead was a long, low building with a tin roof. Its walls were of rough-sided lumber, and it had a porch at either end. A sign on the wall announced the place as Marshside Mama's Restaurant and Bar. As we neared the building I reached into the cooler I carried and handed Patricia a couple of potatoes.

"Here," I said. "These are for a friend of mine. His name is Ned. He's a bit of a local eccentric here on the island. Potatoes are sort of a fetish of his, but I assure you, he's completely harmless. The only thing I ask is that you don't make fun of his teeth. They are in pretty bad shape, and he's sensitive about the way they look. A dentist could probably help him, but he won't leave the island to see one."

Patricia took the potatoes from my hand and gave me a sharp look. "Kennesaw Tanner, what sort of unfeeling, uncaring person do you think I am, that I'd make fun of a poor—"

Just then, Ned emerged from his napping place on the porch. Patricia saw him from the corner of her eye and gave a short startled squeal as she leaped behind me and peeked from around my shoulder.

"What the hell is that!" she gasped.

"Ned!" I called. "Come here, old friend, I've got someone I'd like you to meet."

Ned ambled forward and stopped just in front of us. He looked up expectantly with his deep-set, beady eyes, and as I reached down and scratched him on the head, he made a deep-throated, snuffling sound of greeting.

"Patricia," I said, glancing over my shoulder. "Hand him a potato, he's expecting it."

Warily, Patricia eased herself halfway from behind me but came no farther and made no movement to meet Ned.

"He won't bother you," I said as I took the potato from her hand and presented it to Ned. "Here, buddy. It's all yours. And we have several more where that came from."

Ned gently took the potato in his mouth. He chewed with a great flashing of long yellow teeth and wet grunts of satisfaction. Closing his eyes in pleasure, a look of contented ecstasy came over his face. He quickly swallowed the last of the potato and then took a step forward, to rub the side of his head and neck appreciatively against my thigh. While I scratched him on the shoulders and under the jowls, he reached around and tenderly took the other potato from Patricia's hand.

"Ned is the undisputed king of the island," I said as Patricia found her courage again and came from behind me to take a good look at the huge wild boar in front of us. "Folks say he swam over from the mainland about ten years ago and has had the run of the place ever since. He has a nice shed of his own where he sleeps at night, but most of the time he hangs out down here, where he can see what's going on and meet visitors."

"He's colossal," said Patricia, wonderingly, as I opened the cooler and poured the rest of the potatoes it contained on the ground. "How much does he weigh? And just look at those tusks—they must be six inches long," she said as she reached out a hand and gave him a tentative touch.

"I think he'd easily go four hundred pounds," I replied as I pushed one of the potatoes closer to his snout with my foot. "But amazingly, he's as gentle as a kitten. He walks the kids on the island to the ferry in the morning to catch the school bus, and then meets them when they return in the afternoon. And his closest friend is an old blind hound dog that lives nearby."

I was watching Ned as he finished the last of the potatoes when Patricia suddenly slugged me on the shoulder.

"'Bad teeth. Don't make fun of his teeth. He's sensitive about them,' you said. Oh boy, Tanner. You've got one coming. Just you wait and see."

Patricia chuckled deeply. I picked up the cooler and gave Ned a last pat on the head.

"Come on," I said. "I have some other people I'd like you to meet."

"No more tricks?" she asked as we stepped away.

I gave her a glance as I took her hand. "No more tricks. I promise."

As we followed the road deeper into the island, the live oaks closed in on both sides, their enormous branches intertwining overhead, engulfing us in a cavern of primeval shadow. Within minutes, we were absorbed by the ancient and exotic life of the sea island of Daufuskie.

CHAPTER 4

"THIS IS A PILGRIMAGE I MAKE WITH some frequency," I explained to Patricia as we reached a crossroads and turned right, forging ever deeper into the interior of the island.

"So this is some sort of religious trip for you, eh?" she asked with a teasing smile.

I rocked the cooler on my shoulder. "When you come to realize the purpose of the trip, you might call it a religious experience at that. I come over here to visit the Chambers family. The menfolk are crabbers and have been for generations. And Miss Darcey, the mother of the clan, makes, hands down, the finest stuffed crabs on the face of the planet—perhaps in the entire universe. Plus, I wanted you to meet the family. The Chambers are Geechees, and maybe you know what a special people they are. If not, you soon will."

Patricia gave me a quizzical look before saying, "You

move in a lot of circles, don't you? I know of the Geechees, but can't say I know any of them."

"Well, let me give you a short tutorial, if I may. The Geechees, or Gullahs, as they are also known, are descended from slaves who were brought to the barrier islands and coastal areas of South Carolina, Georgia, and northern Florida, directly from West Africa. When the plantation owners, and other whites, fled the islands during the Civil War, the people continued their lives as they had always done before—farming, fishing, and making their handicrafts. Here, due to the isolation of the region, they were able to retain a great deal of their West African culture, and through the mixing of English and several African languages developed a dialect all their own," I said.

"Uh-huh," she replied.

What I didn't say was that I find the Geechees to be a gracious and very wise people, similar in many ways to the folks I have known, worked with, and lived among along the coastal areas of West Africa. Sadly, they are increasingly under assault by the land developers who covet these once-remote islands. Even Daufuskie, which has no land connection to the mainland, now has a golf development occupying a huge swath of the Atlantic side of the island.

I can only shake my head at what is being lost and ask myself: Are there not enough golf courses and gated mansions in this country already that we don't have to rape the last of our pristine places? And are we not content until we have cut down every ancient tree, paved over every piece of sacred ground, and put up a new mall, so we can wander around in a materialistic stupor, buying things we don't need and enriching the already stupendously wealthy?

I guess the answer to my question is "no." We never seem to care about the things of real value until they are gone. And we care about people—especially black people—least of all. Sometime in this century, the Geechee culture will be little more than a memory, a footnote of history, the subject of a few doctoral theses. When that day comes, we will all be the less for it. But we'll be able to console ourselves with the idea that we'll have some really neat golf courses instead and some fabulous and exclusive island resorts that look like all the other resorts everywhere else in the world.

We reached the Chambers home place a few minutes later. The house sat back from the road, surrounded by a swept yard bordered by a wire fence. Flowers growing in coffee cans lined the porch rails and the oyster shell walk that led to the house. Chickens scratched in the sand of the yard, looking for bugs and pieces of this morning's cracked corn. Under the trees at the side of the house a couple of kids (young goats, that is) stood on top of the woodshed and watched as we approached.

As I opened the gate to the yard and motioned her through, Patricia looked around in delight.

"It reminds me of my grandmother's place when I was a little girl," she said with wonder. "The swept yard—the flowers in cans—it's all the same. Why, it feels—it feels just like coming home."

"I know what you mean," I said as I led us down the walk. "It brings back some memories for me, too."

We were mounting the two steps to the porch when the screen door flew open and there stood Miss Darcey, wiping her hands on a dish towel and smiling a welcome.

"Well, hey, boy. I see you brung a visitor with you this time—and a mighty good-lookin' one, too," she said as she threw the towel across a shoulder and stepped out to meet us.

"I'm Darcey," she said before I could make an introduction. "An' what's yo' name, pretty lady?" she asked as she took Patricia's hand in hers.

"Patricia—Patricia Latham, from Tybee."

"Well, it's glad I am to meet you, Patricia Latham. Welcome to our little place here."

Darcey then turned to me. "And you—come here and give this gal a hug. Why you been gone so long, you?"

Darcey and I embraced, and I took in the sweet aroma of her being and felt the warmth that radiated from this dear woman. After a bit she pushed me back to arm's length and gave me a searching look.

"I've been away for a while, Miss Darcey. But it *has* been too long at that," I said with sincerity.

Darcey glanced at Patricia and then back to me. She held my eye for a second before casting her head back in a small jerk that indicated *back there*.

"She's waiting for you," she said as she released my arms. "Got up early this morning and put on her finest clothes. She was all dressed and made up when I brought in her breakfast. And I said, 'This ain't Sunday. Why you all done up?' And she said, 'My man is coming to visit me today. And I don't want to look like somethin' the cat dragged in when he gets here.'"

I shook my head in amazement, while Patricia shot me a puzzled look. Before I could reply, Darcey picked up the cooler I had set on the porch and took Patricia by the arm.

"Two dozen crabs 'bout enough for you this time?" she asked as she turned toward the door, taking Patricia with her.

"Yes," I replied. "That should just about do it."

"Then you better go on in and see her before she commences to throw a hissy fit," she said as she went inside.

Patricia looked over her shoulder as she was pulled along. I nodded to her and smiled in encouragement as Darcey said to Patricia, "You come with me, pretty lady, and I'll teach you some secrets that you'll never regret the knowin' of."

I followed the women into the house. We entered by way of the living room. Darcey and Patricia disappeared off to the right, toward the kitchen, but I moved through the front room, to a small hallway, and then stopped at a beaded curtain that served as the door of a back room. The pattern on the beads was of a beautiful dark-haired woman holding a parrot on her wrist. As I reached my hand forward to part the curtain, a small voice called from inside.

"I hope you brought me a present this time. I can't stand it when my lovers don't bring me a present. Makes me mad as hell when they don't bring me a present."

I shook my head and smiled, and then, pushing through the beads, entered the room. It was dim inside, the room lit only by the faint light of a single kerosene lamp that sat on a table in the far corner of the room. It was also very warm, with an almost tropical feeling, though there was no fire in the fireplace, nor a heater of any kind in the room. And then, there was the faint but delicious scent of exotic spices that seemed to emanate from the small figure sitting, almost swallowed, in a large, old-fashioned overstuffed chair.

Even in repose, she had the regal bearing of a queen mother. As tiny as a small child, she carried her head held high and her chin lifted in a way that says to the world, "I know who *I* am, and the *someone* I am is very special indeed."

As I approached, she held out her hands for me to take in mine. And as I did, I knelt at the side of her chair and kissed her on both cheeks. Lowering myself to the chair near hers, we looked at one another in silence for some moments.

Miss Cyriah Chambers is a phenomenon of nature.

No one knows her age for sure—except herself, and she doesn't tell. But she is the mother of Darcey's husband, Noah, and Noah, the middle child of twelve, and the oldest still living, is in his mideighties.

Her body is as frail as thin ice, but her voice is still vibrant and alluring. Her mind remains unclouded by the years, and her eyes are those of a girl just entering the beauty of young womanhood. She held me now with those clear, liquid, deep brown eyes, and I felt myself being drawn into them, where I was held suspended, as though I were being turned over and around and examined in great detail. Then I felt myself released, ever so slightly, and sat back in the chair to await her words.

"I'm glad you've come to visit this old woman," she said in her young girl's voice. "I've been seeing you in my mind and was worried. You've been in some bad, ugly places— dry and dusty places—and you have dealt with wicked men."

How she could possibly know this is something I no longer even dwell on. It is simply a fact that Miss Cyriah *sees things*. She sees and knows matters that are hidden from the rest of us. And more than that, she sees into the hidden crevices of others—those places we all have and that we protect from open view, hoping to keep those places and their contents a secret, sometimes even from ourselves.

"You've taken human life," she continued, "but you doubt the wisdom of some of your actions, and your spirit is bruised and feels battered and sore."

I looked into her eyes and nodded. "That is true, Miss Cyriah. Though I've vowed to myself that I would never again inflict harm on others, it seems I always break that promise."

Cyriah sat very still for a moment, the only movement being the ever so slight rise and fall of her chest as the breath of her body ebbed and flowed, as light as the breathing of a small bird.

"There is a balance to all things, my son," she said in a voice that seemed to come from far away. "What we call a harmful occurrence is sometimes the only act that provides a cure. To lance a boil is painful, but the effect is beneficial. It's what lets the poison escape the body so that healing can take place. When you lance the boil of human malevolence, that, too, is painful, but it is also a positive act. The real harm would be to act, even when the cause is a good one, but not to feel regret. For that is the mark of a calloused soul, and therein lies the way of destruction. For this reason you should rejoice in your pain; it is the sign of a healthy life."

I lowered my head and thought of her words, and of the other times I had sought her counsel.

"It may all be as you say, but I wish I could avoid these—these—encounters that seem to lead inevitably to a violent end," I responded. "I wish it were otherwise."

Cyriah smiled and then laughed in the clear ringing tones of a small bell.

"We each one of us live inside a realm we selected before we ever arrived on this Earth. And every one of us has made a sacred agreement with the Master Spirit to play our own little part—our part and nobody else's. Whatever we do with this life and *in* this life *is* our destiny. And that destiny can never be changed. That's why it would be impossible that I could ever live your life, nor could you live the life of anybody else.

"We are fixed in a plane of existence that we alone inhabit. You could no more change who you are and what you do than you could turn yourself into a turtle or a fish. You are here for a specific reason, Kennesaw Tanner, and you must fulfill that reason, whether you want to or not."

I contemplated the meaning of her words. *It's true,* I thought, *we all seem to be established in our own immutable orbits. But I'm . . .*

It was as though I had spoken my thoughts aloud, for Cyriah smiled and nodded in agreement.

"That's right, we all spin in our own true track, but there's more to it than just that," she said. "Each one of us here on this Earth is like a single word on an individual page in a huge book. If all you give the book is just a quick look, all them words and pages seem like they be the same. But each one of them pages say something different from all the others in the book. When you take them pages and bind them altogether they add up to make that one book. But if only *one* of them words from a page is missing, then the book ain't complete. That's why each of us has to be here, and that's why we all be different. Otherwise parts would be missing, and the *world* wouldn't be complete."

I nodded my comprehension, but it was only partial.

"I understand what you say, and it makes sense. But I've never felt that I belong to one place or the other. I'm always seeking something, but what, I don't know. I just know that I'm never satisfied and that I'm never at peace."

Cyriah pointed a finger at me.

"They are exceptions to what I just said, and *you*, dear child, are one of them. *You* don't belong to just any one page of the book. You are the line that goes from page to page, connecting many lives, one to the other. You touch peoples across all the separations of race, and wealth, and power, and position, and you don't see no difference in the worth of whatever person you meet, no matter who they might be. It is a rough and rocky path you're on, one that mighty few of us can follow, but it is yours to tread and yours alone."

"But will I ever find the peace—the relief from things

I've done in the past—from the harm I've done to others?"
I asked.

"No," she said, shaking her head side to side. "Not completely. But the things you do for those in need—for those folks who need your strength, will be a salve to the aches that pain your soul."

We were quiet a few moments as I considered these thoughts. Then Cyriah spoke again.

"But beware, my son. Where you go next is a place of profound evil. Your search will bring you to a realm of hidden foulness. The evil you go against will know you—even now, it knows that you are coming to confront it. It will hide its face and shape from you and strive to make itself seem sweet and innocent. You will not recognize it at all times, for it is clever and has the cunning of the serpent, and it will seek to destroy you."

Cyriah reached into a pocket of her dress and motioned me to come closer. I knelt at the edge of her chair so that we were face-to-face.

"Lean here toward me," she said.

I inclined my head, and as I did so, she reached up and placed a necklace around my neck. The cord against my skin was soft and comforting, and a small pendant of some sort hung from the necklace. I put my hand on the pendant and realized that it was a cloth pouch. Inside the pouch I could feel several items. One of them, when I rolled it between my fingers, felt like a small coin—a penny, or perhaps a dime. Of the other items inside the small bag, I could not be sure.

Cyriah put her hands on each side of my face and, pulling me closer, kissed me softly; first on the forehead and then once on each eye. At each kiss I felt a warm tremor pulse through my body, and I felt lighter, yet somehow, stronger. She then sat back in her chair but continued to hold me by the right hand.

"That necklace you wear will protect you. I made it with my own hands from things I been saving just for a time of special danger. It has great powers, but you must wear it at all times, and you must never let no one else touch it."

I put the fingers of my left hand on the pouch and then felt the cord. It was made of braided hair. Again, Cyriah read my mind.

"Horsehair," she said. "For strength, speed, and a powerful heart. That little bag hanging from it holds the tricks that fools the evil ones—so they can't get a grip on you, nor penetrate your soul."

I nodded. *A trick bag. In the protective arsenal of a hoodoo root doctor, it is the most powerful amulet of them all.*

"Miss Cyriah, I don't know what to . . ." I began, but she quickly interrupted me.

"That girl *was* killed, never you doubt it. She was killed and flung out like trash. But you and that little friend of yours was meant to find her body. You was meant to bring her home, but you was also meant to bring destruction to the evil that took her life. They is others out there, too, Kennesaw, other peoples that is in danger and needs your help. Go help them, son. Go help them, before it is too late."

Cyriah gave my hand a firm squeeze and shook it with a surprisingly strong grip as she said those last words. When she released my hand, I sat back and, looking deeply into her eyes, suddenly found that the world was very quiet. Nothing moved. My body seemed heavy, and the room became very dark. *What was happening? Has the lamp burned dim?*

It then felt as though my spirit was falling within me, falling and yet not falling, but fluttering like a leaf on a capricious breeze. Floating instead, floating until it came to a place of weightless suspension. Then time stuttered, and held its breath, and I was alone in a dark and quiet place. It was a comforting place and I wanted to stay there for a while and rest.

But then I heard Cyriah's words ringing in my mind like a pure echo: *Go help them, before it is too late.*

I took a breath. The room became bright again, and I found Cyriah observing me with a faint smile on her face. I shuddered slightly, and time began again.

"Now what did you bring me for a present this time?" she asked with a coquettish toss of her head.

I stood and reached into my pocket for the small package I had brought with me. Taking the velvet bag in both hands I placed it in Cyriah's lap. She looked at it with curious delight, and then, with surprisingly nimble fingers, she pulled open the snap that held the pouch closed. Reaching inside, she brought forth the bracelet that was hidden within and held it up to view. Turning it over and over in her hand, the bracelet caught the golden glow of the lamp and seemed to throw off subtle sparks of light and a warmth of its own.

"Put it on me," she said as she handed me the bracelet and lifted her left hand.

"It is made of turquoise and lapis lazuli. Made by a great race of people who live in the vast deserts of North Africa. I am told it is very old, and was once worn by a princess," I said as I fastened the clasp on her tiny wrist.

Cyriah held out her arm and contemplated the bracelet closely, a smile of pleasure spreading across her face. She placed her other hand over the bracelet and held it there for a moment.

"The stones are warm," she said in a wondering tone of voice. "They have life and power, and they carry love."

Then she looked up at me with glistening eyes.

"I think the people who made this bracelet are great friends of yours. And I think you feel great reassurance and belonging when you are with them. This is a wondrous present. And I will always wear it here, on my left wrist, the side nearest my heart."

I bowed my head in response.

"Cyriah, thank you for accepting my gift—and thank you for this," I said, touching the necklace I wore.

She sat back in her chair, inclined her head to one side and laughed a deep, clear laugh.

"Now you go on and get out of here, boy. That girl of yours is gonna get jealous before too much longer, what with you spending all this time in here with another woman."

"She's with Darcey," I said as I stood.

"An' that don't make it one bit better," she replied. "Now give me a kiss, and you clear on outta here."

I put a hand on the arm of her chair and leaned over. Cyriah lifted her face to mine, placed a hand lightly on the side of my face, and kissed me on the lips. It was the comforting warm kiss of a mother for a child. When the kiss ended I pulled away slightly to look closely into her face.

She held my eyes with hers for several seconds, her brow knit in concentration, and I felt her looking deeply, searching for something, as though she were worried. Then her face relaxed, as though she recognized whatever it was she had sought.

Patting me gently on the face she said, "Come see me again, chile, when this is all over."

I put my hand over hers and gave it a slight squeeze.

"I will," I said as I started to leave.

Then, turning, I stepped to the door and parted the beads of the curtain. But pausing a second to glance over my shoulder, I saw Miss Cyriah, with her hand lifted in front of her face, turning her wrist back and forth so as to better study the magical blue stones that gathered and concentrated within themselves the subtle light of the room.

I stepped through the curtain and, behind me, heard the faint click of the beads as they swayed and fell into place once again. Then I went to look for Patricia.

CHAPTER 5

THE AIR ABOVE THE SAND ROAD WAS pleasantly warm as Patricia and I walked back to the dock. The small lives in the forest hummed with contentment as we passed by, birds flitted from tree limb to tree limb, and lizards scurried across the track in front of us. We chatted sparingly as we ambled, each of us enjoying the tranquility of the afternoon and thinking of the things we had experienced that day.

Parker was still at the dock when we arrived, and he helped us get under way. He protested slightly, just enough for the sake of politeness, when I slipped him a few bills for watching over *Miss Rosalie* during our absence. Then, pulling away from the dock, I turned around in the broad channel and headed us back to the Georgia side of the Savannah River.

"The tide is falling and will soon be at low ebb," I said to Patricia, who stood beside me in the pilothouse, intently watching the shoreline of Daufuskie as it slid steadily by. "And I don't want to try the channel back the way we came, not at low water. What say we take the Intracoastal back to my dock and I'll drive you to your car on Lazaretto."

"You're the captain," she said as a passing wedge of pelicans winging across our front caught our eyes. "How long will it take us to get back?" she asked.

I checked our position relative to the island. "About an hour and a half," I replied. "Just long enough for you to catch a nap if you like."

Patricia gave me a glance. "Now that, Tanner, is another great idea you've had today. Wake me when we get close to home."

"I'll ring the phone in the cabin," I said. "Have a good snooze. There's nothing like a nap on the boat."

Patricia gave me a smile and, leaving the pilothouse, disappeared into the cabin.

The sun was just at the top of the live oaks on the bluff behind the docks when I eased *Miss Rosalie* to rest. The tide was dead low and the wind was slack, so I had no problem tying her down by myself. I had let Patricia sleep while I got us docked, but now it was time to call her back to the land of the living. I had just snugged down the spring line and turned to go to the cabin when Patricia emerged from below with a wine bottle in one hand and a large tray balanced in the other.

She smiled when she saw me and called, "How 'bout a little help here; I've got my hands full."

I hopped over and took the tray from her hand. It carried a large platter of deviled crabs, oven-roasted potatoes, along with plates and silverware. The aroma of the food made my mouth water with anticipation.

"Follow me," I said.

I led the way to the aft deck where I set the platter on the small table that was just in front of the curve of the stern seats. Patricia set down the bottle and then pulled two wineglasses from the breast pockets of her shirt, followed by a corkscrew she fished out of a back pocket of her jeans. I opened and poured the wine while Patricia arranged the table.

I handed Patricia a glass, presented mine, and made a small toast.

"To an excellent day," I said as we clinked our glasses together.

"Yes, it was," Patricia replied over the top of her glass.

We sat down to enjoy the meal.

"You *are* a surprising girl, aren't you," I said as I dug into one of the crabs. "And I thought I was going to surprise you by fixing dinner."

"Darcey coached me through making the crabs you bought, and then told me just how to cook them. When you told me how long the trip back was going to take, I knew I had just enough time," she replied.

Patricia dug her fork into the open shell and lifted it to her mouth.

"Well, get ready for an experience," I said. "After this you'll never eat another crab unless it comes from Miss Darcey.

We both took a bite at the same time. Patricia had her eyes cast to the side in contemplation as she chewed. Then, as she looked up again she had a smile of near ecstasy on her face.

"My God," she murmured before quickly digging out another forkful and taking a second bite. "I've never tasted anything like this. It's so delicate and yet so rich."

"It's Miss Darcey's secret recipe, but as you saw in her

kitchen, she makes hers of freshly caught crab and spices. The ones you buy in the restaurants and stores are by and large bread stuffing, with little more than a rumor of crab in them," I said, before taking a second bite myself.

We then settled into the meal and held off with the conversation until we had finished. I poured Patricia another glass of wine and then topped off my own glass. We both sipped and then sat back in satisfaction.

I lifted my glass in salute. "Not too shabby, eh?"

Patricia lifted hers in acknowledgment and took a sip.

"What a fabulous day, Tanner. Do you always live like this?" she asked as she lowered the glass from her lips.

"Yeah," I replied. "This is pretty much my normal routine, broken only by the demands imposed by a life of independent poverty."

"Well, I'd like to be included in some of your other excursions now and then; that is, if you wouldn't mind my company," she said in a soft voice.

As we looked at one another I felt an old stirring inside me and realized that I'd like to get to know the tall woman sitting across the table from me.

"I'd like that, too, Patricia," I replied at last. She gave me a warm smile at those words.

"Good," was her reply.

We sat quietly for a few moments before Patricia stood up and announced, "Come on, let's get this stuff cleaned up before I have to leave."

We gathered up the used plates, silverware, and glasses and made our way to the galley. For once, it was a pleasure to do the dishes. With that chore finished we hiked up the ramp to the parking lot beneath the trees. The sun cast long shadows across the ground as we climbed into my old Bronco and I cranked the engine. We then wheeled out to the street and soon were on Highway 80 headed east toward Tybee Island.

We had just crossed the bridge over Bull River when Patricia put her back against the door and turned to look at me.

"Kennesaw, I want to be straight with you about something," she said, in a serious voice.

I glanced over and saw a solemn look on her face.

"Well, please do," I said. "I just hope you're not going to tell me that you're really a man, or that you're married with five kids."

A smile touched the corners of her lips before she went on, "No, nothing like that. But I do want you to know that I ran your record after finding the girl's body."

"Uh-huh," I replied. "Anything I should worry about? Did you find out I'm on a terrorist watch list, or perhaps that I'm a member of a secret organization—like the Masons, or the Rotarians, or something like that?"

"I'm sure you knew that I'd have to dig into your background," she responded. "It's a pretty interesting one, at that."

I looked over again and kept my expression noncommittal. "Anything that worries you?" I asked.

She brushed a lock of hair from her forehead. I'd noticed already that this was a tic of hers when she became serious.

"Not worried, just curious," she replied.

"Is this a professional curiosity, Patricia, or is it personal?" I asked.

"It's profession . . . well, I mean, it's more like both. But it leans to the personal." She hesitated a second, and then added, "I'd like to get to know you, Tanner. I'd like to know you better."

I glanced over again and saw a slight smile on her lips and a soft look in her eyes. My first inclination was to clam up or pitch her a curve ball. But glancing over again, I decided to play it straight, because I realized I wanted to know her better also.

"Okay," I said. "Question away, Detective."

Patricia took a breath and began, "You had a military career but then suddenly got out of the army, just a few years before you were eligible to retire—that's pretty unusual in itself. It also seems that your military records went blank for the last half of your service career. You just disappeared for a period of nine—almost ten—years, and then pop up again only to be discharged. After that, for the next several years the State Department, at the request of the FBI, sends queries to a number of its embassies asking of your whereabouts in various countries. Then, nothing for almost a year, after which you show up here in Savannah and surface when you found that girl's body—at which point, you and I meet."

"That's a pretty thorough background check," I replied. "Now let me fill in some of the blanks for you. For those years that my military record develops amnesia, I was in an organization that doesn't officially exist. And since it doesn't exist, neither do its members." I glanced over again to see if she got my meaning. She nodded her comprehension.

"Toward the end of my years in that outfit, I came across evidence of severely irregular activity being conducted by certain cells within the organization. When I reported this activity to the chain of command I was told to drop the matter entirely. When I pursued it I was threatened with retaliation if I didn't shut up. Being a hardhead, I ignored the warning, brought the matter to the attention of our senior commander—a three-star general—and for my efforts, was promptly accused of disloyalty, excommunicated from the command, and discharged for the good of the service. Within months of my departure, the wrongdoing I had spoken up about hit the news like a clap of thunder."

I looked over at Patricia and saw that she was listening intently.

"Prisoner torture," she breathed. "Were you the one who broke it to the news services?"

I shook my head. "To my discredit, no. I should have, but I knew it would come out eventually, and I also knew that it would be covered up. The military did what it always does—find the lowest-ranking people you can and dump the blame all on them. A few privates and sergeants go to Leavenworth, the higher-ups are cleared, and everything is back to normal again."

Patricia stared at me. "Jesus," she said. "And afterward?"

"After I got out I hung out my shingle as a freelance operative. Bodyguard, private security, military training, asset recovery, anything I could to make a living. Then I found a niche that suited me. After a while, I decided to come back to the States to take care of a few things I needed to address and then move on again. But I wound up here, liked it, and thought I'd stay around for a while. And here we are," I concluded.

"So what is it that you do now, Kennesaw? What is that niche you found?" Patricia asked.

I looked over. "I help people, Patricia. I find things and people—things and people who, for one reason or another, have gone missing. And when I find them, I charge a hefty fee for their safe return. I am discreet, and thorough, and my clients are happy with the results."

"And this recent absence of yours?"

"Was a job for a client," I replied.

"Successful?" she asked.

I thought about it for a few seconds before responding, "Ultimately, yes. It was."

We were at the turnoff to Lazaretto Island. I slowed down, then pulled off the pavement and onto the sand road that led the short distance down to the few buildings at the water's edge. I parked in an oyster shell lot next to Patricia's car and switched off the engine. Turning in my seat, I faced the woman who was eyeing me with such solemnity.

"Clear up some of your questions?" I asked.

She nodded her head and a smile appeared on her face.

"Yeah, enough for now. But the ones in the future will probably be much more personal in nature."

"I look forward to that," I said. "And next time, I just may have a few for you, too."

"I'd like that," she replied in a husky voice.

I reached across to open her door. When I leaned over she lifted her face to mine. Our lips found each other as we enfolded in an embrace.

At length I sat back, and the smile on my face must have mirrored the one I saw on hers.

"It's been a good day, Patricia Latham."

"It's been a really good day, Kennesaw Tanner."

"Call you this week?" I asked.

"You'd better."

I pushed her door open, then climbed out and came around as she got into her car. I handed her a small box.

"Miss Darcey's crabs," I said. "Put them in the freezer, and they'll be perfect when you want them next."

"You shouldn't . . ." she started to protest.

"Don't worry, I kept plenty for myself. Those are for you," I told her.

"Okay, Tanner," she said. "See ya around."

I closed her door. "You bet, Detective."

She cranked the engine, gave me a last smile, and then

pulled away. I waved when I saw her glance up in her mirror. She lifted a hand in return, then pulled onto the pavement and headed for Tybee.

I climbed into my truck, and as the light faded in the west, made my way back to *Miss Rosalie*.

CHAPTER 6

THE NEXT DAY WAS SUNDAY, AND I made a perfectly lazy day of it. I slept late that morning and then went to the Waffle House where I treated myself to a cholesterol-laden, artery-hardening, double-barrel twelve-gauge Southern breakfast. Then, I parked myself on the aft deck of *Miss Rosalie* with a pot of English tea at hand and read every last word of both the *Savannah Morning News* and the *Atlanta Journal-Constitution*.

Afterward I burned a few hours puttering around the boat, tidying up a number of things and inventing some chores. It's not hard to do, because there is always something that requires attention on a boat. And better to attend to things when they are still minuscule than to risk a failure when the seas are running thirty feet high and the situation is about to become critical.

Looking around the deck with the satisfaction that all was right on board, I locked up and went to see if I could find Danny Ray. There was a question that had occurred to me, and I needed to hear what he had to say.

I drove east on Highway 80 until, after crossing the Wilmington River Bridge, the road changes its name to Victory Drive. A few blocks later, in the area known as Thunderbolt, I turned onto Skidaway and began looking for the small street that was my objective. This is an old neighborhood of small frame houses and cottages. The dwellings and the streets are shaded by tall palmettos and live oaks, the trees festooned with the long gray beards of Spanish moss.

I found the place I was looking for and turned in to the sand drive that led around back to Danny Ray's abode. Danny Ray lives in a travel trailer set in the back of an auto repair shop owned by one of his relatives—a brother-in-law, I think. In exchange for rent-free space, Danny keeps an eye on things after business hours. As I parked next to Danny's old pickup I saw him peek warily around the corner of the trailer. But when he saw who it was, a grin appeared on his face, and he came around to greet me.

"K-K-K-Kennesaw," he stammered as he stuck out a hand in welcome.

"Danny Ray, how you doing, my friend?" I asked as we shook hands.

"C-c-c-come around back," he said as he led the way behind the trailer.

I was a step behind my friend when we turned the corner, and I don't think I could have been more surprised at the sight that presented itself. It seemed as though we had stepped into a photo shoot for a *Southern Living* magazine spread of the perfect small garden.

A wooden deck at the back door of the trailer was shaded by an arbor over which grew a tangled mass of muscadine grapevines. From a low stone cliff in a corner of the garden, a silvery rivulet of water gurgled and splashed its way to a fern-shaded pond, where brightly colored fish finned lazily beneath blossoming lily pads.

A profusion of flowers and ornamental shrubs grew in large pots and in rock-lined flower beds. A sandstone path winding about in a serpentine fashion managed to touch every part of the luxurious garden. The entire area was bordered on all sides by small palms, bananas, and other exotic plants.

A green steel glider and two matching chairs—the kind of garden furniture so popular in the 1950s and in vogue once again—were tastefully arranged near the cascade and the pond. A flat-topped black limestone rock that must have weighed a ton served as a table.

Covering the entire garden in a roof of green and gray were the outstretched limbs and leaves of one of the most massive and ancient live oak trees I've ever seen. It was an oasis of delightful tranquility, planted in the most unexpected of places.

When I turned to Danny Ray, I found him standing nearby, a shy smile on his face as he looked at me from beneath the low pulled brim of his Atlanta Braves cap.

"Danny Ray," I said in wonder, "this is magnificent. You created this? You did this yourself?"

Danny Ray nodded his head twice to say yes.

"I've never seen its like before. You should do this as a business," I continued.

Danny Ray shook his head. "O-o-only for friends."

I looked around and nodded in agreement. I knew what he meant. This was something too personal for commerce. It was like a beautiful painting or a sculpture. Only this was a living thing; it was as perfect in its own way as is the beauty of a small child.

I looked at Danny Ray in admiration and thought, not for the first time, what a surprising human being he was.

Danny Ray, pointing to the chairs, said, "H-h-have a seat."

As Danny went to the trailer and ducked inside, I settled into the chair nearest the stream, where I could best hear the lilting song of running water, and made myself comfortable. Danny Ray returned a few seconds later with a bucket of ice that held several bottles of beer, along with a bowl filled with fresh-roasted peanuts.

Danny Ray opened a couple of bottles, passed one over to me, and then leaned over to present his bottle in salutation. We clinked bottles and each took a long pull on the icy brew. I scooped up a handful of peanuts and began to pop open the shells and toss the nuts into my mouth.

Probably nothing goes better together than cold beer and fresh-roasted Georgia peanuts, I thought as I wiped the shell fragments off my hands on the legs of my jeans. I took another swig of beer before speaking.

"Danny Ray, I've been wondering something, and I wanted to ask you a question."

Danny set his bottle on the rock table and gave me a nod. "Th-th-thought so. Wh-what is it?"

"How did Joree find you? Did you know her before y'all came to see me the other night?"

Danny Ray was still and looked at me quietly for a few seconds before replying.

"She's a fr-fr-fr-friend of family. My m-m-mother comes from the same place up th-th-there." Danny pointed north, toward Effingham County, where Joree lived, "P-P-P-Panther Creek."

"Did you know her yourself, her or the girl?" I asked.

He shook his head. "N-n-n-no. Just h-h-h-heard about them."

"Uh-huh," I responded, and then thought for a few seconds before asking, "Danny Ray, can you come up with any reason why Joree would think her daughter was killed? Did she say anything to you when you drove her back to her car?"

Danny Ray cast his eyes downward and after a bit he shook his head slowly side to side before looking up again.

"Th-the g-g-girl was wild. B-b-b-boy crazy—th-they say." He bit his lower lip and looked down again.

I contemplated that response and its significance before asking a last question, or rather, posing a remark.

"So you heard, through some of your family, that the mother was upset, saying that her daughter had been killed and no one would help, and you brought her to me."

Danny Ray looked at me steadily before saying, "I knew—you would talk to her."

It was the clearest sentence I'd ever heard him speak.

I let this sink in before asking, "And what do you think, Danny Ray? What do you think happened to Tonya Causey?"

Danny Ray lifted his bottle and took a long swallow of beer before replying, with a sympathetic shake of his head, "I th-th-think she w-w-was in trouble."

"Yeah, well, it's a sad business, no matter what, isn't it?" I said.

Danny Ray nodded his head in agreement. I stood to go, and Danny Ray got to his feet as well.

"Well, thanks, amigo, you've been helpful," I said as I turned to follow the flower-edged pathway back to my truck.

Danny Ray walked with me and waited as I got in and closed the door. Just as I cranked the engine he stepped near and put his hands on the window ledge. His eyes, beneath the brim of his cap, shifted back and forth across my face several times before he said, "B-b-be careful, u-u-up there, K-K-Kennesaw. Panther Creek—it-it's a b-bad place."

"I will, partner. I'll see you soon—and thanks for sharing your garden with me; it's beautiful."

Danny Ray stepped back as I shifted into reverse and pulled out of the drive. I glanced over as I started away and saw my friend wave a quick good-bye. I lifted a hand in return.

It was midafternoon when I returned to my home dock. I parked my truck under the trees at the top of the lot, and as I ambled down the boardwalk toward the docks I realized that it was well past lunchtime, and in spite of the beer and peanuts, I was hungry. Changing direction slightly, I headed to the far end of the docks where Captain Flynt's Bucket o' Blood bar and restaurant sat perched over the waterfront on its oyster- and barnacle-covered pilings.

The place was wearing its normal Sunday afternoon quiet attitude when I walked in. A couple of wayward tourists held down one corner of the bar, while Big Tee, the bartender, watched Alabama beating up on some other college team on the television. As I strolled past the bar I lifted a hand in greeting.

"Tyrone," I said as Tee looked up. I pointed to the outside deck. "I'll be out there."

"Yah," Big Tee replied, in his normal monosyllable, as he reached into the icebox to pluck out a bottle of beer. In one clean motion, he sent it sliding to the end of the bar, where I intercepted it without breaking stride and kept on walking.

There were a half dozen customers scattered around the deck but with very little conversation to be heard out there. Mostly, people were quietly nursing their drinks and gazing out across the water, soaking up the peaceful ambience as though saving it for a rainy day. Over in a sunny corner I spied my friend Bob Martin. Bob waved me over.

"Hey, young hero," he said as he pushed out a chair with his foot. "Grab a seat and tell me what's the good word."

I sat and looked around. It was unnaturally quiet, and then I realized why.

"Where's Fran?" I asked.

My friends Bob and Fran Martin are a single item. I've never seen one without the other one somewhere nearby. And Fran is such an exuberant personality that to be on the same map sheet with her is to know where she is. It's not that she's loud, it's just that she's a one-woman festive occasion, all by herself.

Bob gave me a grin in reply. "The silence *is* deafening, isn't it?"

I nodded. "Yeah, thunderous."

"She and one of her sisters are visiting an old maid aunt up in Statesboro. The old gal is the last living connection to their parents, so they keep an eye on her," Bob explained.

I looked closely at Bob. He had led a rough life and it was catching up with him. The Korean War had punched some holes in his hide, and Vietnam and Agent Orange had cost him a lung. As thin as a pool cue, Bob walked with a cane, and now that the remaining lung was beginning to decline, he carried an oxygen bottle that fed the clear plastic tube looped across his face and beneath his nostrils. But his voice, with its rich Low Country accent, was strong and vibrant, and his sky blue eyes still sparkled beneath the brim of an old jungle hat.

Bob lifted his glass and, before taking a drink, looked at me slyly over the rim.

"Rumor out on Tybee is that you and a certain po-leece woman are practically engaged," he said with a grin. "Some say it's well beyond that, and that y'all are about to tie the knot."

"Fran, huh?" I replied.

Bob lowered his glass. "Yeah, Fran. One of her spies said she saw y'all out on Lazaretto. Said you couldn't have slid a playing card between the two of you. And well—if Fran knows something, or thinks she does, the tide won't change again before the whole island knows it, too. And as you are probably well aware of by now, *you*, my boy, are one of her favorite topics. You and your love life, that is, 'or lack thereof,' as she puts it."

I took a contemplative pull on my beer before responding, "Women just hate to see an unattached man going happily about his business and enjoying the solitary life, don't they?"

Bob snorted a short laugh. "There is nothing they hate worse than the idea of a single man. I don't know why it riles women the way it does. It can't be explained, it's just one of those facts of female nature."

"Well, Patricia and I are just . . ."

Bob held up a hand in the universal signal of *Stop*. "Whoa, partner, you don't have to explain yourself to me. I'm just filling you in before Fran water boards you. But I will tell you this: Patricia Latham is a remarkable young woman. There's not a finer girl on Tybee Island, or in Savannah, for that matter."

"I think I may find myself in agreement with you there, Bob," I replied.

At that moment Big Tee arrived with a large platter and began to set the table for us. There was boiled shrimp, fried speckled trout, and roast oysters, along with hush puppies, coleslaw, and a large green salad.

When Tyrone had finished, he stood back with folded arms and looked at the table with professional satisfaction, before glaring and pointing a finger of accusation at Bob.

"Eat, Bob. You need to eat this food. You're too damn skinny. Make him eat, Kennesaw. He don't eat enough," he said, casting an accusatory glance in my direction as though I were the source of the problem.

This was a surprise. I'd never heard Tyrone speak that many words all at one time. That amount of speech would usually be about a week's worth for the big man watching Bob with a look of concern on his rugged ebony face.

"Leave it to me, Tyrone. I won't let him up from the table until he cleans his plate," I said with conviction, because I, too, was bothered by how thin our friend had become.

"Good," Big Tee said in his deep bass rumble of a voice.

But as Tyrone turned to go, he hesitated, and then came back to the table, where he filled Bob's plate with something from every dish. He then nodded his head curtly, as though to say, "There, take that," before returning to his post at the bar.

Bob watched Tyrone until he disappeared back inside, then he stared at the plate before lifting his eyes to me.

"Having that man for a friend"—Bob inclined his head toward the direction of the bar—"is like having a two-hundred-forty-pound, black Jewish mother. I'm surprised he didn't come out here with a bowl of chicken soup."

Bob looked at the spread of food on the table and shook his head as though he were contemplating a distasteful task.

"If it's chicken soup you want, I'll go in and tell him," I said as I peeled a shrimp.

Bob picked up a fork and began to pick tentatively at the salad. "No, this will do," he said. "Don't give him any more ideas."

The seafood came fresh off the boat from local waters and could not have been more delicious. I dug in with gusto, and it must have appealed to Bob's palate also, because my friend began to eat with the semblance of an appetite, and before long, I even saw a smile appear on his face. All in all, we did the meal the justice it deserved, and it was good to see Bob enjoy the food.

I gave Tyrone the high sign to let him know it had gone

well when I saw him eyeing us from the doorway to the bar. He ducked back inside and returned to our table with fresh drinks. Dropping the drinks in front of us, he bent down to clear the table.

Picking up Bob's empty plate, he growled, "That's good, Bob. I didn't want to get rough with you 'bout this."

Bob stared steadily at the big man's face until I saw Tyrone make eye contact with the old veteran.

"*Gracias, compañero,*" Bob told his friend in a low voice.

"*No hay de qué,*" replied Big Tee, a fleeting smile illuminating his face for a split second, before his habitual scowl fell back into place once again.

The wide platter, balanced on Tyrone's massive hand as he sauntered away with the grace of a ballroom dancer, looked like a coffee saucer would have on mine.

Bob leaned back in his chair. "I think I could get used to eating again if it was always this good," he said with a contented sigh.

Fran had told me that Bob's appetite was waning and that she was becoming worried about him, as nothing seemed to appeal to his taste. But it looked like Big Tee's pointed concern had done the trick this time. I made a mental note to call Fran and let her know.

"I'm glad," I replied. "Must be the setting and the company this afternoon."

Bob lifted his drink. "Maybe so," he said and took a long swallow.

We sat in comfortable silence for a while before I posed a question. Bob knows the history and geography of the Low Country of Georgia and South Carolina as well as any local university professor. I was hoping he could help me out.

"Bob, you ever heard of—do you know anything about—a place called Panther Creek?" I asked.

Bob raised his eyebrows in surprise before lifting his glass for another drink. After a few seconds' reflection he spoke.

"It's up in Effingham County," he replied. "Why do you ask?"

"It's where that girl—Tonya Causey—was from. The girl Danny Ray and I found in the marsh."

"Uh-huh," he replied. "But still—why do you ask?"

"Her mama came to see me. Asked if I'd look into what happened to her daughter. See if there was something there that the police had missed. She didn't believe the girl had taken her own life."

Bob nodded his head as he listened to my reply. I could see his mind working before he spoke again.

"Up in those mountains you come from, are there any places—small, remote places—where, if you don't live there, it's just best to stay out of?"

I thought, and two names immediately came to mind: Esom Hill and Booger Hollow. Tightly knit settlements, populated by just a few interrelated families, where the principal outlook on life is defined by suspicion of outsiders and a disdain for the rules of society.

"Yeah," I replied with a nod of the head, "I know a few places like that."

"Well, that's what Panther Creek is: a place where nothing good ever happens, and nothing, or nobody, good ever comes from," he said in a level voice, his eyes large behind the lenses of his glasses.

I let Bob's words settle in my mind as I reflected on the rambling litany of Joree Causey's life as she had related it to me the other night: a life infected by poverty, disappointment, and despair. And I also recalled what Cyriah had said, about how we all live on a different page of life, and that those of us on a certain page can almost never get off and move to another page.

I asked myself, *Is that why things, generation after generation, seem never to change for people, regardless of where they're planted in life? Does that explain the rut that most lives appear to be locked into? Is that why the poor, no matter what they do or how they strive, never seem to get ahead? And is that also why the wealthy and powerful, no matter how stupid, or venal, or criminal some of them may be, almost never slip from their positions of privilege?*

Bob spoke again and broke my reverie. "If you want my advice, Kennesaw—unsolicited though it is—drop the whole thing. Tell the woman the police know what they are doing, and leave it alone. If that girl did kill herself, it's sad enough. And if someone pushed her off the bridge, it's even worse. But no matter what the reason, that girl had gotten herself into something mighty ugly. And if you fool with it, some of it's liable to get on you, too."

I took a pull on my beer before setting the bottle on the table and responding to my friend's words of concern.

"I hear you, Bob. And that's good advice."

"But you won't be taking it, will you?" he asked.

I shook my head. "No, I guess not. I promised the mother I'd look into it."

Bob took a deep breath and slowly blew it out as he looked across the water and off into the distance. Looking back at me again after a few seconds, he had a wry smile on his face.

"Didn't think so," he said, shaking his head. "Sheriff up there is the son of an old schoolmate of mine. Want me to call him and say you'll be dropping by to see him sometime soon? His name is Anson Zimmer. I've never met him, but I hear he's a good man."

"I'd appreciate that, Bob," I replied.

"Okay," he responded. "Just do me one favor. Stay out of there after sundown. Even the local cops don't patrol the back roads after dark. And strangers have been known to get lost in those swamps."

"I'll do what I can, Bob. But I'm no more afraid of the dark, or what's in it, than you are. And you might not know it to look at me, but I'm a pretty good navigator."

"I guess I *am* starting to sound like an old woman, huh?" he said with a self-deprecating grin.

"No, partner. You sound like a friend," I returned.

At that instant the shade cast by the building's roof engulfed us in its shadow. And as a chill breeze blew across the waterfront, I saw Bob shiver slightly before zipping up his jacket.

"I think it's time I headed for the house," he said as he got to his feet. "I want Fran to think I've been sitting home alone all day, reading the Good Book, instead of hanging around with derelicts and ne'er-do-wells."

I laughed as I stood and helped Bob sling the pouch carrying his oxygen bottle over his shoulder. As we walked through the building, Tyrone came around from behind the bar and opened the door for us. He put his hand on Bob's shoulder as we passed by and said, "You call me when you get home."

Bob looked up and replied in a snappish tone, "It's only ten minutes away, Tyrone."

"I know where you live—but you call me anyway," Big Tee growled. "I don't want Fran on my ass if something happens to you while she's gone."

"All right, all right," Bob replied in a voice of exasperation. And then, as he cleared the door, he muttered just loudly enough for Tyrone to hear him, "Two-hundred-forty-pound, black Jewish mother."

"Ha!" was Tyrone's snorted reply as he slammed the door behind us.

Bob looked at me with a wicked grin. "I don't reckon any man could have a better friend than Tyrone, could he?"

I shook my head and laughed. "I don't think so."

We walked together to Bob's car. After he drove away I ambled back to my dock where I checked *Miss Rosalie*'s lines before going aboard and walking the deck to make sure everything was shipshape and squared away for the night.

At the companionway to the cabin below, I stood with a foot on the first stair and gazed for a few moments across the marsh and out toward the eastern edge of the continent. I watched as the last of the sun's rays disappeared from the tops of the tallest pines on Tybee Island, leaving the world in a gathering obscurity. And as the final pelicans of the day winged by on dark and silent wings, I followed their example and went below in search of an evening's quiet rest.

CHAPTER 7

A COLD WIND BLEW IN DURING THE night, dropping the temperature by twenty degrees and spreading a heavy gray drizzle over the Low Country. While scooping grounds into the coffeepot I peered out the portholes of the galley and saw that a thick mist hung over the water, blanketing the creek and river in a flowing stream of cottony white that ebbed and eddied on a faint and uncertain breeze.

Setting my cup of java aside for a moment, I opened the settee in the salon that served double duty as a clothes locker, found an old wool sweater and pulled it on. I slipped on a canvas jacket and, now snug against the inclement weather, went out on deck to check the boat lines and take a closer look at the day.

The sounds of the morning were muffled and distant, and even the seagulls muttered to themselves in lowered tones as they drifted through the haze on almost invisible wings. The sound of the cars, dribbling steadily over the Highway 80 bridge from Tybee, carrying commuters to their jobs in Savannah, was unnaturally hushed, and the vehicle headlamps cast wide halos of dim light in the vaporous atmosphere.

I turned my face toward the Atlantic and felt the chill air spilling inland from that great ocean wash over me, leaving a taste of salt on my lips and a sheen of moisture on my face. I could visualize the surface of the sea today. It would be gray and forbidding. Not yet angry and hostile, but a veteran seafarer, recognizing the signs, would know of a building violence soon to come and take heed.

Looking downstream I could just make out the upper mast of a sailboat anchored in a small cove on the western shore, the hull of the boat hidden in the whiteness. Standing under the awning of the aft deck, I felt the chill of the morning wash over me as though it were a cold bath, and a shiver ran down my back. For some reason I thought of the last time I was in Lima, Peru, that city of cold ocean and perpetually dreary skies, and unexpectedly, my lips spoke the word *llovizna*—Spanish for drizzle or light rain.

It was a good day to stay inside, turn up the heat, wrap up in an old army pancho liner, and read a novel between intermittent naps. But this was the day I intended to visit Joree Causey at her home and see if I could find a thread that would help lead me to the discovery of her daughter's whereabouts for the last year and a half.

So, finishing my coffee, I went back inside and busied myself with chores in the engine room while waiting for the fog to lift and the morning traffic to die down. A couple of hours later, I locked up *Miss Rosalie*, fired up the old Bronco, and began to wend my way northward.

I think Savannah is just about the most beautiful city in North America, and that's no adman's pitch. Even on a day such as this, she shows her charms with a rare style and grace. Savannah, when founded in 1733, was the first planned city on the continent. Laid out around a series of small parks, or squares, shaded by monumental trees covered with Spanish moss, the stately old homes are dreamlike in their tranquil beauty.

River Street, and Factors Walk, down near the riverfront, are living pictures of a time long gone, but here, they continue to live as they ever have. And to drive over some of the old streets, paved with the ballast stones of ships from the age of sail, is a history lover's—and a romantic's—delight.

Like all other cities, Savannah also has its rougher side. But in contrast to many American cities, in Savannah, the poor and the affluent live almost side by side and cheek by jowl, with little or no buffer space between.

Traffic was thin, but as I threaded my way through downtown the mist drifting from the lowered sky increased to a light rain. Turning right on Abercorn, I went toward the river before turning north on Liberty and making my way to Highway 21. Crossing old U.S. 17, I cast a quick glance to the right and saw, rising high over the broad waist of the Savannah River, the great piers and suspension wires of the Talmadge Memorial Bridge. From its center span, 185 feet above the river's surface, Tonya Causey had plunged with finality, to the rapidly flowing and darkly fatal waters below.

Once, on a night jump, I'd had a total parachute malfunction. And to this very second, I can recall the electric jolt of terror that blasted through my being as I struggled to cut away the useless main parachute. And I can recall, just as vividly, the overwhelming sense of relief that flooded my body when I felt that lifesaving reserve parachute yank me back from the maw of certain death. But Tonya Causey had nothing in reserve. Tonya knew the full horror of that fall—all the way to fatal impact.

Once above the industrial and port area of the city, Highway 21 turns almost due north. For the most part, it runs parallel to the Savannah River, staying well away from the broad swamps that flank that great stream. But the land lies low, and as often as not, the terrain is characterized by the coffee-colored, tannic waters of the meandering creeks, cypress and gum swamps, and the curiously elliptical water-filled depressions known as Carolina bays. Dry land in this region is generally known as "the Hill." But true hills, here in the lower coastal plain, are nowhere to be found.

To the sides of the highway, the land, where not immersed in water, alternates between wide, flat fields of cotton, corn, soybeans, deep grass pastures of cattle, and forests of pine. To see these magnificent conifers standing straight and proud, limbless for the first seventy-five feet above the ground, is to understand the meaning of the phrase "tall as a Georgia pine."

Soon I crossed from Chatham County into Effingham. For the first decade of the new millennium, Effingham County has been one of the fastest-growing places in the nation, its population almost doubling during that period. But even with that rate of growth, the number of people residing within its boundaries is still slightly less than forty thousand souls.

The town of Rincon, lying closest to Savannah, has experienced the most growth, followed by the town of Springfield. And with that growth has come a certain sense of cosmopolitanism, and along with it a recognition of the slightly wider world to be found not so very far away. But out in the countryside, far down the dirt roads leading through the swamps, deep woods, and fields, little has changed over the last thirty years. If anything, attitudes and expectations have regressed during that period of time, as people have lost jobs, and hope, and become more and more hardened. Panther Creek is the poster child of that phenomenon.

The rain was starting to beat harder as I turned off the main highway and, following the map I had drawn, began to navigate my way through the country by a series of unmarked dirt roads. Crossing a low wooden bridge that spanned a wide creek where the water was almost up to the road bed, I was beginning to wonder if I should proceed any farther when I saw a mailbox with the hand-lettered name Causey painted on the side. I turned in at what looked to be a driveway leading back into the thick woods.

The rutted sand track led a hundred yards to a clearing, across which were scattered three old trailer homes, an ancient tumbledown wooden shack, and a number of old sheds and animal pens. To the sides and behind one of the trailers were twenty or thirty blue plastic barrels lying on their sides, each with a hole cut in one end. There was a stake driven into the ground in front of each barrel, with a line leading into the interior. Most of the inhabitants were sheltering inside, but here and there a fighting rooster was out in the rain, scratching the ground or straining at his tether, trying, with hostile intent, to reach his neighbor.

At the edges of the woods, overgrown with weeds and brush, sat, in various stages of decomposition, a dozen or so derelict cars and trucks. An old pickup, one that must have been there since the fifties, even had a tree growing through it. All sorts of other castoffs were strewn across the clearing in a careless and haphazard manner. Broken washing machines, air conditioners, lawn mowers, and other unidentifiable remains of twentieth-century consumerism littered the ground. And I thought, not for the first time, that no one else loves their junk the way we Southerners do. We like to keep it close at hand for our own admiration and for the benefit of visitors.

At the trailer to my left sat a new pickup truck, and to the side of the trailer, parked carefully beneath a metal carport, was an eighteen-foot bass boat with a two-hundred-fifty-horsepower motor on the transom. A quick glance around the area told me that the truck and boat were worth more than everything else in sight combined.

I doubted that Joree lived in that particular trailer, and also that she was in the one surrounded by the fighting cocks, so the process of elimination indicated that I should try the trailer on the far side of the clearing; the one sitting by itself, with a small porch sheltering the front door. I pulled on my hat, turned my collar up against the rain, and stepped down from my truck.

Crossing the muddy yard, I climbed the two steps of the porch and knocked on the door. I could hear a television, the sound blaring loudly, inside. Then the noise of the television went silent, but no one came to the door. The person, or persons, inside had frozen. I knocked again and then stepped back as far as I could on the porch, to give whoever was there a chance to get a good look at me. Hopefully, I didn't look like a bill collector or someone serving a warrant.

After what seemed like a full minute, the door opened a few inches and a man's face appeared, his body remaining hidden behind the door frame. He was bearded, and from what I could see he wore a yellowed and dingy T-shirt stretched tight over a swollen beer belly. His puffy eyes flitted from my face to my truck, and then back across the clearing, before coming to my face again and eyeing me with suspicion.

I started to introduce myself, "My name is . . ."

But he cut me off with a slurred, "What d'you want?"

"I'm looking for Joree," I replied as I gave the man a close look.

He cast a glance across the clearing and lifted a hand, extending it out the door and pointing a finger.

"Over there, in that one," he said, indicating the trailer with the new truck and boat.

"Thanks," I said woodenly as the door closed in my face.

I slogged through the rain, back across the mire of the yard, but when near the other trailer, I glanced over my shoulder and saw the man watching me from the corner of a window. I expected him to step away from view but he held his place of observation and continued to watch me with what could only be called disinterested interest. Turning again, I proceeded to the trailer he had pointed to as being Joree's.

There was no porch at the door, only some steps made of loosely stacked concrete blocks. I stepped carefully to the top of the blocks, and with rain sluicing from the brim of my hat, knocked on the door.

A television was on here also, but it wasn't as loud as in the other trailer. A woman's voice said something inside and was responded to by the deeper tones of a male. I couldn't make out the words but it sounded as though the woman had given an order of some sort and the man had replied in a surly whine.

The sound of the television lowered. Then, rapid footsteps approached, the corner of a curtain in the nearest window was pulled back, and Joree Causey's face came into view. A look of surprise registered in her eyes when she saw me. Then the curtain fell back into place and the door was thrown open.

"Lordy, Mr. Tanner—Kennesaw," she cried out. "What

are you doing standing there in the rain? Get yourself inside—come in, come in."

She stepped back and held the door open for me as I took off my coat and hat, and shook them off outside, before stepping in.

"I didn't hear you pull up, what with this rain a-drummin' on the roof like all creation," she said as she closed the door.

She took my coat and hat and placed them on a chair at the nearby dining table. Then, turning, she spoke to a young man slouched in a recliner at the far side of the small room. He looked to be in his early to midtwenties. A scraggly rust-colored beard crawled across his face, with a thin mustache adorning his upper lip. He was dressed in the standard country-boy uniform of hunter camouflage and boots. Medium height, thick and flabby, with a Georgia Bulldogs cap pulled tight on his skull, he was practically indistinguishable from a few million others just like him between here and the Tennessee River.

"Junior, come say hello. This here is Mr. Tanner. You know. He's the one I told you about. The man that's gonna help us find out about Tonya."

Junior did not respond other than to pick up the television remote control, turn the sound up again, and begin flipping through the channels.

"Junior!" Joree called sharply. "Put that damn thing down and say hello! You act like I never taught you a bit of manners!"

Junior looked up in disgust, clicked off the television set, threw the remote control at the nearby sofa, and bounding to his feet, stormed into the next room, slamming the door behind him.

Joree looked at me with a grimace of embarrassment on her face.

"That boy," she said with a tone of exasperation. "Sometimes, I just don't know what I'm goin' to do with him. He don't pay me no more mind than the man in the moon."

I merely pursed my lips and nodded my head in commiseration. I could see this was just part of the background in the household, because in the next blink of her eye, Joree seemed to have forgotten about it entirely.

"Come sit down here," she said, indicating the vacant recliner. Instead, I sat at the nearest end of the sofa.

Joree sat at the other end and lit a cigarette before jumping up and saying, "Shoot, 'bout lost my own manners there— it's so seldom I have any real company. Would you like something to drink? A Co-Cola maybe, or a cup of coffee?"

"No, thanks," I replied. "Perhaps later."

"Well, I hope you don't mind if I have somethin' myself," she said as she stepped to the refrigerator.

"No, not at all," I said as she popped the top on a soft-drink can.

Returning to the sofa, she plopped down at the other end. Putting her back against the armrest and pulling her feet up underneath herself, she took a long drink from the can before setting it down and giving attention, once again, to her cigarette.

"You didn't have no trouble findin' the place, did you?" she asked, blowing a stream of blue smoke toward the ceiling.

"No," I responded. "Your directions were excellent."

"Well, that's good. That's real good," she said, almost absently, as she took a long drag on her cigarette.

She acts as though she has no idea why I am here—or as though she wishes I weren't here. Well, that's immaterial. It was time to get with the program, I thought. The woman sitting here had come to *me* with her problem, not the other way around, and now was the time for answers and not speculation. It appeared there was nothing for it but to dive right in.

"Joree, why do you think someone harmed Tonya? What gives you cause to think that?" I asked.

Joree continued to smoke and stare at the wall.

"Well," she said, before pausing again for several seconds. "She was out there amongst some bad people."

"What bad people? Who were they? What were their names?" I queried.

Joree smoked and continued staring at the wall, seemingly lost in thought. She took another pull on her cigarette, and as she exhaled, she shook her head and tears came to her eyes.

"I don't know who they are," she said in a small voice. "Only thing I know is that the last time I talked to her, she said she was worried that they was gonna get her."

"Did she say who *they* were? Did she say *why* they were going to get her?"

Joree shook her head. "No, she didn't."

"When was that, Joree—the last time you spoke with your daughter? Was it here? Did she come see you? Did you meet somewhere? Or was it a phone call?"

She shook her head again as she stubbed out her smoke and then took a drink from the can before saying, "No, I didn't see her then. It was a phone call. She called me late one night, long after I had already gone to bed. That was about two months ago."

I thought for a second. At least this was something.

"Joree, do you have a house phone, or do you use a cell phone?"

She looked at me for the first time. "Just a cell phone," she said. "We ain't got no house phone."

"Do you still have the bill from that month? Can you find it?"

"Yeah, I b'lieve so," she said, rising from her seat and looking about the room. "I should have that bill around. . . ."

At that instant the door to the next room burst open and Junior came crashing out. He was struggling into a jacket as he stormed through the room.

But turning to his mother, his face reddened with emotion, he shouted in a choked voice, "You need to leave it alone, dammit! Just leave it alone! She's gone, and no matter what you do, she ain't comin' back!"

"Junior! Honey! Wait. Don't go. Stay here and tell Mr. Tanner what . . ." she called impotently to his back. But Junior had already slammed the door behind him.

Joree ran to the door and, throwing it open, was just in time to see her son jam the truck into gear and, wheels spinning wildly, shower the side of the trailer with a geyser of gray mud.

Joree stood in the door and watched the truck slewing crazily across the yard, mud flying in all directions. Tearing down the drive, Junior and his new red truck were out of sight in just seconds.

Joree closed the door with a sigh of resignation and, giving me an embarrassed glance, crossed the room to sit once again at the end of the sofa. She lowered her chin to her chest and mused a bit before saying, more to herself than to me, "I've done everything I can think of for that boy, and nothing seems to work. I just don't know what else to do."

I, too, was thinking along similar lines, wondering how the chain of pathologies within dysfunctional families can be broken, and whether or not it can ever be changed for the better. The only answer I could come up with was: No. It seems to go on and on without end.

Poverty, combined with a disdain for education and willful ignorance, a life view based almost solely upon immediate satisfaction of the base appetites, layered with the loss of real jobs and consequently a loss of hope—all these factors have coalesced to produce an American underclass that is almost impervious to help of any kind.

This unassailable culture of failure, passed intact by each generation to the next, infects the young, before they can even talk, with a social disease to which there appears to be no immunization and no antidote.

And those exceptional few, the lucky ones, who by sheer native intellect, tenacity, and stupendous power of will, do manage to claw their way up from the abyss of despair, are from then on under continual assault from their families and former associates in a perverse attempt to grapple the escapees back into the fetid social cesspool from whence they came. For to escape the colony and succeed at life is to be a living reminder to the lepers that it can be done, and that the failure to try is the greatest failure of all.

No, I thought. *Junior is an apt student, one who has learned his lessons exceedingly well. He is the logical end point of all the human history that has gone before him in his line of ancestry. And if he lives, he will most likely beget more of the same.*

"Joree," I said, pulling her back to the present. "It seems to me your son is old enough to look out for himself. Let's you and I talk about Tonya."

Joree turned to me as though she were seeing me for the first time. Then, as she let go the sad thoughts of Junior, recognition came across her features, and she turned her mind again, to the even sadder memories of her lost daughter.

"Yeah, I reckon so," she said in a forlorn tone of voice.

"Tell me about Tonya's friends," I prodded. "Who was her best friend at school? Did she go to church? Who were her friends there?"

"Well," Joree began, lighting another cigarette. "She

and Sandy Willis was real close—they had been since they was little girls in grade school together. The Willises lived just down the road a ways back then. The girls rode the county bus together from elementary all the way through high school."

We're getting somewhere at last, I thought.

"And they both went to church down at the crossroads— at that new church. You passed it on the way here. Well, it ain't exactly new," she continued after a puff on her cigarette. "It'd been sitting empty for a long time, 'til that new preacher come and opened it again. The girls liked to go there. I know Tonya was there every time the church doors was open.

"She tried to get me to go with her, and I went just the onct—with Tonya that is. But I didn't much care for it. I just don't take to carryings-on like that in church—what with them drums a-beatin', and electric guitars a-frailin', and all that shoutin', and dancin', and a-speakin' in tongues and all. I just don't think it's dignified, myself," she concluded with a sniff of disapproval.

A Holiness church, I thought. The raw exuberance of the services always attract a young audience, in addition to the old true believers who grew up in these, the most fundamental of all the Christian sects.

"So Sandy was Tonya's best friend. Do you know if she had contact with Tonya, after she left home?"

"I don't know," Joree replied, shaking her head and appearing to slip back again into a state of mental lethargy. "She might have, but I just don't know. I ain't talked to Sandy in a long time. But I hear tell she still works at the convenience store out on the highway."

"Well, I can speak to Sandy and see if she has anything to tell that may be helpful." I rose to go. "And do you think you can find those phone bills for me?"

Joree looked at me with puzzlement on her face and then started with a sort of recognition.

"Oh yeah. The phone bills," she said as she stood quickly and glanced around the room. "They ought to be . . ."

She walked to the part of the room that was the kitchen and began opening and closing cabinet drawers.

"I think I put them in—yeah, here they are."

She reached into a drawer and plucked out a disordered ream of papers. Waving them aloft as though she had just won a prize, she turned and placed them triumphantly in my hand.

"Here ye go," she said. "They're in that stack—somewhere."

A quick glance told me that the jumbled mess of papers I held were just that: a mess. But maybe one of them would turn out to be the phone bill that could help pinpoint Tonya Causey's location, at a given time, on a certain night. At least it was something. I folded the papers as best I could and put them inside the front of my shirt. Crossing the room I retrieved my jacket and put it on.

"Joree," I said as she handed me my hat. "I'll call. And if you think of anything else—maybe one of Tonya's friends who might have seen her in recent months—call me immediately, okay?"

"I will," she said, looking me in the eye, a sad expression on her face. "And I hope you don't think too badly of Junior. He really is a good boy. It's just that, well—he's just been mighty tore up about Tonya. And he don't know what to do."

"I understand," I replied as I pulled my hat down low over my eyes. "You just call me—with anything at all—no matter what the time."

"I will," she said.

I leaned over to exchange a quick hug, and as she gave me a kiss on the cheek, she breathed, "Thank you."

I opened the door and dashed out into the driving rain. As I turned my truck to drive away I looked up and saw Joree's face and open hands pressed against the window pane, the rain streaming down the glass like a flood of tears.

CHAPTER 8

THE NAME OF A FRIEND, A CHURCH, a school—these were all useful. Tonya Causey had lived the majority of her short life here in Effingham County, Georgia. And someone here—maybe several someones, for that matter—would have information, whether they knew it or not, that would point in the right direction. That would lead to the essential answer of what happened to bring about the tragic and sorrowful end to a young girl's life.

The slanting gray rain came down with a steady power that filled the low places and was already sending the many streams and branches over their low banks. I drove slowly over the muddy roads and even slipped the truck into four-wheel drive a couple of times in some of the worst places. The last thing I wanted was to slide off into a cypress swamp on a day like this.

I came to an intersection of two roads, and off to the right, surrounded by a grove of towering pines, was a small white clapboard church. Off to one side and slightly behind the building I saw the headstones of a small cemetery. I swung the truck into the churchyard to get a better look. Splashing across the chain of rain-filled potholes, I pulled up close to read the hand-lettered sign fastened to the front of the porch above the doors.

The sign, painted in a surprisingly good hand, read:

**PANTHER CREEK
FULL GOSPEL
EVANGELICAL PENTECOSTAL HOLINESS MISSION
PASTOR TRUMAN RAINWATER
ALL PEOPLES WELCOME**

Well, I thought as I read the sign. *The pastor's name is certainly appropriate for a day such as this.* And when had anyone ever seen a "Partial Gospel" or a "Half-Gospel" Holiness church? Probably the only thing the sign left out was: **FOOT WASHINGS AND DEMON CASTINGS, EVERY FOURTH SUNDAY**.

That was getting a little irreverent of me, I'm sure. But I grew up going to a church pretty much like this one. My grandmother dragged me with her, every Sunday morning and evening, and also to Wednesday-night prayer meetings, until I became old enough to rebel and get away with it. How many countless hours had I squirmed my bottom on that hard pine bench, wishing I were somewhere else, daydreaming about what I would be doing were I not sentenced once again to another interminable Jesus pummeling.

But churches are the center of the social life in rural communities. And if Tonya had attended here, someone would know why she slipped away and, just possibly, what became of her. It was also quite likely Brother Rainwater could provide some insight that was lacking in others. In the country churches the pastor often fulfills the function of private counselor and special confidant, much like the priest of a Catholic parish. He was the one person who, no matter what, would not hurt you, or turn you away.

The churchyard was empty now. No one else was here; just me, the dripping pine trees, and the silent residents of the graveyard. But I made a mental note to return and have a confidential talk with the pastor. If anyone was likely to be helpful, he was probably the one.

I turned the truck slowly, splashing as softly as possible across the growing pond of the rain filled parking area, and pointed my bows eastward again. Another twenty minutes sailing over the sand and mud roads brought me once again to the asphalt pavement of the state highway. And sitting at the intersection was the convenience store where I hoped to find Tonya's friend, Sandy Willis.

I pulled in and sidled up to one of the gas pumps that, thankfully, was under the protection of a high metal roof. Looking around as I filled my tank, I took in what there was of the local scenery. This was another one of those chain places that was identical to the thousands of other convenience stops all across the nation. But just off the property, at the far end of the lot, sat the original version of the rural gasoline station and store.

The building was a faded white, two-story clapboard structure sitting in a sea of knee-high weeds and ankle-deep rainwater. Extending from the front of the second floor was a portico covering the place where the gas pumps once stood. The upstairs would have served as the home of the owner and his family while the first floor was the business section of the building.

Though the pumps were long gone, it was a good bet that the originals were the old gravity-fed models. The ones where the customer ordered so many gallons and the attendant then cranked a hand pump, filling the large glass jar that sat on top to the appropriate level. When the right amount of fuel was visible in the see-through container, the attendant stuck the nozzle in the neck of the tank, pulled the lever on the handle, and gravity did the rest.

When I was a boy, an old abandoned gas station near our home had one of those pumps, and it was a continual source of fascination to me. Years later I found them liberally scattered around the world, in remote locations that were not yet blessed by connection to the electric grid. I still think it's a clever idea.

Looking at that old station, I thought of what it must have meant to the family that had lived there and made their living from that business. A man in charge of a business he owns himself—what a marvelous thing. How many kids had been raised in that upstairs apartment? How many lives had been nurtured and fostered by that little place on the side of the road? And then, to compare that with the sterile entity that stood before me—one where none of the people working inside were either nurtured or enlarged; surviving, at best, as twenty-first-century wage slaves.

My gas tank filled, I stepped across the island and made my way across the oil-stained and littered pavement to the door. Parked at the side of the building were a couple of older cars, both with muddy tires, and one with missing hubcaps. Stationed closest to the door was an '80s model small Japanese pickup with a cracked windshield and a Confederate flag prominently displayed on the back window. I often think the people who fly that banner in public do so in order to dispel any doubt as to whether the owner is a bigoted ignoramus. This way, by virtue of the emblem, you know so at a glance.

A customer, who I took to be the owner of the truck,

was at the counter as I entered. He had a twelve pack of beer at hand and was in deep conversation with the cashier as he made his selection from a rack of lottery tickets. I roamed the aisles for a couple of minutes, picking up a few items, and killed time until the man had concluded his transaction and departed. Then I stepped to the counter.

The cashier was a slight young woman almost hidden by the cash register and the racks of impulse items and other chingadera stacked atop the counter. Her head was down as I approached, but when she looked up, her face, framed by short honey blond hair, was cute and bright, but as she saw me, her eyes took on a glaze of suspicion.

"It's really coming down today, isn't it?" I remarked as she rang up my items.

"That's twenty-three dollars and forty-two cents," she replied in a flat tone.

I handed her a couple of twenties, and as she made change I asked in a quiet, friendly voice, "Aren't you Sandy Willis, from over on Panther Creek?"

At my words, a flicker of curiosity touched her face, and as she handed me the change, I introduced myself.

"My name's Kennesaw Tanner. Joree Causey told me I might find you here."

With a closely appraising eye, the young woman looked me over for a few seconds before answering, "Yes, I'm Sandy. What can I do for you, Mr. . . . ?"

"Tanner, but please call me Kennesaw."

"Yes, sir—Kennesaw. But what can I do for . . . ?"

And then a startled look came on her face.

"Joree's okay, isn't she? She's not hurt or anything, is she? Lord, tell me she's not in trouble. God knows she's had enough of that already."

"No, Sandy. Joree is fine," I reassured her, "but she thought you might be able to help me with something I'm looking into. She tells me that you and Tonya were good friends—best friends, in fact, and that you might be able to tell me something about where Tonya may have gone after she left home. Perhaps where she was living, and what she had been doing recently."

The worried frown returned to Sandy's face and a far-away look came into her eyes.

"Tonya," she whispered. And as though it had been poised there all along, waiting for the right moment of release, a single tear spilled from each eye and rolled down her cheeks.

Sandy wiped her face with the back of a hand and then fixed me with a searching stare.

"What is it that you're looking for, Mr.—Kennesaw? What exactly is it you're trying to do?"

From outside came the sound of tires crossing the wet parking lot. Then a car door slammed.

"I want to know what happened to her, Sandy. I want to know how and why she came to her end."

"And just how is that any of your concern?" she asked in a clear and forthright voice. "Why do you care—when practically nobody else does?"

She did not avert her eyes from mine but held a gaze that lasted several seconds. And with the measuring look that passed between us, I knew Sandy Willis had backbone.

"Because I found her body, Sandy. And because until Joree knows what happened to her, Tonya is still out there—she's still lost and alone."

At that instant came the distinctly implosive *ploosh* of a car window shattering. I looked out the door just in time to see a huge man with a baseball bat in hand as he took a powerful swing at the passenger window of my truck—the back glass was already gone.

Plooosh! The window exploded inward, shattered glass flying throughout the inside of the truck.

I dashed outside yelling, "Hey! Stop that!"

The man paid me no mind but took a few steps forward as he now turned his attention to the windshield. *Craccckkk!* The bat rebounded off the thick glass of the windshield.

"Hey, you!" I yelled again as, coming up behind him, I grabbed the sweet spot of the bat and gave it a yank, just as the man was limbering up for another try.

The bat was at full backswing when I locked on to it with both hands and heaved with all my strength. He was off balance in that position and the bat should have come away, but instead, he gave a tug that sent me flying against the front fender of the truck and brought me face-to-face with the mad batter.

"Man, what the hell's the matter with you?" I yelled, in an attempt to change his focus and stave off another swing at my truck. He paused a second, dropping the bat to his side as he peered at me, and now I had a good look at him.

A mountain of flesh, he was six and a half feet tall and weighed at least three hundred pounds. In spite of the chill, he was dressed in a pair of jeans and a T-shirt with torn-off sleeves. His head was shaved bald, which accentuated the small ears that stood straight out to the sides. But it was his eyes that grabbed and held my attention: They were the dead eyes of a psychotic—utterly devoid of intellect or compassion—and I knew for a fact I was dealing with a madman. There was that, and his following words.

"That thing there is Satan's fiery chariot," he pronounced in a squeaky falsetto voice, pointing the bat at my truck. Then as he looked at me, a spark of recognition came into his eyes—that, and a new sense of mission.

"And you are the devil's own driver," he hissed, taking a mighty swing at my head.

I bent low to the right as I leaped backward and felt the bat go sizzling past my ear. He missed my head, but his follow-through caught the windshield again, the blow sending a network of cracks ripping across the glass.

I danced hastily backward as the giant came at me again with the quickness of a cat. When he cocked the bat for another whack, I feinted to my left and dodged right, just barely avoiding a stroke aimed at my midsection.

"Look, partner," I said as I tried to reason with him. "You don't need to do this. I think you've got the wrong truck here, and you surely have the wrong man. If anybody loves Jesus, it's sure as hell me."

"Spawn of Lucifer," he hissed as he fired an overhand blow that whipped just in front of my face with the blinding speed of a samurai's sword.

Sandy came running outside, screaming at the man, "Stop it, Leon! Stop it! You're gonna kill him!"

She must have tried to jump on his back, because I saw him give his shoulders a quick shrug. Sandy sailed through the air and hit the pavement behind him. He came on again, his eyes now lit with a maniacal glee.

I circled the hood of the truck, trying to put enough distance between us so that I could get to the driver's door. If my timing was right, I could throw the door open between us and grab the little .22 caliber automatic from inside the console. Maybe a few rounds of snake shot into his legs would bring the man to his senses. Pain sometimes has a way of doing that, and if not, the rest of the magazine was loaded with solid points.

"I am the strong hand of the Lord," Leon sputtered as I slid backward, down the driver's side of the truck. "The Lord is angry, and he has sent me here to wreak vengeance upon his enemies," he intoned as with two flicks of the wrist he casually took out the headlights.

Then, coming around the bumper, he delivered a shrieking swing of the bat that tore the side mirror from its roots. I flung the door open, and keeping my eyes on Leon, made a quick grab at the console lid. But before my hand could find the gun, Leon launched a powerful swing at the window. I was just able to get a shoulder up to protect me from the slamming door, but the blow hurled me backward, almost to the rear bumper of the truck, while shattering glass rained over me like a storm of sleet.

Leon came on again. But dammit, I'd had enough. It was time to end this silliness here and now! I stopped my retreat and squared on him, my knees slightly flexed, while holding my hands loose and relaxed, just in front of my chest.

Leon realized that he had me trapped between the truck and the gas pumps. He lifted the bat above his right shoulder and lunged at me. As the bat swung down in a blurred and vicious arc, a gurgling scream of madness burst from his throat.

I sprang forward, getting inside the range of his arm, and smashed my chest into his upper abdomen. The air whistled again as the bat passed my head, and a massive arm crashed over my shoulder and across my back. The blow had missed its intended target by only a few millimeters.

As our bodies clashed, I let my knees fall from beneath me while simultaneously launching both hands and arms upward to full extension. At the precise microsecond that my body was falling away with the full force of gravity, the heels of my joined hands smashed directly into Leon's granitelike chin.

His teeth and jaws slammed together with a loud clack, and I felt the shock of the blow I had thrown course the length of my body. For a split second nothing happened, then I heard the ball bat hit the pavement behind my feet. Leon went limp, the air hissed from his lungs, and he toppled over on top of me. He hung there momentarily, until I gave the inert body a shove, pushed the heavy arm off my shoulder, and watched the behemoth crash to the ground like a side of beef.

Just as I stooped to check his pulse the place was lit by a flash of blue lights, and from behind me came the *whoop-whoop-whoop* of a siren. I stood up again, lifted my hands above my head, and slowly turned to face the witness of my most recent antisocial act.

A lean, broad-shouldered constable of the law got out of the car and stood silently as he straightened his hat and looked the area over. Shooting me a glance, he then looked at the body on the ground.

"Officer," I said in a calm and even voice—one that I— in spite of the evidence lying on the ground before us— hoped sounded like that of a good citizen, "I think you should call for an ambulance."

"I seen it all, Sheriff," Sandy said as she came around the back of my truck. "This man was defending hisself. Leon went crazy. He was smashing the man's truck with a baseball bat, and when this feller tried to get him to stop, he went after him."

The sheriff gave Sandy a glance, then looked at me again for a second before he reached to his shoulder, keyed the mike of his radio, and said a few words.

Releasing the mike, he stepped forward to take a look at the man on the ground, and as he leaned over he said to me, "You can put your hands down, Mr. Tanner. I saw everything that happened from the time you came out of those doors."

The sheriff checked the carotid pulse of the man on the

ground and then stood and looked me over, a wry smile tugging at the corner of his mouth.

"When Bob Martin called to say you might be coming up this way, I had no idea you were going to make such a dynamic entrance. I just hope for all the rest of the good citizens here in Effingham County that you take it easy the remainder of the day. And as for Leon Wren here, why I've been looking high and low for that boy for the last several months. So it appears like you've done us a favor."

A noise that sounded like a saw blade hitting a pine knot erupted from the insensate Leon. We looked down and saw him shiver a few times, like a freshly caught mullet thrown on ice. Then, he let out another groan, rolled clumsily onto his side, and tried to sit up. He didn't quite make it the first try and had to lie back down again. From there, he blinked his eyes, took a few shuddering breaths, and on the second attempt came to a wobbly sitting position, his chin dangling on his chest, with his hands flopped loosely across his thighs.

Sheriff Zimmer took the handcuffs from his belt and stepped closer to the man.

"Leon? Leon? Can you hear me, boy?" the sheriff asked in an authoritative tone.

Leon sat with closed eyes and gave no indication that his brain was yet reconnected to his ears.

"I'm gonna cuff you now. But if you give me any grief, I'll sic this man on you again and let him whup you good this time. You hear me?"

Leon lifted his chin from his chest and, opening his eyes, gave me a watery and wavering stare. Then, as the sheriff tapped him on the shoulder, Leon made a clumsy attempt to put his hands behind his back. I guess when it's a movement you're well accustomed to making, the body can function even through the cloudy haze of a concussion.

Sheriff Zimmer quickly and efficiently got the cuffs on Leon, but from the sound they made when being closed, I could tell they just barely went around the man's thick wrists.

"Leon, why don't you just lie back down 'til the ambulance gets here. It won't be long now, and you'll feel better," said the sheriff as he took the giant by the shoulders and guided him gently to the ground. Leon complied like a sleepy child. He curled on his side, let out another groan, and closed his eyes once again.

In the distance, the first warbling notes of approaching sirens came fluttering down the highway. A sheriff's deputy arrived just a few seconds before the ambulance pulled in. As the two EMTs strained to load an unresisting Leon into the ambulance, Sheriff Zimmer gave his deputy instructions.

"Travis, once you get Leon to the hospital, keep a watch on him. I suspect the doctor on duty will probably want to keep him overnight for observation. If he does, place a continual guard on him and make sure he's shackled to the bed. It took long enough to lay hands on that boy this time, and I don't want him skipping off again. When the doc releases him, bring him straight to the jail. We'll talk to him there. Meantime, I'll get the charges filed. Clear?"

"Got it, Sheriff," replied the burly deputy.

Zimmer turned his attention to me. "Mr. Tanner, why don't you follow me? We can talk about this"—he nodded toward the departing ambulance—"and whatever else you have on your mind at my office."

I looked at my truck. Three side windows and the back window were smashed in, and the windshield was shattered. I picked up the destroyed mirror and tossed it inside.

"Sheriff, I can't drive my truck in this condition. What say I park it off to the side and call a wrecker to pick it up and take it to a shop. Is there a rental agency in town where I can get a car?"

"Sure," he replied. "We can help you with that."

"Also, there's one other thing I need to tell you. I have a firearm in my truck, and I don't want to leave it here."

A faint smile touched Zimmer's lips. "Is it a big one or a little one?" He asked in a teasing fashion.

"Rather small," I replied.

"You got a carry permit?"

"Yes, sir, I do."

"Well, if the sovereign state of Georgia thinks well enough of you to issue a concealed gun permit, I guess I can play along, too. Get it and come on, though. I'm tired of standing around in this cold and damp. It's beginning to depress me."

As I pulled my wounded truck to the side of the building, Sheriff Zimmer looked across to Sandy, who was standing quietly nearby.

"Sandy, I don't want you having to lose time from work on account of this mess, but I need a statement from you, too. So why don't you come see me when your shift is over. All right?"

Sandy nodded her head. "Okay, Sheriff. I'll be there right after three o'clock."

"I'll tell Evaleen that you're coming. She'll show you right in. I just ask that you don't talk to anyone else about this until you talk to me. Can you do that?"

"I can, Sheriff," she replied.

"Good girl," he said as he got into his car.

With my body between her and the sheriff, I handed Sandy one of my cards and spoke in a quiet voice, "I still want to hear your thoughts about Tonya. Call me and let's set up a meeting—will you?"

Sandy looked closely at the card, then lifted her eyes to

my face and nodded her head. "I'll call," she whispered, and then turned and scurried back inside.

I opened the door and climbed into the sheriff's cruiser. The sheriff drove swiftly and surely along the rain-blackened, arrow-straight highway that ran straight as a knife blade through the darkly dripping pine forest. The fog and misty rain had settled even lower upon the terrain, hiding the top half of the trees and covering the land in a blanket of cold and foreboding dreariness that seemed to carry within its ghostlike folds the guilty permanence of sin.

CHAPTER 9

WHILE ZIMMER HANDLED A PHONE call, I took a sip of the surprisingly good coffee and looked around the office. Most official sanctums I've been in have at least one I Love Me wall, decorated with photos of the office holder being honored by other people of even higher rank and position. Sheriff Zimmer's photos were all of other people. Friends and family, I could only assume, or perhaps, simply people he admired.

On the corner of a nearby bookshelf sat a small framed black-and-white photo of a group of combat soldiers in the desert, posed self-consciously in front of a still smoldering tank. The men in the picture were filthy with the grime, dirt, and stress of combat. They looked exhausted, but the grin each man wore on his face told the real story—they had lived through a deadly fight they probably hadn't expected to survive—and were ecstatic with the joy of finding themselves still among the living. A closer look told me it was a squad of marines, and that the man in the middle of the group was Sheriff Zimmer in younger days.

Zimmer finished his call and gave me his attention at last.

"My deputy tells me that Leon will indeed be spending the night in the hospital, at county taxpayer expense, as usual."

It didn't seem that I needed to reply, so all I said was, "Uh-huh."

Sheriff Zimmer looked at me quietly for a few seconds. I believe he was letting the silence build, hoping I'd say something. I didn't and merely held his look.

"What the hell did you hit Leon with?" he asked, breaking the silence at last. "That boy went down like he'd been poleaxed."

"It's called a drop punch," I replied. "I learned it from an old cop in Yonkers, New York."

"Well, it seems to be right effective. Maybe you can show me how it works sometime," he said, leaning back in his chair, crossing his legs, and placing both hands over a knee. "But first, why don't you tell me what brought about that little altercation. Most people don't walk away from a fracas with Leon Wren. In fact, I've got two outstanding assault warrants on him right now—this one makes three. And if I could dig up some witnesses or other proof, I'd have him up on a murder charge or two."

My hand drifted to my throat and a finger lightly touched the tiny bag that hung beneath my shirt. *Cyriah's gift.* Perhaps it had worked some protective magic after all. I let my hand fall to the arm of the chair.

"He's one of your bad boys, it seems," I remarked.

Zimmer leaned back in his chair and ran a hand over his closely cropped hair. "He comes from a bad clan, Mr. Tanner. The only law the Wren family recognizes is what they make themselves. There's hardly a low-down, crooked, or thieving undertaking they're not involved in. My predecessor made it his mission in life to see 'em all behind bars or flushed out of Effingham County, but it was a task he was never able to fulfill."

"I take it you feel the same way, Sheriff," I replied.

Zimmer nodded. "I do. That Panther Creek bunch has had their way around here for too long now. Cockfighting, whiskey running, robbery, stealing cars, marijuana, now methamphetamines, and whatever else they can find to get into. I figure a substantial part of the criminal activity in this area centers on that crowd out there. But it's damn near impossible to get anyone to talk. What few witnesses there are always seem to come down with a case of lockjaw—a few of them, fatally. So maybe you can tell me what brought you up here and led you to cross paths with Leon Wren."

I contemplated what to say and realized that in this case nothing was better than the truth—just how much of it to dispense was the only question I retained. So I quickly and succinctly told him of my initial meeting with Joree Causey and my visit to her home this morning. But I left Danny Ray's name out of the tale, and for some reason or other, I said nothing about the fit of anger thrown by Junior Causey when he stormed out of the house.

While I spoke, Sheriff Zimmer sat quietly in his chair, rocking slightly, and tapping his lower lip with steepled fingertips. When I finished my story he stopped rocking, but remained posed in quiet contemplation for several seconds more.

"So, what do you think happened to the Causey girl, Mr. Tanner?"

"Call me Kennesaw, please," I replied.

Sheriff Zimmer pursed his lips and a smile came into his eyes. "Is that *Kennesaw*, like in the mountain up by Marietta?"

"Spelled and pronounced exactly the same," I responded.

"Okay," he said. "But again—what do you think happened to Tonya Causey?" he asked.

"Sheriff, the only thing I know for sure is that she's dead and that her mother thinks it was no accident."

Zimmer was silent for a few seconds again, as though he was giving careful consideration to his next words.

"Would it surprise you to know that the Causeys and the Wrens are pretty closely related? Joree Causey herself was a Wren before she married. And I can't begin to count the many ways those families are intertwined."

It was my turn to sit silently and think for a bit. *Did it matter at all? And was it just coincidence that Leon Wren should show up at the convenience store while I was talking to Sandy Willis? No, that was a chance encounter, the crossing of paths with a dangerous lunatic. Leon had attacked my truck in a fit of madness. If it hadn't been mine it would have been someone else's. It was just an unexpected and inexplicable event, like running across a rattlesnake coiled on a busy city sidewalk. You can't account for it, but those kinds of things sometimes happen.*

"No, Sheriff, that wouldn't surprise me very much. There are people in my own family that we just call cousins and leave it at that. If you try to follow the lines of relationship it becomes too complicated and confusing. But I do wonder this, is Leon Wren crazy? I mean, is he mentally deficient or unhinged in some manner? Has he done this sort of thing before?"

Zimmer frowned and shook his head slightly. "Leon Wren is an utterly vicious and completely cruel man—he has been all his life. But crazy—no," he said, shaking his head again. "I wouldn't call him intelligent. In fact, in many ways he's stupid, but he does have an animal cunning about him that is surprisingly powerful. Some people say he took over the operations of the clan after his uncle Lazlo Wren burned to death in a trailer fire last year. Some people also say that Leon might have had something to do with that fire. But nobody says it out loud, and no one's ever said it to a grand jury.

"But if you'll press the charges," he continued, "I think I can see that Brother Leon goes to Reidsville for a few years. This makes him a three-time loser, and by God, this time, *I* was the witness."

"Of course, Sheriff. I'll file. But I think you need to get a shrink to run an evaluation on him. The entire time he was swinging that bat he was babbling a bunch of crazy religious talk—all about being the avenging hand of God, cleansing the Earth of Satan's spawn, and such lunacy. And I can tell you for certain, the man I saw behind those eyes was sincerely crazy."

"It might have been a big dose of crystal meth doing the talking," Zimmer replied.

"Yes," I said upon reflection, "it could have been at that. But it could also be something deeper and more permanent."

Zimmer nodded. "I take your point, and I'll get the doc to have him evaluated. Now, all this aside, what can I do for you?"

I asked what he knew about Tonya Causey and her family. What he told me pretty much paralleled the story I'd been given by Joree. Tonya had been the recipient of a grim upbringing. A shredded family, deprived childhood, surrounded by dysfunctional adults, she'd quit school at sixteen, worked at a few dead-end jobs in the local area, and then just drifted away. Which wasn't that unusual for girls in her circumstance. She had never been in trouble of any kind, so she had never popped up on the local police radar—that is, until her body was found. And sad to say, her death had been the most noteworthy occurrence of her short life.

"As for Tonya being gone for the last year, as her mother says, well, nobody ever reported her missing. So, apparently Joree wasn't all that concerned for the whereabouts of the girl after all—at least until the money stopped coming in. I wonder if she might not be laboring under a case of regret for *things that might have been*. Maybe that's what's driving Mrs. Causey's belief in foul play. Perhaps it's a way of escaping from a sense of fault and self-blame," Zimmer concluded.

I turned that over in my mind. Sheriff Zimmer may have touched on something there. It was an angle I hadn't considered before.

"I don't know, Sheriff," I conceded. "But it's something that certainly bears looking into."

I glanced up as a tall, voluptuously built black female deputy sheriff stepped to the door. A streak of white hair ran, like a lightning bolt in a dark night, from her forehead back across her curly tresses. I couldn't tell if it was a natural phenomenon or if it was contrived, but the effect was certainly captivating.

"Sheriff," she said as she returned my glance with a smile. "Mr. Tanner's car is here. The boy that drove it over has some papers for him to sign."

"Thank you, Evaleen," Zimmer said as he rose from his chair. I stood also and followed as he led us into the hallway.

"Let's see about making you mobile again, and then I need to get your statement about that little dance you were performing with young Leon. After that," he said, checking his watch, "it's lunchtime. And since you're my guest,

I'd like to take you to a barbecue joint here in town. They treat me pretty good there—my mama runs the place."

"Lead the way, Sheriff," I said. "If barbecue is in the offing, seems this wasn't a wasted trip after all."

And as we followed the lovely Deputy Sheriff Evaleen down the hallway, I could only think how there is that certain *something* about a well-built woman in a police uniform, that *something* about her, that just makes you want to take the law into your own hands. I'm sure you know what I mean.

THE RAIN CAME IN WAVES OF VARYING intensity as I drove back to Savannah. While the wipers beat a mesmerizing cadence on the windshield I tried to make sense of the day's events. I had gotten little from the sheriff that I didn't know already. But I hadn't expected to learn anything really earth-shattering. Joree had been vague, as though she had rethought whether it had been such a good idea to come to me in the first place. But Junior was scared, and so was Sandy Willis. Those two knew something—but what? Did they have knowledge of the same things or did they each carry with them a little something about Tonya that no one else was aware of? As for Leon Wren—related to the Causeys or not—he was a lunatic, and of no consequence in the matter.

So I tallied up the cost of this little inquiry so far. My truck had every window except one knocked out of it. Poor thing looked like it had been stolen by gangbangers and used for a joyride, before being brutalized and abandoned on the wrong side of town. And I had damn near had my head torn off by a madman. I was okay, but new glass for my old Bronco might be pretty hard to come across. I thought

I'd keep this one to myself—no need to upset my insurance company. I had my doubts that they'd understand.

And if Joree Causey was no more interested in the death of her daughter than she had indicated this morning—if she had undergone a change of heart about the matter—then maybe it was time to pull the plug and forget about it before I wasted any more time and effort.

The afternoon was late, the sky was low and dark, and the traffic heavy and sluggish as I came back into town. I cruised slowly down Bull Street, watching closely for the sudden flare of brake lights ahead of me as I negotiated the fitful stop and go of the bumper-to-bumper crush of cars. Savannah may be a city of many superlatives, but its drivers are some of the worst in the nation. They bumble through the streets with all the elegance and smooth capability of a bunch of mindless tadpoles swarming around in a mud hole. At the eastern end of the old city, I worked my way over to Victory Drive, and before long was soon in the village of Thunderbolt and at the auto shop of Danny Ray's brother-in-law.

There was my truck, sitting inside an open bay, looking like a broken-down club boxer who has fought his last match. I parked and went inside. The young man running the place said the glass had already been ordered but that it would probably be the next day before it came in. "It was a special order from Atlanta," he made a point of telling me several times over.

I asked if Danny Ray was around and was told that he had not returned yet, but maybe I could find him down at the docks where he often worked. I didn't bother to reply that I lived there myself. I left some cash to cover the cost of the new glass and then headed home.

As I pulled into the parking lot I noticed that the light on that end of the lot was out, and I remarked to myself how rapidly the days shorten this time of year and how much denser the obscurity of the nights seem to be. When I was at the top of the stairs that lead down from the board-walk to the dock itself, I spied a lone figure, sitting slump-shouldered on an upturned bucket at the end of the dock.

He was leaning head down, with his forearms resting on his knees as if asleep. His face was turned slightly away and was hidden by the hood of his rain jacket. Something about his presence made my hackles rise. I put my hand into my coat pocket where it automatically found the pistol that nestled there. I let my finger rest lightly outside the trigger guard but put my thumb on the safety and stepped forward to find out who the visitor was.

The man must have felt the dock sway underneath us. He instantly looked up and, seeing me, called my name.

"Kennesaw."

It was Parker Wells. He stood and stepped forward, extending a hand.

"I was beginning to wonder if you'd return today. I've been sitting here staring at the water until I must have dozed off," he said.

"Parker? What's going on? You've been looking for me?" I asked, a bit puzzled by his presence.

"Yeah," he said, his long head nodding seriously on his equally long neck. "Miss Cyriah sent me."

"Oh," I replied. "Well, come on inside. You can tell me there. Besides, I need a drink and I'll feel better if you'll have one with me."

"I'd be delighted," he replied, a smile lighting his face.

I had Parker shuck off his rain gear and once inside gave him an old sweater to pull on. Parker is as skinny as a blue heron and I knew the chill of the evening had to touch him to the bone. I flipped on the heat to drive the damp from the cabin, and then poured us each a liberal glass of Irish whiskey. Parker lifted the glass in salute and took a long, appreciative drink.

"Ahh," he breathed before taking another sip and then resting the glass on his knee. "Our Celtic brethren across the waters certainly know a thing or two about the art of whiskey making, don't they?"

"You know the old saying," I replied as I lowered my glass. "God invented whiskey to prevent the Irish from conquering the world."

Parker lifted his glass to the light and looked at it with consideration. "Then he is a wise and benevolent deity indeed," he said reverently, before taking another slow sip.

We sat in silence, each glad to be out of the gloom of the darkened day and snuggly belowdecks, warming our insides with the golden goodness of mellow drink.

Parker sat his empty glass to the side and politely waved me away when I pointed at the bottle and lifted an eyebrow in query.

"No, thanks," he said. "One is plenty—and on occasion, more than enough—and I forget my reason for coming."

"You said Miss Cyriah sent you," I said, a feeling of foreboding tightening my gut.

"Yes," he replied in an earnest voice. "She says you must move your boat away from here. Take it away someplace where no one will find it. She says, and I quote, 'The truly mad wear the mask of sanity, and the mad in appearance are but children in his hand.'"

I nodded slightly to indicate that I had heard the words. Parker sat quietly and looked courteously to one side, as though to leave me with the privacy of my thoughts. Most people would have immediately asked about the meaning of the message. But Parker, by the casual manner in which he had repeated the warning, seemed no more mystified than as if he had only reported the current weather forecast.

"When did Cyriah give you the message?" I asked.

Parker looked at me again. "This morning, about ten o'clock, but it was around one by the time I finally arrived here. I hope I was not too late."

I marveled. Cyriah had summoned Parker and sent her message before I had arrived in Panther Creek. I shook my head in amazement and wondered, who was the one she had actually spoken of in her prophecy? And did it have real meaning? Well, that was just something else to ponder. Time alone would tell if her message had genuine significance.

Parker stood. "Well, I think it's time I was returning."

"How did you get here, Parker?" I asked.

"I came in my skiff," he replied.

"Hombre, there's no way I can allow you to make that trip at night in a skiff. It's bad enough in daylight during this kind of weather. But in the dark—that's just out of the question. You'll stay the night."

He started to wave in protest, but I didn't allow it. "You'll stay here, Parker Wells, and that's the end of it. What kind of a host do you think I am? And do you think for even one minute that I want Miss Cyriah to know that I sent you out on a night like this? She'd take the hide off me for sure—or turn me into a frog, if not something worse."

Parker grinned and sat again. "Thanks, Kennesaw. I was hoping you'd offer. I wasn't looking forward to that trip."

"Great. That's settled then. And besides," I continued, "I was intending to make a carbonara for dinner, and I never can seem to make it for just one person."

"Well, that being the case," he said, "I think I'll avail myself of the whiskey I just turned down."

I handed him the bottle.

"And you may not believe it to look at me, but I'm a

pretty accomplished cook in my own right," he said as he refilled his glass.

"I'll take your word for that. But seeing as how this is my galley and my recipe—handed down to me, by the way, by an Italian countess with whom I am intimately acquainted—you can sit there with a drink at hand and regale me with a story—it can be any version you like, I'm not a stickler for the facts—while I prepare a meal fit for human consumption," I said with a theatrical flourish.

"Be glad to oblige," he said. "But first, can you tell me where to find the head?"

"Sure thing," I said, pointing toward the bow. "Head is the first door to the left in the passageway. The next door on the left is your cabin. You'll find towels, soap, toothbrush, and all that kind of stuff in the cabinet next to the bunk. The light switch is to the right side of the door frame. Make yourself to home."

When Parker returned a few minutes later I was already elbow deep in the preparation of dinner. I directed Parker to the wine cabinet where he found a bottle of Chianti, and we switched from Irish whiskey to Italian peasant wine.

While I diced the ham and got it ready for the pan, my guest leaned against the galley counter, and by way of introducing his tale, he asked, "You have been in the military, haven't you?"

My hands occupied with dicing a large slice of ham, I nodded. "For a substantial part of my adult life and a pretty fair portion of my adolescence, I served in Uncle Sam's army."

"Then this will mean something to you," he began.

Parker told of how he came to his present circumstance in life. I knew he was well educated and had felt that he was even an accomplished man. But to pry into the life of a fellow saltwater nomad was something that just isn't done around here. Those of us who mark time near the high-tide line tend to live in the present moment, and we extend to others the same courtesy.

If a man or woman wishes to reinvent themselves and create or start a new life—well, this is the place to do it. Our creed is: *Cause no harm to others, be a good citizen, mind your own business, and your privacy will be respected. Your past belongs to you and you alone, and no one will dig into it.* So when Parker began to tell me something of his life, I knew it had to be important.

Parker had been educated at a very prestigious university. He was an engineer and had spent his professional life working in the defense industry. A good and diligent worker, with each passing year he had been tasked with more and higher responsibility. Then came a time when his company landed a major contract with the military. It was to create and build a new armored vehicle for the combat forces. But when the contract was awarded and work began, Parker, to his consternation, realized that something was direly wrong—the specifications were flawed. Flawed in such a manner that it would lead to catastrophic failure in the field. The vehicles his company was building were death traps.

So Parker, being an engineer, and trusting in the empirical evidence of hard engineering data, conducted an evaluation and submitted his concerns in the form of an engineering study. The study was promptly lost. He resubmitted his study. It was ignored. He spoke with his boss and was told that the matter was being looked into by the powers on high. Parker asked, "By whom?" but got no answer. Still nothing happened, and in the fullness of time the flawed vehicles began to roll off the assembly line.

Parker was more alarmed than ever. This couldn't be right. Soldiers were going to die, and die needlessly. He went to the plant manager and professed his concerns in convincing and irrefutable terms. After all, he had hard data to back up his fears. The manager told Parker that though he was a superb engineer, he should leave the final marketing of product to others. Parker said he would take his concerns higher.

That's when life began to change. He was reassigned to another, lesser job. Soon, he found that people were reluctant to associate with him. Still he persisted. He knew if only the right person would listen to him the mistake would be rectified. And that's when he was enlightened, and as he stated it in biblical terms, *He put away childish things*.

Parker was invited to the top floor—the Citadel, the Holy of Holies, if you will—of company headquarters, for an interview with one of the *senior* vice presidents of the firm. The man he met was cordial—even polite—but in very few words he made it perfectly clear to Parker that if he wished to continue with the company—or, for that matter, with any other American defense firm—he would immediately and completely shut up.

The man went on to tell Parker how the business really works: that contracts are always underbid, with the certain knowledge that once work is under way it is an easy matter to pump more money out of the military. And it was also ludicrous to deliver a perfectly functional system, when one with minor glitches would ensure years and years of additional funding to polish up those little problems. Properly managed, a single program could last a man his entire career.

Parker pointed out that the problems he had enumerated were anything but minor. The vehicles, supposedly providing protection against all classes of small arms, and most battlefield antitank rockets, would light up like roman candles if hit by even medium-caliber weapons.

The vice president replied that it was a matter of opinion, a personal one, and a wrong one at that. Parker's response was that they would see about that. When he rose to go, the VP delivered a clear and unmistakable warning. *Repeat your unfounded and un-American slanders and find yourself in a difficult legal position. Or, be quiet, like a good and loyal worker, and find yourself rewarded.* It was Parker's choice to make.

So Parker chose. He tendered his resignation. Still believing in Santa Claus, he sent his findings to his congressman. The response was an injunction forbidding him to speak publicly of *any* matters pertaining *whatsoever* to his former employer. Next day the FBI came to his home with a warrant authorizing a search for classified defense materials. They found none, but to console themselves in their failure, they did manage to trash Parker's house and confiscate his computer.

Parker got the message. He sold his house and car, cashed in his 401(k), closed his bank account, and bought a sailboat. Then one fine moonlit evening when no one was looking, he quietly set sail, leaving the sunny shores of California fading in his wake. His course took him down the coast of Mexico and Central America. He was in no hurry, with no real destination in mind. When he found a port that had a good feel he tied up for a while. After a journey of two years—his Spanish now pretty good—he eventually made his way through the Panama Canal and into the Caribbean.

When Bush II launched his war in Iraq Parker was sickened to see his predictions come true. Soldiers died by the scores in the fatally flawed vehicles. But by now he was not surprised when no one was held accountable. The only outcome was a new contract to retrofit the vehicles, and hence, as the VP had forecast, the money continued to roll in.

When Parker finished his tale he just sat for a while, looking at me with his large eyes. I wish I could have told him how shocked I was. But I wasn't. It was just another sad tale, one that fit within the litany of my own experience. What he had not said was the extent of the complicity and corruption. How military contracting officers go along with the charade, the promise being: Play along, and there's a cushy job waiting for you after your active service days are over. Retired general officers sit on the boards of the arms manufacturing conglomerates for the same reason. Lobbyists gleefully fill the troughs where the greedy swine of Congress come to feed. Everyone gets a piece of the pie. Everyone, that is, except the soldiers, their families, and the American taxpayers. As always, they get the shaft.

"What would you call a situation like that?" Parker asked, a sad look on his face.

"Treason," I replied without hesitation. "There's no other word for it. No matter how hard the guilty may try to dress it up, it is a crime against the people of this nation."

"Yeah," he responded in a subdued tone of voice. "I've never quite admitted to myself that it's that bad, but it is. There's no other way to put it."

I took the pan of pasta from the stove and pointed Parker to the small galley table. "Pour us some more wine while I fill the plates. You better be hungry, because I don't want any leftovers," I remarked as I heaped our plates with the marvelous concoction of pasta, ham, and Parmesan cheese.

We sat, and as I reached for the wineglass, Parker bowed his head, folded his hands, and closed his eyes. I paused with lowered brow as Parker silently gave thanks for the meal.

"Amen," I said when he lifted his head and looked across the table with a smile.

"This is the nicest meal I've sat down to in quite a while. Thanks, Kennesaw," he said.

"Thanks for the company, amigo. Now dig in," I rejoined.

We ate in contented silence. And when Parker's plate ran low, he offered no resistance when I filled it again. I realized as I watched him put away the food that it had probably been a while since he'd had a really filling meal. I had a thought.

"Parker," I said when the dishes were washed and put away, and we had settled down with a glass of port. "What kind of engineer were you? I mean, what was your specialty?"

"Oh," he said after taking a sip of the port and nodding his approval. "I was a mechanical and electrical engineer. I was also a metallurgist—I say *was*, but I guess I still am. I just haven't had cause to work in the field in some time."

"Well, what I mean is—were you a theorist, a planner—or were you a hands-on type?" I inquired.

"Ultimately I was a designer. But I am also a first-rate machinist; the dirty hands aspect of engineering is something I've always enjoyed."

"I guess that's what I was getting at," I admitted. "I have a reason for asking," I continued. "There are some things I want done on my boat and I just don't have the time right now—that, and some of it is beyond my capability."

Parker sat forward in his chair. I saw that I had his interest.

"Some of it is pretty simple. The main engine and transmission need servicing. You know, fluids, filters, and such. The hydraulics could stand a very thorough going-over. I also want to replace all the old belts and hoses with new rubber. But the main project I want done is an upgrade of the electrical system. I'd like to couple a wing generator to the main engine for use while under way, and I also want to increase the capacity of the battery bank—so that when at anchor I can power the air conditioner and the lights, and run the radios and radar without having to fire up the generator. Additionally, I want to extend the roof of the pilothouse so that it covers the aft deck—and that would require a fair amount of metal fabrication and welding. Could you do those things?"

Parker rubbed his chin as he thought. "It sounds like you're contemplating a long trip," he said with a smile.

"I'm *always* contemplating a long trip," I responded. "But would you do it? Would you do the work for me?"

"It's all rather routine. Just a matter of attention to detail," he said, more to himself than to me.

"You can live aboard and I'll pay you the going marina rate for the work," I said, hoping to help make up his mind.

"What make is the engine?" he asked.

"She's a Gardner. A model Six LS, if that means anything to you," I explained.

Parker sat upright in his chair. "A Gardner!" he almost shouted. "Those are probably the most exquisitely engineered diesel engines in the world. In this case the English manufacturer excelled even the Germans. As the saying goes about Gardners: *Designed and built by geniuses, for use by idiots*. I would almost pay *you* for the opportunity to work on a Gardner."

"Then you'll do it?"

"Sir," he said, extending his hand. "It is an honor and a privilege to accept your kind offer."

"Great. I have something that's occupying me right now, so I won't be able to help much. But I have a trusted friend—Danny Ray Pledger—who is a skilled worker and is familiar with the boat. If you could start tomorrow— look everything over and come up with a parts list and a schedule of work—then I would appreciate it no end. I'll give you an advance so that you can pick up odds and ends as you get started."

"I will, Kennesaw," Parker replied. He hesitated a second and then added, "You don't know how timely this is. I was almost down to scavenging for a living. In fact Miss Darcey had been seeing that I had something to eat on a regular basis. This means a lot to me. And I know who Danny Ray is. From what I've heard of him, I couldn't ask for a better companion."

"I'm glad," was all I could say. "But I'm gonna turn in now, and you might want to do the same. We'll talk about it more tomorrow."

Parker went to his cabin, but I went out on deck to check the dock lines and give everything topside one last look before locking up for the night. Walking the deck, I thought of all that had happened during the day.

In the trip to Panther Creek I had stepped back in time, back to the era of *Tobacco Road* and *God's Little Acre*. My truck was beaten into a state of poor health, and I'd nearly had my head torn off by a bat-wielding giant who thought he was an Old Testament prophet. *There is no such thing as coincidence,* I reflected. *Nothing happens to any of us for no reason at all, though that reason is sometimes impossible to comprehend.*

The gentle man bunked in the cabin below had been living in the grounded hull of a derelict boat on Daufuskie Island. Surviving on scarce odd jobs and handouts, barely keeping body and soul together, he had come near the end of his tether. But now I had a capable hand to perform some very necessary work, and he had a comfortable paying berth. Funny, sometimes, how things work out.

And then the vision of a tiny old woman came to my

mind; a woman with a soul as old as humanity itself. An ancient woman she is, but one with the brightly flashing eyes and the musical voice of a young girl.

Cyriah, I thought, *how well you know us, the people in your life.*

With that thought echoing in my mind, I went below for the night, seeking the rest and repose that is found only in the unconsciousness of sleep. But in that final instant of waking cognizance, just as my mind made the short slide into oblivion, I heard an echo of the words spoken by a famous Georgia girl from a time and place long ago: *Tomorrow is another day.*

CHAPTER 10

I FOUND THAT PARKER, LIKE ME, WAS an early riser, and that also he was a quiet house companion. We must have each heard the other rustling around, and by the time we met in the salon I had the coffee going, and sliced fruit, warm bread, and marmalade on the galley counter. We took our breakfast up on deck. Bundled in jackets and hats, we sat under the forward canopy, eating in companionable silence while staring out across the waters of the creek; watching as the early morning breeze stirred and ran its fingers through the marsh grass with an invisible but chilly hand.

After breakfast we made a technical walk around of the boat. I took Parker from one end to the other, and he, with a pad and pen in hand, made notes of the work I wanted accomplished. Following that, we went below to the engine room, and there, Parker was in a near state of bliss. Again, he made notes and sketches in his book, and even pointed out a couple of areas needing attention that had caught his engineering eye but had evaded mine. Returning to the galley we freshened our coffee cups and then went, one by one, down the list of items in the notebook.

Parker took a sip of coffee and, setting down his cup, directed my attention, once again, to the several pages he had written.

"First, I'll draw up a list of materials and determine their costs. I should have that available for you by the end of the day. Then, I'll prioritize the schedule of work. That way, you can determine which areas are the most critical tasks to accomplish and what is the most cost-effective. Once you give the okay to the scope of work, I can begin."

"Sounds good, Parker. I'll stop by the marina store this morning and tell them you'll be coming in. Harold Jones is the manager, and if there's anything they don't have, he can order it for you. I'll let him know that you are handling this for me and that you have authority to put everything on my tab."

Parker gave me a smile. "That's pretty trusting of you, Kennesaw."

"What are you going to do? Run off with some steel plate or rubber hoses? Besides, I know where you live," I bantered in reply.

Parker reached down and picked up the end of his beard. He waved it in my direction.

"Wouldn't happen to have a pair of scissors handy, would you?" he inquired.

"You're not getting rid of that beard, are you? Why, it's your trademark," I replied. "People wouldn't know you without it."

"Can't work and wear a beard this long. If it gets caught in some machinery you're liable to find me in the engine room with my head torn off. Besides, now that I have a job, and am once more found in the ranks of the gainfully employed, I need to look like a professional," he said with another smile.

"You'll find a pair in the top drawer of that cabinet," I said and pointed.

"Also, I'm going to make a run back to Daufuskie this morning, to let Miss Cyriah know I made it, and to pick up a few things. I should be back by noon," he explained.

I slid a key across the galley table. "Here," I said. "It fits everything on the boat—all the hatches, doors, and lockers."

Parker picked up the key and looked at it closely. As he did, I took a few bills from my wallet and put them in his hand. "A few of the elusive spondulix to get you started."

Parker looked from the money in one hand to the key in the other. His voice was a little tight when he said, "Thanks, Kennesaw. I haven't felt this trustworthy in a long time."

I nodded. I understood how he felt. "Great. I may be out most of the day, so I'll see you this evening when I return."

"Will do," he replied as we both rose to leave.

Out on the dock, I persuaded Parker to take my sea skiff for his trip to Daufuskie. It has a center console with a windscreen and a T-top that would give some protection from the weather. It was still heavily overcast and drizzly, with a forecast for more of the same.

I gave the bow a shove away from the dock and watched as Parker carefully pulled away. After clearing the no-wake zone, he shoved the throttle forward, brought the boat quickly up on plane, and then throttled back to a neat cruising speed that was easy on the engine but would still gobble the miles.

Very well done, I thought as I watched him handle the boat. Then, just before rounding the bend that would put him out of sight, he looked over his shoulder and gave me a wave. I touched my fingers to my forehead in salute. And as Parker disappeared into the arms of the salt marsh, I turned and mounted the steps to the parking lot.

I intended to make a trek to police headquarters to pick up a copy of the report of Tonya's death, but the traffic heading into town was still heavy, so instead, I turned east for Tybee Island. After crossing the Bull River Bridge, Highway 80 traverses a low causeway that rises just barely above the level of the marsh. Paralleling the north side of the road is the bed of the old rail line that once was the only land connection to the island. But a hurricane, years ago, had put an end to the train, and the rail bed now is a bike and pedestrian pathway. I come out here often to run.

On days like today, with the tide running high and an onshore wind piling in the water, the road itself comes near to going under. I haven't seen it yet, but locals tell me that it isn't all that unusual for Highway 80 to meet the Atlantic Ocean in the marsh near Bull River, about ten miles west of its usual terminus at the south end of Tybee Island.

But it was still above water today and in less than a quarter of an hour I was on the island. I slowed at the landmark I was looking for, a huge live oak on the corner, where I turned south on to a residential street. Bungalows and Tybee cottages flanked either side of the narrow street. This was a neighborhood that naturally made you want to slow down. It was tree-shaded, quiet, and friendly. Anyone outside automatically waved when a car passed by. Finding the place I was looking for, I pulled into the drive.

Bob and Fran's house is a yellow, wood-framed, two-story cottage. A massive oak layered in Spanish moss shelters the front walk, with a luxuriant growth of flowers bordering the property on all sides. I stepped to the kitchen door at the carport, and before I could knock, it was thrown wide open.

Fran stood there in her house robe. A hand on one hip and a cup of coffee in the other, she thrust out her notable bosom, lifted her chin, and struck a pose.

"I've told you before, young man," she breathed in a sultry voice. "Never to call on me this time of day. You know *very* well that my husband is still home."

She held the pose a second longer, then let out a cackle, grabbed me by the back of the neck, and pulling me close, gave me a smack across the lips.

"Hey, Fran," I said as I pulled back a step and unconsciously lifted a hand to wipe the lipstick from my face.

"Don't you dare wipe that off," she ordered, pointing a finger in my face. "I want Bob to see it and know he's not the only man in my life." She laughed.

I sheepishly lowered my hand. "Okay, Fran. How you doing?"

"I'm doing fine, honey. But I know you came to see Bob and not me. You'll find him out back in his workshop." She pointed with her cup. "Probably out there looking at girly magazines—why, I don't know, when he has all this inside." She lifted a leg and pulled up the hem of her robe, exposing a thigh and giving me a lascivious grin.

"Fran, too much of anything—even that—isn't good for a man," I returned with a grin of my own. "And cover that leg, before I forget your old man is at home, and I do something I shouldn't."

"Nothing but promises." She sighed. "It's the story of my life. See you this week at the club?"

"You bet, Fran."

"All right, lover. I guess I can wait 'til then—but just barely. And bring that policewoman with you. I'd like to give her a sniff and make sure she's not trying to beat my time."

Fran pushed out her lips in an exaggerated pout and then gently closed the door. I shook my head and walked away, but as I did, I heard her throaty laugh from inside.

Bob's shop sat at the back of the yard, almost at the edge of the marsh. It was built of rough-sided sawmill lumber and roofed with tin. A dirt-floored porch ran the length of the near side. The building had been constructed entirely of scavenged materials. Twenty feet away a boardwalk ran thirty yards out to a small dock that sat perched over a tidal creek. It, too, was built of wood that had been recovered from a thousand different locations and patiently hauled, piece by piece, to become a part of Bob Martin's backyard domain.

I stepped under the roof of the porch and lifted my hand to rap on the door when Bob's voice called out from within, "Come on in, Kenny Boy—the door's open."

I walked in and closed the door behind me. Bob sat on an old bar stool over against the far wall, chewing on a toothpick and contemplating a long wooden boat that lay perched between us on a series of sawhorses. Bob pushed his hat to the back of his head and pointed to the center of the boat.

"Hardest part is now. Where exactly to position the mast step? If I don't get it just right, she'll sail like a dead cow, and I'll have to haul her out and try again."

"Don't you have any plans to go by?" I asked.

"There are no plans, never were. These were always built by eye—and this will be the first one launched in more than fifty years," he replied. "I've been going by my memory and the advice of some old-timers from up and down the coast."

I cast my eyes the length and breadth of the boat. She was maybe twenty feet long and perhaps six feet wide, at her widest. It was an open boat with four plank seats.

A rudder with attached tiller was hung in place on the squared transom. The sides of the boat, I noted, were made of a single, very wide plank of wood. As I stepped closer and looked inside I saw the bottom was made of just two planks. Bob anticipated my questions and answered before I could speak.

"She's an old style sailing bateau. Only four planks of wood went into making her hull. And I can tell you, I had the devil of a time finding the cypress to build her of. There're precious few of the old big trees ever timbered anymore. I found this one down on the Ogeechee River where the state was widening a bridge. If I hadn't hauled her to the sawmill, they would have chipped her up for mulch." Bob shook his head at the thought of such a travesty.

"I've seen one or two of these in old photos," I remarked as I admired the simple lines of the boat.

Bob nodded and replied, "People out here on the islands, and up and down the rivers and creeks, have built and sailed this type of boat since the white man landed on this coast. This was how people got about until decent roads were finally built. I remember seeing them when I was a boy. The Geechee women from out on the islands used to bring their produce and handicrafts in to Savannah on these bateaus.

"I can see it like yesterday—the boats piled high with fresh vegetables, baskets, tubs of crabs, and cages of chickens—even live fish in the fish wells. A teenage boy or young man handling the tiller and sail—sailing in on a rising tide—with the old women sitting under their parasols— dressed to kill and looking like the Queen of Sheba done come to Jerusalem. It used to be a colorful sight."

I had an image then of Cyriah landing at River Street back in the years gone by. What I would give to have seen that.

"So what's the plan here, Bob? Is this for a museum or something?" I asked.

Bob stared at me a moment. "It's a little something to leave behind—for when I'm gone," he said in a gentle tone of voice. "So it won't be completely lost. I'd like to think that one of these old boats survive and maybe someone will get to enjoy it."

Bob and I had talked about this subject before—not the boat—but the realization of his mortality. Bob felt he had only a little time remaining, and he still had things to accomplish. And though I would never say it aloud—I had to agree with him. His body was beginning to fail more rapidly now. He had been hospitalized several times in the last year, and finally, after the last occasion, he had said, "No more. That's enough."

Bob told me he was tired of the indignity of it all, and that when it was time to go, it would be here, at his home—and the doctors be damned.

I had no reply, all I could do was nod my head and clear my throat, "Ah-hmmm."

We were silent a few moments, and then Bob leaned over the side of the boat and ran a hand across the smooth cypress bottom. "So what do you think? This look like the right spot for the mast step?" He indicated a point on the floor just in front of one of the seats.

"What kind of sail rig you going to use?" I asked, grateful to change the subject.

"Sort of a modified sliding gunter. That way I can use a short, unstayed mast—one that's easy to get up and down and handle by one person. If there's no wind, the rig stays rolled up and you use the oars. I thought about hanging a small outboard on the transom but came to the conclusion that it would be damn near sacrilegious."

"That being the case," I replied, "the center of effort is

pretty much over the center of the boat. I'd think the mast has to go farther forward." I indicated a spot. "Say, about here."

Bob stepped back and gave the boat an encompassing sweep with his eyes. "I think that might be it," he said pensively. "I'll figure the square footage of the sail and that should give me the final answer.

"But you better be right," he announced as he looked up with a grin, "'cause you're gonna be the one to take her out on her maiden voyage."

"I'll be glad to, Bob—as long as you ship aboard as admiral."

"All right," he replied with a short nod. "So, now that's settled, come have a seat and tell me what's on your mind. You didn't come here just to admire a boat."

Bob led the way to a corner of the shop that was set up as a lounge area. A few old deck chairs were arrayed around an irregularly shaped table made of a single slab cut from what must have been a huge cypress log—I guess the one Bob had used to build his boat. Off to the side was a counter with a sink and a two-burner gas stove top. Bob pointed to a coffeepot that sat perking on the stove and raised an eyebrow. I shook my head no and had a seat as Bob poured himself a cup and then joined me at the table.

That slight amount of movement had winded my friend, and for several seconds after sitting, he held the oxygen tube closely beneath his nostrils, gasping like a beached fish. At last he looked up and gave me a sheepish smile.

"Getting old is not for the weak. I suggest you avoid it if at all possible," he joked. He took another deep breath and then asked, "Now what is it you want to talk about?"

"There are a couple of things I need your advice on." I then told Bob the story of my visit to Effingham County. It sounded, in recitation, even weirder than the experience had actually seemed at the time. Bob sat quietly as I spoke, sipping his coffee, and now and then emitting a noncommittal, "Uh-huh."

As I finished my tale I found myself leaning forward in the chair with my arms braced tensely on the table. Relaxing my pose, I sat back and crossed my legs. Bob was silent a few more moments. He was staring fixedly at a spot on the wall behind me, but I could see his mind working. He spoke at last.

"You've stepped off into some craziness there—you know that, don't you?" He gave me a sharp look.

"I believe so," I replied.

"So why don't you just withdraw and declare victory? It worked for Nixon and Kissinger."

"No." I shook my head in response. "I gave my word to the mother—Joree—that I would do what I could."

"Well, right now you have precious little to go on, so what does your gut tell you?" He solicited.

"The girl was in trouble of some kind. In her mind it was so bad that she had to cut off contact with her family. Her friend Sandy Willis seems to know something about where Tonya had gone, but I'll have to tread very lightly there; she's as skittish as a colt." I reflected a moment. "No, that's not quite true—she's afraid; of who or what I don't know, but she's frightened."

"And the brother?" Bob asked.

"He's hiding something, Bob. He's scared also. And he's into something dirty of some kind. I doubt that he works a job, but he drives a tricked-out pickup, and there's a new bass boat sitting in the yard."

"Have you come to any conclusions?" he prodded.

I shook my head. "No. I don't have enough information yet and I don't want to cloud my thoughts with unfounded supposition. I'm going to the police department today to get a copy of the nine-one-one report; maybe there's something hidden there. After that, I have to find a way to get Sandy Willis to speak candidly with me."

Bob was looking at that spot on the wall again. "Ever hear of something called Occam's razor?" he asked.

I thought for a second. "Yeah," I replied. "I think it goes, 'Plurality ought never be posited without necessity,' or something close to that."

Bob nodded. "Uh-huh; if several theories will give you the same result—pick the simplest one. Now, how did we say that in the army?" He smiled.

Now it was my turn to smile. "The old KISS formula: Keep It Simple, Stupid."

"Exactly," my friend returned. "And it works with everything *except* people. The answer, when you find it, to *what* happened to that poor girl, will be simple. The reasons—the answers to the question *why*—will be anything but simple, because it has to do with people and their emotions. We like to think of ourselves as rational animals—and in some ways we are. But the decisions we make are almost always emotional ones."

It was my turn to be silent and think for a minute. There was much wisdom in Bob's words. And I had to ask myself if the *why* of the matter made any difference to me. The answer to my question was: Yes, it did—to me, if to no one else. And I had to admit that for me it *was* a decision based on emotion.

I looked again at my friend across the table. He spoke before I did.

"I don't think there's anything I can help you with there, Kennesaw. My advice is to quit, but you've already shrugged that off. I just want you to be careful up there in Effingham. People—outsiders—can disappear if they rub someone the wrong way; it's happened before. And remember—everybody hides something, all the time—it's the nature of the human animal. Now, you said you had a couple of things on your mind; what was the other one?"

"I may need to move my boat, Bob—for a little while at least. To somewhere out of the way and out of sight, but not too far from town."

A huge grin came on Bob's face. "Amigo, I got just the place for you. Did I ever tell you about my old fishing camp out on Dutch Island?"

"Bob, there are no fish camps on Dutch Island, just millionaire mansions," I replied with a surprised voice.

"Millionaire mansions, yes—and one old shotgun shack," he replied with glee. "It was my daddy's place. He bought it before the war. We used to go camping out there when I was a boy. Once I was grown I realized it was Daddy's hideout when he and Mama would get in a tiff. Over the years we built a cabin and a dock on the property. Now, it's the last undeveloped lot left on the island. I check on it every week or so and think of how much those two acres of deep-water frontage will be worth when I'm gone. It's my insurance policy for Fran."

Without doubt, I thought, there was a veritable phalanx of real estate agents and developers salivating, this very day, over the prospect of getting their hands on that piece of dirt. And I knew enough about Bob's nature to realize what a perverse joy he would take in turning them down.

"The cabin has electricity and running water. It's set up like a bunkhouse and has all the comforts of home," he explained. "The dock is in a deep cut in the bluff, and there's ten feet of water there, even at the lowest ebb tide—so you shouldn't have any trouble getting your boat in there.

"But the channel coming up the river, and then the creek, can get pretty tricky. It shifts with every season and every spring tide. But Danny Ray knows the way in. Get him to pilot you up, and you'll have no trouble."

"Bob, I didn't mean for you to—" I began, but he interrupted me with the wave of a hand.

"No, it'll be good to have someone out there for a change. You know how a place will fall in if it doesn't have a human in it now and then. I don't know what it is, but somehow or other buildings know when they're not appreciated. You'd be doing me a big favor."

"Well, since you put it that way—I'll accept your kind offer," I responded with gratitude.

"Great," he replied as he took a key from the ring in his pocket and pitched it over.

He then wrote on a scrap of paper and passed it to me. "That's the address and a map to the place. The key fits the gate and the lock on the cabin. The place is covered with trees, so if a limb is down in the drive you'll find a chainsaw in the shed behind the cabin—key fits the lock on the shed, too."

I picked up the piece of paper and rose to leave. "I'll call and let you know how things look when I get out there," I said.

"I'll get ahold of Danny Ray and see if while he's there with you he can patch up the things that need fixing," Bob said as he, too, stood.

I held the key aloft and twitched it at him. *"Gracias, viejo."*

"De nada, joven," he replied. "Now, clear on out of here. Some of us have work to do, and I can't spend the whole day jabbering with you.

"See you, Bob," I said as I turned to the door.

"Later," he replied as he went back to where he was when I entered and resumed his perch on the stool.

As I closed the door I glanced over my shoulder and saw my friend sitting with head lowered and face downcast—his chest heaving wildly as he struggled to catch his breath.

CHAPTER 11

TRAFFIC WAS LIGHT, OR AS LIGHT AS it gets in Savannah, as I made my way to police headquarters downtown. The building sits in the historic district at the intersection of Broughton and Oglethorpe streets. I circled the place once and started to turn in to the indicated parking area, but for some reason, I turned down a side street and parked a block away. I guess it was one of those emotional decisions Bob had spoken of.

Before I got out of the car, I gave myself a good going-over. Only thing I had on my person that I needed to jettison was my folding knife. I slipped it from its accustomed place in my waistband and deposited it in the console with my pistol where I locked both away.

Getting out, I pulled my old weatherproof canvas hat on at a low angle to ward off the weather and headed down the sidewalk. The fog and mist, if anything, was even heavier here in town. Except for the palms, live oaks, and Spanish moss, a visitor could be forgiven for thinking they were in London. But then again, the original settlers of the city had done their best to re-create another London town here in the subtropics. Within a few minutes I turned the corner, and there I was, 201 Broughton Street.

Entering the building, I immediately encountered the screening area. Automatically emptying my pockets under the watchful eye of an older police officer, I then passed through the metal detector. The officer monitoring the machine gave me a perfunctory nod of hello as I passed through. Scooping my change and keys from the small plastic basket and redistributing them in my pockets, I turned to the officer and said, "I always expect to hear buzzers and sirens go off."

He laughed and replied, "Everybody does."

I then asked, "Can you tell me where I can find the records section? I need to pick up a copy of a police report."

Before he could answer a voice spoke up behind me, "Not here, buddy. Records section is on the other side of town."

I turned to that familiar voice. It was Detective Patricia Latham. She flashed her badge to the officer on duty and walked around the screening kiosk to where I stood.

"Hello, Detective. I didn't expect to see you here, but I'm glad I did," I said.

Patricia looked to the officer standing nearby and gave him the hard eye. "Rayford, I hope you checked this man especially well. He's a known troublemaker and not to be trusted under any conditions."

"Nothing but the best, Detective. He got the full treatment," he replied with a chuckle.

"Maybe so," she said, "but just in case—Mr. Tanner, I think you better come with me."

"If you insist, Detective," I replied to her order.

"Oh, I do," she responded.

Then turning slightly, and with a quick tilt of the head, she indicated the direction we were to go. I fell in step beside her as she paced away. With Patricia in the lead we made a couple of turns in the hallway and then arrived at a room divided into the standard office gopher cubicles. She made her way through the room with a "Hello, Dave" and a "Hi, Jim" here and there, until we came to her warren in the far corner of the room.

She hung her jacket on the back of a chair, and as she sat down she smiled and, pointing to the other chair in the booth, announced, "Sit."

I did as she directed.

"So—what's this business about a police report? You don't have to go to such lengths just to see me," she quipped.

I raised my hand in a facsimile of taking the Boy Scout Oath. "I *am* glad to see you, Patricia," I said in a solemn voice, "but also, I do need a copy of a police report."

She paused a moment before replying in a lowered voice, "Good to see you, too, Kennesaw. Now—what's this about a report? Because you really are in the wrong place for that; records section is in the Chatham annex, over on the west side of town."

"You know, if I had a friend in the department they could probably get the report I need and save me a trip," I said in a deadpan manner. "In fact, I'm not above offering a bribe—say, perhaps—lunch."

Patricia snorted a short laugh. "And I'm not above accepting. Now, tell me the report you want."

"I need a copy of a nine-one-one call-in, and the follow-up police reports. I'd also like a copy of the autopsy if that can be managed. It's a case you're familiar with."

The smile left Patricia's face and a serious tone entered her voice. "The Causey girl?"

I nodded my head. "Yes. That's the one."

Patricia looked at me a moment, her eyes searching mine. Then she turned to the computer on her desk and made a few keystrokes. She scanned the monitor and made several more entries. Reading the screen again she nodded her head and then made two more taps on the keyboard. Then she stood abruptly and grabbed her jacket. "Come on," she said as she left the cubicle. "We'll pick up the report on the way out."

I followed her to a small office not much bigger than a good-size closet where we found a printer busily spitting out pages. Patricia plucked a sheaf of papers from the tray, glanced at them quickly, slid a paper clip over the top, and handed them to me. A few seconds later the machine went dormant again, and I had the complete report.

"You owe the City of Savannah twenty-five cents a page for that report," Patricia pronounced. "And as a duly appointed officer of the law, I can accept payment in cash or kind."

I started to make a remark, but she cut me off just as I opened my mouth. "But we can take care of that over lunch. Come on—you can take me to my favorite place."

"Lead on, Detective. I place myself entirely in your capable hands," I replied.

She gave me a quick smile. "Then I must warn you, Tanner—be careful what you say. I may just hold it against you."

I let the double entendre hang in the air before saying, "Okay. Let's go to lunch."

As we exited the building Patricia asked where I was parked. When I told her, she said, "We'll take my car. Just don't play with the radio or the siren."

"Yes, ma'am," I replied as we walked a short distance to a row of parked cars where I saw a sign on the walkway announcing: Detectives.

"But maybe on the way back we can turn on the blue lights."

She looked at me over the top of the car as she opened the door. "Get in, Tanner."

"Yes, ma'am," I responded as I heard the door lock on my side click open.

I got in and fastened my seat belt. As we headed over toward River Street we chatted about odds and ends, both of us avoiding the contents of the report I had stuffed inside my jacket. The car tires clattered roughly down the cobblestoned ramp that leads off of Bay Street, past Factors Walk, and down to River Street. I thought we'd have to search around, but as if by magic, Patricia found a parking spot right in front of the café.

In the river, to our front, a huge container ship from China was slowly beating its way upstream, a pair of tugboats tethered to her stern as insurance against accident. She would soon cross beneath the Talmadge Bridge on her way to the ports just upriver. This was the second bridge, I recollected, the old one having been hit by a ship a decade or so ago. I had to admit: The new bridge was a vast improvement, aesthetically and otherwise, over the previous one.

I stared up at the center of the arch and tried to imagine what it would look like from up there, gazing down, so very high above the surface of the river. From here, the cars on the bridge looked like toys—a person would appear as no more than a tiny stick figure. I vowed to myself that I would go up there. I would walk the bridge and stand at the spot where Tonya Causey had pitched to her death. Why, I don't know. I guess it was another one of those emotional decisions Bob had spoken about.

"Hey, you coming in, or you gonna just stand there in the street, gaping like a tourist?" Patricia called from the sidewalk, snapping me out of my reverie.

"Yeah. Sure," I said as I hustled around the car and opened the door to the restaurant.

The interior of the building was warm and welcoming. The large window fronting River Street let in the gray light of day, and the old-fashioned lamps threw splashes of yellow illumination that gave the place a relaxing feel.

I helped Patricia out of her jacket just as a pretty, young waitress with short-cropped blond hair came over to greet us.

"Hello, Detective." She smiled as she picked up two menus.

"Hi, Rhonda. Is my favorite table available?" Patricia inquired.

The girl was already turning away. "You bet," she said over her shoulder. "Right this way."

"I'll give you a few minutes to look the menu over," she said as we slid into the corner booth. "But how about something to drink first?"

We both ordered iced tea—sweet, of course, this is the South after all—and Rhonda bustled away.

I gave the room a quick scan—habit, you know, and when I looked back across the table Patricia was looking directly at me. We held the gaze a second before she said, "I was hoping to see you, Kennesaw. In fact, I was thinking I might stop by that bar at your dock and try to catch you at happy hour."

"Yeah, I'm glad we ran into each other. And I'll just tell you this—I want to see more of you, Patricia—it's as simple as that. And I'd like to call with no other reason than to talk with you and hear your voice," I said as I slid a hand across the table and placed my fingertips over hers.

She looked down at our hands, and when she looked up again it was with a warm smile on her face.

"I'd like that, too," she breathed as we held the look a bit longer.

Then she withdrew her hand and picked up the menu and gave it a cursory look. "And since you're buying, I think I'll have a Low Country Boil. Eddie—the chef here—makes one that's the talk of the town. And when the weather is as dreary as it has been, it's a dish that'll put a little cheer back in your soul," she announced as Rhonda set the tea glasses on the table.

"Make that two of them," I said to the waitress as she looked from Patricia to me.

"Two Low Country Boils it is," she replied.

We waited until the girl was gone and then Patricia spoke, "So what's your interest in the girl?"

I took a sip of tea and began my tale. Patricia sat quietly and listened without interruption as I told her of my initial meeting with Joree Causey, and her concern that Tonya had been killed by "them sons a bitches."

When I finished that portion of the story Patricia nodded and said, "I tried to find the callers who reported a jumper."

"Tried?" I asked with surprise.

"Yeah—tried. It was from a prepaid phone that was a throwaway."

"But there has to be a record of the purchaser," I hastened to respond.

"Paid for with cash—no record of who bought it," she answered with a flat voice.

I thought a second. "Both nine-one-one calls were from a prepaid phone? That's mighty odd."

"What's even more odd—the calls were from the same phone. The voice of one caller was a woman's, and the next call that came in was from a man, but the call was from the same phone."

"Who uses prepaid phones?" I wondered aloud.

"Teenagers whose parents are limiting their calls—and

criminals. But in my experience, mostly criminals in the drug trade," Patricia replied.

I looked out the window and watched as an empty freighter, riding high in the water, its black bottom paint exposed, slid silently yet swiftly down the river. When I looked back across the table Patricia was waiting for me.

"I made a few more inquiries after that, but the decision had been made by the powers that be that they didn't want the waters muddied. 'It was a suicide, Detective, leave it at that.' But to tell you the truth, Kennesaw—I also have some doubts," she concluded.

I nodded my comprehension as my mind took in the possibilities of what she had just told me.

"What do you think of it all now?" I asked.

"As you said while we were standing on your dock after I had taken your statement: 'It's bad juju.' More than that, at this time I have no idea. But I'm no longer so sure that it was a suicide," she said, pushing an imaginary lock of hair back from her forehead, in what I knew was a gesture of exasperation.

Our food arrived just at that moment. Patricia assured the waitress that we needed nothing else and we were left alone once again. I leaned over to take in the delicious aroma arising from the large bowl, and as I picked up a spoon I said, "There's more to tell."

We ate steadily, and between mouthfuls, I told Patricia of my strange trip yesterday, and of the impressions I had taken away. She listened carefully, her eyes holding mine so as not to miss any of the unspoken meaning, and I thought, not for the first time, that this woman sitting across from me was a formidable police officer.

When I had finished my tale and our bowls were empty we both dabbed our lips with our napkins and sat back in the booth. I glanced outside and saw that the rain was falling heavily now—the drops so close together they appeared as long continuous streaks, bouncing from the tops of cars in the street and pounding a dimpled face on to the moving surface of the river.

"Where do you look next?" Patricia asked, bringing me back from my reverie.

"I need to speak to the Willis girl—Sandy," I said, looking again at Patricia. "And tomorrow evening, I'm going to church—to a Wednesday-night prayer meeting, in fact, to meet that preacher I told you of. He may just have a little insight into Tonya's state of mind before she left home."

And then, as an afterthought, I asked, "Want to come with me?"

Patricia gave me a quick smile. "Yes, I'd like to come with you. And anything I can do to help—unofficially of course—I will. But is this one of those 'speaking in tongues' churches?"

"Yeah," I said, nodding in affirmation. "I'm pretty sure it is. So it may get a little wild if everyone gets worked up, and in the spirit."

"Okay, but next time you ask me out, I get to pick where we go."

"You've got a deal," I replied with a smile of my own.

At that instant I felt my phone vibrating in my pocket. Very few people have my number, and I never interrupt a conversation with a live human to stop and take a phone call. So I just let the phone buzz until it went dormant again. I would see who it was later.

"Shall we go?" I asked, looking around for our waitress.

"We'd better," Patricia replied as she glanced at her watch. "I need to start earning the big bucks the City of Savannah is paying me."

I settled the bill, and afterward a smiling Rhonda ushered us from our table and wished us a speedy return. The rain was still pounding relentlessly as we dashed to the car and dove inside. While Patricia drove I retrieved the phone message. I listened to it once, and then to make sure that I had heard correctly, I listened again. I closed the phone and put it back in my pocket just as Patricia stopped at a light.

"Anything wrong?" she asked, glancing over.

"I don't think it's anything good," I said, meeting her eye. "That was Sheriff Zimmer. He was calling to let me know that Leon Wren bonded out of jail a little while ago."

Patricia stared at me. I saw the light turn green. "Go," I said.

Patricia gave her attention to the street again and asked, "Who got him out? That's always worth knowing."

"That's the really interesting part," I replied. "The person who posted bond was Joree's son, Junior Causey—Tonya's brother."

"What do you do now?" Patricia asked as she maneuvered around a double-parked delivery truck.

"I think it's important that I speak with Sandy Willis. I think it's possible Wren might try to intimidate her."

"For what reason? You told me the sheriff saw the altercation between you and Wren—so she's not important as a witness," Patricia responded.

"I know. But I have a feeling he's the type who likes frightening smaller folk. And I'll bet he especially enjoys scaring girls."

Patricia pulled to a stop behind my car. "Anything I can do at this point?" she asked as she turned slightly and we faced each other.

I smiled and shook my head. "No. Not now. But how about I pick you up at your place tomorrow? We need to leave about six. What time do you get off?"

"Won't work," she replied. "That's when I usually leave the office—unless something is going on. Why don't you meet me at the security checkpoint where I stumbled across you earlier today. I'll see you there at six. If it looks like I won't be able to make it, I'll give you a call and let you know."

"All right," I said as I leaned over and we exchanged an embrace and a small kiss. "See you then."

"Yeah," she replied as I pulled on my hat and zipped up my jacket. "See you then."

I gave her one last smile and then threw open the door and dashed from the car into the pelting rain. Patricia waited until she saw I was in my car, and then, with a wave, she pulled away. I sat and watched until she turned the corner at the end of the block and then I reached for my phone. I listened to Zimmer's message again and then started to call.

And as I touched the icon to make the call, I wondered how Zimmer had gotten my number—because I had purposely not given it to him.

CHAPTER 12

EVALEEN INFORMED ME THAT THE sheriff was in a monthly meeting with the county commissioners that afternoon and would be unavailable for the rest of the day. But she would certainly let him know I had called, and was there anything she could do in his stead? I thanked her and answered that it was nothing important and that I would call again.

I then looked up the number of the convenience store where Sandy worked and gave them a call. The girl on duty at the counter told me that Sandy hadn't come in to work that day. When I informed her I had some important information for Sandy, she gave me her cell number without hesitation.

I called and got no answer but left a message on her voice mail. I told her that Leon was out of jail and that should he show up, wherever she might be, she was to call the sheriff immediately. I also asked her to call me so that we could arrange a meeting.

I thought it best I get back to the dock and see if Parker had returned yet. I also needed to stop at the marine supply store and let them know that a Mr. Parker Wells would be stopping in now and again, and that he had my authorization to pick up supplies and equipment on my account. But first, I wanted to check on the condition of my truck. Just maybe the glass had come in and it would be ready today. I drifted through traffic over to the Truman Parkway and from there to Thunderbolt.

The rain lessened a bit as I drove, so that when I arrived at the auto shop it had subsided to a desultory patter. When I went inside I saw my truck sitting forlornly in the work bay—still with all the windows knocked out. But the young man on duty at the counter happily informed me that the glass would be delivered later in the day—in fact he was waiting for the truck to arrive any time now—and that as soon as it arrived they would get right on it. I thanked him and turned to leave. Though I wanted my truck back as soon as possible, I could wait another day without complaint. This was a good shop, and I knew they were doing their best.

As I stepped outside, to my surprise, I found Danny Ray, leaning against the shop doors, sheltered by the canopy that ran the front of the building. He looked at me from beneath the brim of his Braves cap and gave me a shy grin.

"Tr-tr-truck t-took a beating—huh?" he stammered, but with the grin still on his face.

"You tried to warn me, Danny Ray, but I wouldn't listen to you. That *is* a bad place up there, and now, just look at my truck," I replied with a grin of my own.

"Wh-what ha-ha-happened?"

"Some crazy guy—a huge dude named Leon Wren—tried to tear my head off, but instead he only managed to cripple my truck," I bantered.

The grin left Danny Ray's face only to be replaced by a look that was serious, and maybe even a little startled.

"Tha-that family is b-bad—real bad."

"I heard about the uncle. And I can testify that the nephew—the one I met, is no pillar of the community, either," I replied, still with a light tone of voice.

Danny Ray shook his head. "N-n-no. I mean—b-bad. K-killin' bad."

"Do you know Leon Wren? Have you ever had anything to do with him?" I asked.

Danny Ray shook his head again. "N-n-no. B-b-but I've heard. W-watch out."

I looked at my friend. It would have been easy to make light of his words of warning, but now that I realized how serious Danny was, that would have been the wrong thing to do. Danny Ray was concerned for me, and I could only acknowledge his concern.

"I will, Danny," I replied. "I'll watch out. Now," I said, changing the subject. "I have a man doing some work on my boat and I was hoping you could come over and give a hand. Should be about a week to ten days' paying gig. Also, I'm thinking of moving *Miss Rosalie* to another spot, for just a little while. Bob Martin's letting me use his place out on Dutch Island, and he said you might be able to pilot me there. Could you do that? Could you come give me a hand?"

Danny nodded his head and said, "T-t-tomorrow. I-I can come—tomorrow. 'Z-'zat okay?"

"Yes, Danny, that will be fine. And I'm much obliged—for your help, and also your advice."

Danny ducked his head at the compliment but then lifted his brow and gave me that shy grin again. He didn't speak but nodded his head in response. I knew the sign; it meant *thanks*.

"Okay, my friend," I said as I prepared to depart. "Come on by tomorrow whenever you can. I'll see you then."

Danny Ray nodded again. "'Kay," he replied.

I skipped across a large puddle and got in the car. As I pulled away, Danny Ray lifted a hand in departing salute, which I returned with a wave of my own. As I turned the corner just a short way down the block, I looked back toward the shop and saw Danny still watching. He waved again, and then scampered around the corner of the building toward his trailer.

I had a few errands to run before I went back to the boat. First stop was the supermarket. I needed to lay in a good stock of food as there was going to be three of us at the boat for the next couple of weeks. I wanted Parker and Danny Ray to be well fed, because as we all know, happy workers are good workers. My next stop was at a nearby sporting goods store, and my intention there was not what you would call a friendly one—it was more in the line of sober preparedness.

I already have one shotgun aboard *Miss Rosalie*, but I wanted a second one so I could stow them in two different places. When cruising, I keep a shotgun in the pilothouse, where it is ready and at hand, since that is where I am almost always to be found. When in port I keep it under my bunk, so that if I hear a suspicious sound at night I have it nearby and ready for action. But lately I had felt it would be a good idea to have one in the pilothouse *and* another in the cabin—just in case I was in one place or the other and something untoward should arise.

Why a shotgun? Because, for close-up work, there is nothing else quite like a twelve-gauge pump gun. It is a compact and naturally pointing weapon. The pump action never fails. And as all cops will tell you—even if a person has never heard it before, they know exactly the sound of that pump action racking a shell into the chamber. It is a sound well worth the heeding, one that will often discourage a prowler or would-be antagonist.

Rather than buckshot or slugs, I keep mine loaded with number 2 shot, often called goose shot. The number 2 shot is devastating for the length of *Miss Rosalie*'s deck, but it won't go flying away into a neighbor's boat or through a body and into an unintended victim. The sound of a shotgun, being fired at close range, is horrific, and at night it belches out a truly impressive muzzle flash. A good shotgun, if not heeded as a deterrent, is a weapon that will put a rapid end to any heated exchange.

I was in luck. The store had in stock just what I was looking for, a straightforward, no-frills shotgun. It has an eight-round tubular magazine underneath its twenty-inch barrel. The barrel and receiver are clad in a weatherproof coating that protects it from water and salt air, and the synthetic stock is impervious to the elements. I also bought a butt stock shell holder for the shotgun, a couple of boxes of twelve-gauge shells, and some pistol ammo. As an afterthought, I picked up a nylon sling for the shotgun, in case I ever wanted to carry it slung over a shoulder during a trek ashore.

My purchases complete, I now headed back to the dock. The afternoon was wearing on, and the gray daylight was beginning to darken noticeably. In ten minutes I was back at the waterfront and gazing down on *Miss Rosalie* resting quietly at her tether.

To save myself some steps, I parked as closely as I could to the top of the boardwalk. I took my gun store purchases to the boat on my first trip so I could stow them away as soon as possible, then I hustled back to the car to get the groceries in. Near the top of the boardwalk I thought I heard a sound— something like a low whine, but as the rain was beginning to come down more heavily again, I gave my attention to the task at hand.

It took two more trips to get everything unloaded and dropped off in the galley. But first I would move the car back to the parking area under the trees and then put the food away in the pantry and the fridge. At the top of the walkway I heard that sound again. It was coming from somewhere beneath the boardwalk. I quickly parked the car and then came back to investigate.

Quietly and slowly, I walked down the slope at the head of the walk, and when I reached the edge of the sea grass, I stood still, looking and listening. A few seconds later, I heard it again. It was the sound of an animal in distress— sort of an exhaled whimper or groan. I cocked my head to one side and tried to zero in on the source of the sound.

It came again, more faintly now, but it seemed to be from underneath the boardwalk and on the other side. I looked to where the sound seemed to emanate, but couldn't see anything unusual. However, there was a large tree limb lodged against one of the piles on the other side that must have floated in on the last high tide. Maybe whatever was making the sound was over there.

I scrambled back up the muddy slope and slid down the steep bank on the other side. Again, I stood at the edge of the grass and listened. Nothing, but then I saw a slight movement out on the tree limb—just behind where a broken off branch was sticking up.

What the heck is that? I wondered. It was a dark ball of something. *Is it a small raccoon?* I asked myself. Raccoons and possums often prowled the edge of the marsh, hunting crabs and scavenging for dead fish. Then whatever it was lifted its head and turned its large green eyes directly toward me. It was a cat. A small wet cat.

I tried to coax it to me but to no avail. I thought of

returning to the boat to fetch it some food but rejected that idea—it might slip away while I was gone. I had to bring it in out of the weather. Seeing there was nothing else to do, I pulled off my shoes and socks and threw them up on the boardwalk. Then, rolling my pants up to the knees, I eased myself into the mud.

"Hold on, little fella. Don't run. I won't hurt you," I cooed to the soaking creature as I slogged closer and closer.

I fully expected the poor thing to make a dash to avoid me, but it waited patiently until I was within arm's reach. I slowly bent forward and reached out to pick him up, speaking soothingly all the time. When I touched him with a tentative hand, he gave me a pitiful meow, hopped into my arms, and buried his face in my chest. I stroked him softly as I turned and struggled back to the walkway through the grasping, gumlike marsh mud.

Reaching the boardwalk at last, I retrieved my shoes and carried them in one hand while I cradled the small cat in the crook of my other arm. Near the boat, I dropped my shoes to the dock and, holding on to a pile with one hand, alternately lowered each leg over the side of the dock and swirled it around in the water to sluice off the mud. Then I retrieved my shoes and went aboard and to the main cabin below.

I quickly nabbed a couple of towels and as gently as possible began to dry the little guy. As I ran my hands over him I realized I could feel every bone in his body. I have never seen or felt an animal so emaciated and still alive. I anticipated he would put up some resistance, but instead he sat quietly, even though every few seconds he was racked by a shiver that shook a pitiable churring sound from deep within his thin frame.

When he was somewhat dried off I wrapped him in a dry towel and carried him to the galley. Setting him at my feet, I found a can of tuna in the pantry, which I quickly opened and dumped onto a saucer. Kneeling down, I placed the meal in front of my guest. I fully expected to see him hurl himself onto the fish, but instead, he looked me in the eye for a second as though surprised by the gift, and then ducked his head and began to feed.

I looked him over as he ate like only a starving animal can—in great gulping, choking bites. In appearance, he was an old-fashioned tabby cat—the type of feline that most closely resembles his wild ancestor. His coat was a dark gray—tending to black—with reddish markings on the chest and under the throat. Several light brown, almost blond, stripes ran from between his eyes to the back of his head and a similar colored stripe made a perpendicular blaze across his back, just behind the shoulders. There were more stripes on his flanks and around his legs, and alternating rings on his tail that closely resembled the markings of a raccoon.

I ran my fingers lightly over his body as he ate, and though he was as scrawny as a war refugee, he didn't seem to have any injuries.

"You're lucky that old one-eyed boar 'coon that hangs around here didn't find you before I did, little fella," I said as I completed my examination. "That old rascal would have made mighty short work of you."

He finished his tuna and, looking up at me, blinked his eyes and licked each side of his upper lip. In what I took to be a gesture of satisfaction, he came close and rubbed his head against my knee. I let my hand run the length of his body, and then, picking him up, carried him to the salon where I gently placed him in the corner of the settee. He immediately curled himself into a ball, and as soon as he was settled, promptly closed his eyes and went to sleep.

Just then, I heard the sound of an approaching outboard

motor and, grabbing my hat and jacket, went out on deck. It was Parker, finally returning from his trip to Daufuskie. I lashed the skiff to the dock as he unloaded his meager gear. It consisted of an old surplus navy sea bag, a large box of tools, and a cardboard carton.

We quickly hustled back inside where Parker jumped into a hot shower to get the chill of the day out of his bones. When he came back in again I passed him a steaming cup of coffee and handed him a bottle of Irish whiskey to top it with. Parker gratefully accepted both the cup and the bottle and when his coffee was properly doctored he held it under his nose and with closed eyes let the vapor waft over his face.

"I didn't intend to be gone so long, Kennesaw," he said as he lowered the cup from his lips. "But I had loaned out some of my tools and it took me a while to round them all up again. I just didn't want to start a job without my own tools."

"Of course," I replied.

That was understandable. No workman wants to be without his tools. And when you own very little in the way of personal belongings, they become either very important to you or very unimportant.

"There's also a message from Miss Cyriah. She says to tell you this, 'It's moving, and it knows who you are.'"

Parker looked away after delivering Cyriah's warning, as though he did not wish to see the impact of the words.

I nodded. "Thank you, Parker."

"Oh, by the way," Parker said with a start, putting down his cup and crossing the galley in one long stride. "Miss Darcey sent these."

He reached into the cardboard carton and, lifting out a quart jar in each hand, held them aloft to catch the overhead light.

"Homemade vegetable soup. She calls it her summer

soup because she makes it from the vegetables in her garden every summer. She said we were to have some as soon as I returned."

I looked at the jars as he presented them for inspection. Through the shimmering glass could be seen every vibrant color of a vegetable garden: red tomatoes, white potatoes, green cabbage, purple peas, yellow corn, orange carrots.

My grandmother used to make soup like that every year. She prepared it over an open fire in an old cast-iron wash pot in the backyard. One of my earliest and fondest memories from childhood is of helping her when she canned her produce and made soup. In the depths of the winter I would look at all those jars arrayed row upon row in the pantry, and I would think of them as being filled with the captured warmth and essence of summertime. I knew exactly what Darcey meant when she called it her summer soup.

Looking at those jars in Parker's hands, I could feel my mouth water—and more than that—I felt the warm hand of a caring woman as it touched my soul.

"To the galley!" I cried out.

I reached into the pan cabinet and handed Parker a pot for the soup. Then I pulled out a ten-inch cast-iron skillet and sat it on the countertop.

"This is a special occasion," I said with enthusiasm. "You tend to the soup, and I'll make us a pone of cornbread."

Parker was unscrewing the lid of one jar but paused to cast me a glance.

"And none of those questioning looks, you doubting Thomas, you. I'll have you know that I make the finest cornbread you'll find anywhere along the Atlantic seaboard—or, for that matter, within the Gulf of Mexico and also the Caribbean," I boasted as I got out a mixing bowl and set it on the counter.

"Tasting is believing," Parker said with a smile. "As an

engineer, I put my faith in empirical data. Mere talk is of no relevance whatsoever."

"Then you don't scald the soup—and hand me the buttermilk from the fridge. And if it's proof you demand—just give me a little elbow room and thirty minutes—then we'll see what you have to say."

An hour later we pushed our chairs back from the galley table. A small scrap of cornbread remained on the plate in the center of the table. We eyed it at the same time, but when Parker looked up with lifted eyebrows, I shook my head, waved a hand side to side, and patted my stomach to indicate, *I can't; it's all yours.*

Parker quickly reached out a hand and popped the morsel in his mouth. He closed his eyes and lifted his head slightly as he chewed and swallowed the last of our supper. Then, with a contented smile on his face he looked at me across the table.

"I admit the veracity of your claim. That was the best cornbread I've ever tasted. In fact, before this, I was never a fan of the dish. But I believe you've managed to change my attitude," he said with a sigh.

"Well, bread made with sawdust and sand would taste pretty good with that soup," I pointed out. "But thank you for the compliment. I'm glad you enjoyed it."

Parker looked to the cat still curled asleep in the corner of the settee.

"Unless I missed seeing him earlier, it appears you have a new guest."

"I found him under the boardwalk when I came in. I think he must have been abandoned—he's not wild. But he's been on his own for a while and is in pretty poor condition," I explained.

"Have you graced him—it is a him, isn't it—with a name yet?" he asked.

I shook my head. "No, not yet. In fact I haven't even thought about keeping him. But as poor as he is, it wouldn't be right to try to shuffle him off somewhere else."

"Then it looks like you've picked up another stray, Kennesaw. And if that's the case—he needs a name," Parker replied.

I looked at the little sleeping ball of fur and thought for a second. *What's a good name for a tabby?* I asked myself. *What's a good name for a little waterfront cat? A salt marsh cat—an island cat.* And then it struck me.

"His name is Tybee," I pronounced.

"Tybee," Parker repeated. "Tybee—yes, that's an excellent name. Tybee."

"And if you'll lend a hand with the cleanup, I need to run out and get him a few things," I said as I rose from my seat.

"No, I'll take care of the washing up—it won't take but a minute. You go get the little guy what he needs for his new home, and we'll see him properly settled in when you return.

"All right," I said. "You need anything while I'm out?"

"No." He shook his head. "I can't think of a thing I need."

"I won't be long—you make yourself comfortable," I said as I grabbed my hat and jacket. "And help yourself to the Irish—you know where it is."

I was back within a half hour with everything a cat needs to set up housekeeping. Tybee was still asleep when I came back into the cabin, but when I popped the lid on a tin of cat food, he leaped from the settee and came and curled himself around my ankles.

I only gave him half a can of food this time. I was afraid of feeding him too much at first. I know what it's like to overeat after you've been almost starved to death. It's a jolt to the system and in some cases is harmful. I would watch his intake carefully over the next few days and bring him along slowly.

Everyone now fed and comfortable, we settled in for the evening. I had some correspondence to catch up on—I still write letters—and Parker gave his attention to drawing up the list of materials he needed to get started with his work. Tybee stayed curled in the corner of the settee but when either Parker or I moved around a bit, or made a sound, he would open a sleepy eye and look about the cabin before drifting off again.

But something was tugging on my mind, and there was a question I had to ask. I put down my pen and looked in Parker's direction. He must have felt my attention upon him. He looked up and caught my eye.

"Parker. Twice now you've delivered a message from Miss Cyriah, and neither time did you demonstrate the slightest interest in the meaning of those words. Most people would have had to ask what it was all about, but you didn't. Why not?"

Parker sat still. He shifted his gaze to the bulkhead behind me and after a few seconds back to my face again.

"I never intended landing on Daufuskie. It just so happened that my worm-eaten boat sank from beneath me out at the mouth of the Savannah channel. I climbed into my dingy as the boat went under the waves, and let the tide and wind wash me ashore on Daufuskie. I was a derelict in a strange place, a man with no money, no job or family, and no hope.

"It was early spring, and for a while I lived on the beach under the upturned dingy, wondering what I was to do. And then one day, early in the morning, I decided on a course of action. I would take the long swim. I would just wade out into the Atlantic and start swimming for Africa. By the time I became exhausted I would be too far out for anyone to notice. I am told that drowning is an easy death. Then, just as I stood up to walk into the water a boy showed up—a deaf-mute boy—Ronnie. Do you know him?"

I shook my head in the negative.

Parker continued, "He and his family live near the Chambers place. Anyway, this boy shows up. He takes my hand, and by various signs, indicates that I am to come with him—that I have been summoned. He then led me to the Chambers house where I found Miss Cyriah sitting on the porch—waiting for me, she tells me."

Parker looked away again, and cleared his throat before continuing his tale.

"Well, I sat with her on that porch all morning and listened. I say I listened, but most of the time there were no words—at least, not spoken words—but there was a message given just the same. And she made me realize that I was not here by accident, neither on this planet nor on the island. She told me that my present condition was no accident, either, but was meant to clarify my mind and my soul; and that this morning, in the depths of my despair, I had finally arrived at the place where I could hear, with an open ear, what it was that the world needed of me."

Parker paused again and gave me a searching look, his eyes shifting back and forth over my face.

"I won't go into all the rest except to tell you this: Miss Cyriah saved my life. I believe her and I believe *in* her. I've never met anyone else remotely like that dear, remarkable woman, and I'm sure such a person comes along only rarely. Sometimes I am privileged to act as her messenger. And when I do, I take it as a sacred duty, because I have a realization of the importance of her words. So, no, Kennesaw, whatever I deliver to others from Miss Cyriah causes me no curiosity. I know it is something for the greater good, and I am content to be a vessel that helps convey that good."

I nodded my head in acceptance of his words. "I think you and I are very fortunate to have found ourselves in her realm."

"I think so, too," he replied.

With that, we lapsed back into a contemplative quiet. The rain continued to beat a persistent cadence on the deck above our heads, and it wasn't long before I found my eyelids beginning to droop. I wasn't the only one hypnotized by the pattering drops. Parker was slumped in his chair, the clipboard and pen resting in his lap, and his chin on his chest. I roused him as I turned out the cabin lights, and with that, the passengers and crew of the *Miss Rosalie* called it a good night.

CHAPTER 13

THE WEATHER HAD CLEARED A LIT-
tle during the night, and the next morning a few shafts of
sunlight managed, here and there, to find their way through
gaps in the clouds.

I had slept all right but had been awakened once by a
recurring dream. It's one that has its source in my days as
a young soldier.

It is December 19, 1989, the first night of my first war,
and we are in a vicious firefight in Chorrillo district, the
wooden slums of the old city of Panama. The buildings
have caught fire from the tracers and the detonating shells
and are burning furiously. Thousands of civilians, fleeing the conflagration and crazed with fear, run screaming through the streets, oblivious to the battle that rages
around them.

My squad fights its way deeper and deeper into the heart
of the city. We pause in a narrow street, and then, above us,

I hear screams. I look up, and there on a third-story balcony I see a person—a man or woman, I cannot tell. But the flames of the burning interior are licking out over the person and I see smoke as the clothes begin to scorch. I'm horrified at the sight and feel helpless to assist.

"Jump!" I shriek at the top of my lungs, trying to make myself heard above the raging firefight. "Jump!"

But then I see that the person is trapped. The balcony is wrapped in iron burglar bars—bars meant to keep out intruders but now separating the person from safety and life itself.

I want to look away, but I can't. I now see that it is a woman. She grabs the iron bars and shakes them with her entire body as she tries madly to escape the greedy flames. Then, she throws back her head and howls in agony as a broad tongue of fire reaches out, and her hair goes up like a torch.

"Do something!" I scream in impotence and terror. "Somebody do something! She's burning to death! She's burning!"

Blamm!

A single shot rings out from behind me. The woman's hands fly from the bars and she smashes to the floor of the balcony and out of sight; her frenzied screams of tortured agony silent now—replaced by the roar of the raging fire.

I look over my shoulder, and there stands my squad leader, Sgt. Marcus Evans, his rifle still to his shoulder, and his face drenched in a greasy sweat. His stares fixedly at the balcony—empty now but for the flames gushing obscenely from the door behind.

Evans slowly lowers his rifle and then looks imploringly, hungrily, at each one of us huddled there in the narrow street of the burning city. We stare back at him with empty eyes—seven soldiers, stunned by the dawning comprehension of his merciful yet horrible act. We are mute, and time stands still.

Evans turns his face to me. "Move out, Tanner," he says in a quiet voice, one I can barely hear above the roar of combat and conflagration.

I give a last glance at the balcony, just as the wall of the building collapses into the street, sending sparks and cinders flying heavenward. Thankfully, I do not see the woman's body. It has been consumed in the flames, and what is left is indistinguishable in the rubble.

"Move out, Tanner," Evans repeats, and he points his rifle in the direction I am to go.

I look down the street ahead and see a storm of tracers shredding the air at the intersection of the next corner. Explosions reverberate and echo in the streets, while brilliant flashes reflect off the smoke-filled sky above.

I bring my rifle up to the ready and pull my head down into my shoulders, like a man without a hat, steeling himself to run out into a heavy rain. I take a first hesitant step—and then find myself awake in my bunk, bathed in a cold sweat.

But I remember more now that I am awake. Afterward, none of us in the squad ever spoke of that moment—that act. *Never*. Young as we were, we instinctively knew that it was taboo, and thus, it was the great untouchable. It was a subject so far beyond the emotional pale as to put it in the realm of dark unknowingness.

But there were times, usually in moments of unexpected repose, when nothing else was going on, that I would steal a surreptitious glance at Evans and find him sitting off by himself. Silent, and still as a statue, his eyes lifted slightly above a private horizon, staring into the infinite distance of the great beyond—*el más allá*, as they say in Panama.

And in those moments I could see expressed quite plainly on his face—on his whole demeanor—the soul-corroding poison he carried within, and would carry with him forever, for that one, that bone-chilling act of incomprehensible courage.

I marveled that a man could wield such awful courage. Marveled at, but also feared it, as one cannot help but fear the unknown. And now, more than twenty years later, I find that I marvel at it still and am still afraid.

Danny Ray arrived in time to join us for breakfast, and that gave him and Parker a chance to break the ice and begin to know one another. Danny is painfully shy, and will either quickly warm to someone he meets or not at all. He makes his decision within minutes, and if he doesn't warm, he'll disappear. But after a bit, and by the time we were having a final cup of coffee, I began to see Danny cast a few glances in Parker's direction, and at last saw a slight smile find the corner of Danny Ray's mouth as he listened to Parker speak of what he intended for the day. It was going to be all right. Danny had come to the decision that he could trust Parker, and I was certain the two of them would become friends.

"Parker," I announced. "Danny Ray knows *Miss Rosalie* probably as well as I do."

I cast a quick glance at Danny and saw him duck his head and pull at the brim of his cap.

"So if you two will go back over the boat with your list, Parker, and afterward, if you both agree to the scope of work, take Danny's truck and pick up the supplies you need to get started. While y'all are doing that, I'll take Brother Tybee to the vet for a good going-over. Sound okay?" I concluded.

"Good idea," Parker said. "It's always best to take a second look before setting to work, and I'd like Danny Ray's opinion on a couple of things."

Danny looked from Parker to me and nodded his head. "Y-y-y-yep," he said.

After finishing his breakfast Tybee had made his first short tour of the cabin of the boat and was now curled once again in the corner of the settee. I let him snooze there while I put a towel in the bottom of the cardboard box that had contained the jars of soup.

"Come on, buddy," I said as I bent and picked up the little cat.

I held him in the crook of my arm as I stroked him gently and was rewarded by a soft purr. *God, he's skinny,* I thought again as I carried him to the table and set him in the box. As I folded over and closed the top of the box, I thought he would try to fight me, but he merely curled up and closed his eyes again. He rode quietly in the box all the way to the vet's office.

I told the girl at the desk that I wanted him to have a complete checkup—shots, parasite treatment, the works, and if he needed to stay overnight, that was okay.

Next I swung by the auto shop to inquire about my truck and had a little good news. The glass had been delivered and they would get on the job today. But first they would have to do a little touch-up on the paint. When Leon had knocked the mirrors off, the doors had sustained some deep scratches. I gave the approval for the work and left the shop in a better mood than when I had arrived.

As I drove back to the docks, I saw a few more rays of sunshine finding their way through the clouds. I had checked the marine forecast first thing this morning, and it looked like we were to get about a twelve-hour respite from the rain. I thought I would take advantage of that for a few hours and accomplish a minor task.

I parked the rental car in my accustomed place under the live oaks and walked down to Captain Flynt's Bucket o' Blood. Fortunately, the garbage truck hadn't arrived yet this morning, and I had a little Dumpster diving to do before Tyrone came in and caught me at it. Somehow or other, rooting around in a trash container is just something a man prefers to do in private.

When I went around back of the building where the Dumpster sits I saw that Dolores was back from Atlanta. Her red Cadillac Eldorado was parked in her regular spot near the back door. I would have to work quickly and be quiet about it unless I wanted to be cornered and forced to give a report of my last trip.

I opened the door of the container and peered inside. Yeah, there, over to one side, was what I was looking for: several flattened cardboard boxes. But they were out of arm's reach and I really didn't want to climb inside. I looked back outside for something to extend my reach. By the edge of the lot was a limb that had fallen from a nearby black gum tree. *Just right,* I thought as I picked it up and returned to the Dumpster.

I leaned inside as far as I could and raked the first box to hand. I pitched it to the ground outside and was leaning in again—I had to reach farther this time—when someone smacked me across the backside and called loudly in a rich and throaty female voice, "Kennesaw Tanner, just what in the hell do you think you're doing in there?"

I came out of the Dumpster and faced my interrogator.

"Hey, Dolores. I was looking for some boxes," I deadpanned.

Dolores stood with her fists planted on her shapely hips, tapping a toe, and slowly shaking her head. She arched her brows and gave me a questioning look.

"Boxes, hell," she said with a toss of the head and a skeptical tone in her voice. "I think you've been spying on me. That's what I think you're really up to. I think you're out here looking for love letters I might have thrown away or maybe pictures of some of my old beaus." She lifted a hand and flounced her flaming red hair. "That's what I think you're really doing. I've seen how you look at me when you think I'm not aware of it."

I hung my head in a gesture of guilt. "You've caught me, Dolores. I may as well declare myself." I lifted my head, threw the stick I held to one side, and reached out my arms. "Come here, you fabulous stack of woman, you. Just let me get my hands on you!"

Dolores squealed a peal of laughter, leaped backward a good two feet, and pointed an accusatory finger at me. "You wash those dirty hands of yours first, and then we'll see about that."

I stopped and looked at my hands. They had gotten pretty filthy at that.

"If you really cared, you'd invite me up for a shower," I bantered.

She gave me a saucy grin. "Keep it up, big boy, and I'll make you show those cards one day."

"Now that will be a hand to remember," I replied before changing to a serious tone. "I understand you were just up in Atlanta, something about your son. Is he okay?"

The smile left Dolores's face as she looked at the ground and shook her head in consternation. "That dumb-ass boy of mine," she said, almost to herself, before looking at me again. "Lets his little head do all his thinking for him. I swear, those kids of mine are gonna put me in either the madhouse or the poorhouse. It's just a matter of which one comes first."

"I'm sorry, Dolores. Anything I can do?"

She brightened again. "No, sweetheart, not about that. But come by this evening and have dinner with me after happy hour. I'll tell you all my troubles, and you can tell me yours."

"Can I take a rain check on that? I'm already booked for this evening."

"Got a hot date?" she teased.

"No, just something I have to take care of is all."

"Well, yeah. First chance you get, come on by. I've got something I want to talk over with you," she replied.

"I'll do that, Dolores."

"Good, now get your boxes and get out of here," she ordered with a dismissive gesture. "I don't want you trashing up the place. What will people think? Besides, it's bad for business."

"See you, Dolores," I said as I bent to pick up the flattened boxes.

"You better," she responded as she turned to walk away.

That's one helluva woman, I thought as I tucked the boxes beneath my arm and headed back to the dock. A smart guy would do well to pay serious court to her. Several had, but Dolores had sent them all packing. She told me that after she had lost her husband, Bill, she just didn't want to go through the difficulty of getting to know someone again, or of getting close to another person—she didn't feel it was worth the effort and energy. It was a sentiment I could understand. And then a picture of Patricia came to my mind. *Well, maybe,* I thought. *But I'm in no hurry. And if things develop in their own good time . . . Well, we'll see.*

Danny Ray and Parker were just pulling away in Danny Ray's truck as I crossed the parking lot. And as they turned onto the street I could see Parker gesturing with his hands and talking animatedly, with Danny Ray nodding vigorously in response.

On the dock, I dropped the boxes and went inside to get a few tools. Back on the dock again I opened the boxes with my pocketknife and then cut each flat sheet of cardboard into two pieces. I then retrieved several one-by-four planks I'd been saving and stapled the planks to the cardboard sheets along one side. Standing one of the narrow planks on end I checked my work. *Yep,* I thought, *these would do nicely.*

I went below and retrieved the shotgun I had bought yesterday, along with a box of shells and a pistol—my nine-millimeter CZ 75. I threaded my belt through the Band-Aid pistol holster, placing it cross-draw style on the left side of my waist. After checking it for fit and comfort, I then zipped up my jacket.

Back on deck I pulled a pair of rubber sea boots from a storage locker and exchanged them for the deck shoes I was wearing. In just a few seconds I had everything loaded in the sea skiff and ready to go. While the engine warmed, I gave the boat a quick once-over. Everything was the way it should be. The instruments looked good and the automatic bilge pump had gotten rid of the rainwater that had fallen. I cast off the dock line, slipped the engine into gear, and quietly pulled away.

I swung wide out into the creek and coasted along for a bit, looking at the docks, *Miss Rosalie*, and the Bucket o' Blood. *This is a good place,* I thought as I saw Tyrone come out on the club's outside deck and check for anything amiss after the night. I gave him a wave when he looked up, which he returned with a scowl and a shake of the head, as if to say, *Something is wrong with this picture; here I am at work and there you are larking about.* But then, he gave me a short wave of the hand before returning inside.

Clear now of the no-wake zone, I shoved the throttle forward and headed downstream. Soon the creek met up with Bull River, and I turned toward Wassaw Sound and in the direction of the open Atlantic. But it was an island I was headed for today and not the ocean. A few miles farther on, I turned into the wide mouth of a side creek and slowed to half speed. I turned right at the next stream, a smaller one, and slowed now to just above idle.

Ahead, around the next bend, rose the bushy palmettos, stunted oaks, and taller sea pines of a small island—a hammock. I pushed the bow of the boat gently up on a sandy spot on the end of the island, just between the arms of two salt creeks. The tide would rise for about another forty-five minutes to an hour, so I should have no problem getting off again. I pitched the anchor up into some bushes and unloaded my cargo.

I had used this little island as a shooting range on several other occasions. It is about three acres in extent, shaped sort of like a tadpole, and oriented in such a way that no boats could get in behind, as there was nothing in that direction but open salt marsh. It was about as remote a place as one could find and still be in the geographical limits of Chatham County. I knew the sound of gunfire could be heard only by me and the other animals here on the island and in the nearby marsh.

I carried my stuff about twenty meters into the center of the island and looked around. Some brush had grown a bit since I was last here. And I was dismayed to find a pile of discarded trash and a stack of empty beer bottles. For the life of me I cannot comprehend why anyone would befoul such a beautiful and tranquil place. *Oh well,* I thought, *trashy people have trashy ways. There's just no other way to explain it.*

I paced off another twenty meters and then shoved three of the stakes in the ground—each about three feet from the other. I went back to where I had begun, and reaching in my pocket, took out a pair of foam earplugs and stoppered up my ears. Then I loaded the tubular magazine of the shotgun, but left the chamber empty.

I put the butt into my shoulder with the muzzle down in the ready position, and lined my body up on the leftmost target. I closed my eyes and swung the shotgun into firing position. Opening my eyes, I checked to see where the gun was pointed. It was off to the right just a bit. I shifted my feet slightly to the left and went through the motion again. This time, when I opened my eyes, the muzzle of the gun was pointed directly at the target.

I quickly cycled the pump, shoving a shell into the chamber. And as I saw the target centered again on the bead sight, I slapped the trigger.

Bloooom!

The butt of the shotgun punched me solidly in the shoulder and as I rocked backward with the recoil, I cycled the slide, ejecting the spent shell and chambering a fresh one. As the muzzle of the gun came back level again I shifted my feet slightly to the right, saw the next target on the bead, and slapped the trigger again.

Bloooom!

The shot roared and the gun recoiled. I jacked in a fresh round, fired at the next target, and then, slipping the safety to on, lowered the gun back again to the ready position.

The action feels good, I thought as I walked to the targets. *A little stiff, maybe, but I can smooth that out with a polishing stone.* The pattern of the shot was perfect when I inspected the targets. The mass of pellets had perforated the center of each of the cardboard sheets. At that distance the shot pattern covered the width of a man's chest.

I shucked the remaining shell from the magazine and then checked the chamber. With the action open, I looked inside and then stuck a finger in the chamber for the "blind man's test." Next I stapled new cardboard on the targets and stepped back this time about ten meters.

Putting down the shotgun, I drew my pistol and squared on the right target. I stared at the center of the target and, keeping it in clear focus, swung the pistol up in front of my face and tapped the trigger twice, as fast as I could. I lowered the pistol back to the ready and checked the target: two holes, a half-inch apart, in the center of the cardboard.

I expended several magazines of pistol ammunition on the targets. I fired first on single targets, and then worked them as multiples. Then I walked as I shot, and after that, I ran—always closing with the targets—always firing on the move.

Satisfied that the old habits were still there, I holstered my pistol, took a plastic garbage bag from my pocket, and picked up all the shotgun shells and nine-millimeter brass. After that, I gathered up the targets and returned to the boat.

The boat had floated a bit on the rising tide, but I pulled her into shore with the anchor rope. I loaded my stuff and grabbed a couple more bags from the bow storage locker. Returning to the center of the island, I picked up the trash that had been left behind. Then I walked to the end of the island to look at man's residue from another era.

At the very tip of the island, hidden in a thicket of palmettos and gallberry bushes are three shell mounds—piles of oyster shells left behind by the Indian inhabitants of this area.

These are the remains of who knows how many shellfish feasts, consumed and enjoyed long before Europeans ever saw this land. In the center of each mound is an indentation—a hole. And each mound I've discovered out here on these islands has a similar hole in the center. For a while I couldn't fathom why it was there and then one day it occurred to me: It was left when the tree that was originally in the center of the mound rotted away. For some reason, it seems, the Indians always made the mounds around the base of a tree. Maybe someday I could find an anthropologist who could tell me why.

But just looking at these mounds—the remains of a distant and extinct people—caused me to reflect on the bounty of this region and realize once again what a precious Earth we inhabit. Everything we require for life comes from the Earth and her waters. And when we treat it badly—abusing and spoiling its gifts by reason of avarice and stupidity—we harm only ourselves.

You can trash a house with filth and refuse until it becomes unfit for habitation and you have to move someplace else—or sicken and possibly die of the consequences. But this is the only planet we have—there is no other place to go. And if we don't clean up our act in a serious way, and soon, it is the Earth itself that will slough us off like a snake shedding a dead skin.

The canaries are dying in the mine shaft. The blue crab is disappearing from these very waters, and the oysters are beginning to sicken. The dead zones off the mouths of the major rivers—areas so depleted of oxygen by runoff pollution as to no longer being capable of sustaining life—are becoming larger, more numerous, and longer lasting by the year.

Around the globe, fish stocks are crashing from overfishing. The once inexhaustible North Atlantic cod fishery—a resource that once fed millions—has been exhausted and is close to extinction. The big fish—the bluefin tuna, the swordfish, marlins, and the big sharks—are being taken in such numbers that they are now unable to reproduce and replenish themselves.

What we are doing is the equivalent of a farmer eating his seed corn and giving no thought to the next season. And it's all being done in the name of greed—for the enrichment of the few and the paupering of many. When we finally manage to upset the balance of life in the ocean, we may well have sealed our doom.

It starts small. I doubt that the people who threw their trash on this remote and beautiful small island are bad people. More than anything, they are guilty of being lazy and unthinking. But it is that on the larger scale that allows the truly callous and venal to get away with their depredations. When we all wake up and look around and realize the consequences of what we are doing, then we will demand a change. We will hold ourselves accountable for our actions. I just hope it happens before it is too late to make a difference.

I retrieved the bags of trash, along with a few other cans and stuff I'd found, and returned to the boat. Danny Ray and Parker had not yet returned by the time I arrived back at the dock. I unloaded the boat and put my gear away, then carried the bags of trash and my shot-up targets to the Dumpster back of the Bucket o' Blood, where I made a deposit instead of a withdrawal. This time no one caught me in the act.

CHAPTER 14

BACK ABOARD THE *MISS ROSALIE*, I made another phone call to Sandy Willis, and this time, as before, received no answer and had to leave a voice message. I called the convenience store again, and the girl I had spoken to previously told me that no, Sandy still hadn't come to work, and that if I spoke with her first to tell her that it was causing problems in the schedule and she needed to call Mr. Harold and let him know when she was coming in. I replied that I would relay the message and hung up.

The boys returned from their trip, and I helped unload the supplies they had brought back. After taking a break for lunch we gave ourselves to the task at hand, and under the capable direction of Parker we began to make headway in preparing the scheme of work he had devised. First, we would concentrate on the rigging and other exterior work, and following that we would move belowdecks.

It was a joy to lose myself in manual labor, but while

taking a short break I happened to glance at my watch and realized that the afternoon had flown by.

"Friends and neighbors," I announced. "I hate to break this off, but I've got a function to attend this evening. I hope you won't think too badly of me if I bow off the stage and wash some of this honest sweat from my brow."

Danny Ray tugged at the brim of his cap and flashed me a grin. "Z-z'okay."

"Not at all, Kennesaw. Danny and I can handle the rest of this. We only need to cut out a few more spots on the bulwarks and weld in the new metal. But we'll probably work on into the evening. I want to get this portion done while the weather holds off."

"Y-y-y-yeah." Danny Ray nodded in agreement.

"Okay then," I responded. "It's all yours."

Thirty minutes later I emerged from belowdecks, cleaned, curried, and dressed. Neither of the men looked up from their work as I departed. They both had their heads down, shielded by welding masks, bathed in a shower of sparks and flickering blue light.

Driving into town was a snap. All the traffic was flowing out as I was coming in. I pulled into the police headquarters parking lot just as Patricia was walking out the door. I cruised up alongside the walkway, lowered the passenger window, and leaned over.

"Looking for anyone in particular, miss?" I asked.

Patricia looked in the window. "Yeah, I am, but until he comes along, I guess you'll do," she quipped as she opened the door and got in beside me.

"Hey you," I said as I reached over and squeezed her hand.

"Hey you," she replied as she returned the squeeze.

"How was your day? Filled with the normal mayhem and carnage of life in the city?" I asked.

"By and large. A little short on carnage, and about average on the mayhem."

"That's one of the things I'll never understand about being a cop, and probably why the life never appealed to me," I said as I glanced over at Patricia. "How you can wade, day after day, through the most sordid acts committed by man, picking up the fetid, smoldering pieces of human wreckage, and still retain your emotional equilibrium, your sanity."

"Some cops don't," Patricia replied in a sympathetic tone of voice. "Some become drunks. Some beat their wives. Some abuse the people they deal with in the course of duty. Some quit for another profession. Some go off the deep end. And some blow their brains out."

"And you?" I asked, glancing over again.

"Oh, me?" she replied with a smile. "Every once in a while, I take stock of where I am and give myself a great big psychic enema. I flush it all out, until I feel clean again."

"How do you do that?" I asked, genuinely interested and concerned.

"I read once about a god of the Aztecs," she said. "His name was the Filth Eater. Even though he sounded really rotten he was actually a very beneficent god. You would visit him at his temple with every nasty thing in your life. You told him of all the dirty, wicked, vicious, and disgusting things you had done, or witnessed, or that had been done to you. The Filth Eater would consume all the foulness you brought to him, and he would eat it entirely—leaving you clean and whole once again. In my own way, I have a Filth Eater. And sometimes, I have to give him the things I've collected."

I glanced over again. "I'm glad," I said. "And I think that's probably what's wrong with us as a species—too few of us have a Filth Eater—and eventually, the filth consumes *us*."

"I see it every day," she replied. "Every case I've ever

had, you can follow a string of events as far back in a person's life as you care to go, and still not know where it really started. But hey!" she said brightly. "Enough of that stuff, tell me about this church we're going to."

"Well, it probably puts the capital *F* in the word *fundamentalist*. So if you've never been to a Holy Roller church before, get ready for some excitement."

"And your reason, again, for going?"

"I want to meet the preacher, Brother Rainwater. He may know something about Tonya Causey. He might be able to fill in some blanks and tell me something about her state of mind. It's possible he knows something the mother doesn't."

"And you think he'll tell you if he does?" Patricia queried.

"I don't know." I shrugged. "But it's a potential handle. And you know how it is—it's sort of like dancing with the fat lady."

"How's that, Tanner?" She snorted.

"It's not that you can't do it," I said, glancing over again. "It's just a matter of where you grab hold of her."

"Ohhh, you are such a funny man," she said in a mocking voice as she gave me a punch on the shoulder. "And such a chauvinist."

"It's merely a means of illustrating a concept, Detective. And I'll have you know I am nondiscriminative. I like women of all shapes and descriptions."

"Oh, you do, huh," she replied in a cool tone.

"Yes, I do," I answered. "But mostly, I like tall women. Tall women with auburn hair and freckles on their noses, and with a pistol on their belt. I think, right now, that's my favorite type of woman."

Patricia was silent a few seconds, and I wondered if I'd said too much. But she reached over and squeezed my hand again.

"Thanks," she breathed. "That was nice."

It was now my turn to return the squeeze of her hand. Then my phone rang. Glancing down and recognizing the number, I lifted the phone to my ear while pulling off the street and into a nearby parking lot.

"Sandy," I said as I switched off the car engine. "I'm glad you called. When can we get together and talk?"

"Can you meet me tomorrow?" she began without preamble.

"You just tell me when and where, Sandy. I'll be there."

"Meet me at the bus station in Savannah at two thirty in the afternoon," she said in a rushed voice.

"I'll be there, Sandy."

"Good. Just don't be late, Mr. Tanner. It has to be at two thirty."

"I'll be there. Don't you worry."

She clicked off without another word.

"What was that all about?" Patricia asked. "You look puzzled."

"It was a friend of Tonya Causey's—Sandy Willis, the girl I had stopped to see when I had the encounter with that head case who beat up my truck. She agreed to meet me, but she sounded strange—worried, maybe. Or perhaps scared, I don't know." I shook my head in thought. "Everybody I've met since I've touched this thing is—well—different, I guess, if I were to put it generously."

"Want me to come with you and lend a hand?" Patricia asked.

I shook my head again. "No. That might spook her. It's taken several days for her to surface, and I don't want to lose her again."

Patricia nodded her head. "Just let me know if you need any backup."

"I'll be the first to yell for help," I said as I cranked up and pulled into traffic again.

"Somehow or other, I kinda doubt that," she replied.

"Yeah, Detective, I know. But I had to say it. For politeness' sake, if no other reason."

That garnered me another slug on the shoulder.

Traffic thinned as we drove north on Highway 21. The sunlight was gone by the time we passed through the town of Rincon. And when we turned off the highway and onto the pine-bordered dirt roads that ran through the swamps and woods, it felt as though we were driving down a darkened tunnel. Then, at the next crossroads, we were at the church.

The parking area in the churchyard was surprisingly full when we pulled in. Most of the vehicles were pickup trucks, with a smattering of older sedans, a new tricked-out SUV, and over to one side, sitting by itself, the hulking cab of an eighteen wheeler, minus the trailer.

A single bare bulb on the porch illuminated the entrance to the church, but a bright light shown forth from the windows, and I could see the shapes and figures of people moving about within.

I parked on the outer fringes of the yard. As Patricia and I stepped onto the porch I took her arm and stopped for a second.

"Things may get a little wild here tonight. If you feel uncomfortable, let me know and we'll leave," I told her.

Patricia gave me an amused smile. "You make it sound like some kind of a witches' coven. Don't worry, Tanner, I'm game if you are."

She then reached out her hand, opened the door, and stepped inside. I followed close behind.

The room was abuzz with voices. There were six wooden pews arrayed on each side of the aisle. Seated on the pews were the children and the older folks. The center aisle was full of people talking, laughing, and gesturing to one another—these were the adults and the older teenagers. As we stepped in an old man dressed in freshly pressed bib overalls and a red plaid flannel shirt grabbed me by the hand and nodded to Patricia.

"Hey, y'all. Welcome, welcome to Panther Creek Holiness Church. I'm Brother Alvin Turhune, and we're mighty glad to have you here tonight. Won't you come on in and make y'self comfortable? We about to get started any minute now."

Brother Alvin's dark brown face and African features glowed with the gentle smile of a farmer, a man of the earth, as he gestured to a pew in the back row.

"Thank you. We're glad to be here," I said as I ushered Patricia to the pew.

I studied the congregation as Patricia and I took our seats. The mix was about evenly white and black. Some of the older women were just as I recalled from my childhood: long hair piled high in a beehive hairdo, long-sleeved cotton print dresses that came down below the knee, and great open-faced smiles as they talked to their friends and fellow congregants.

The teens huddled in a couple of groups of their own, while the men seemed to walk throughout the building saying a word here and there, and then moving to another person. Several people came over to speak to Patricia and me, and everyone was friendly and welcoming.

The voices grew louder and louder as the crowd became more animated. Then a man stepped onto the raised platform that spanned the front of the building, where he picked up an electric guitar and slung the strap over his shoulder. He plugged the cord into the base of the guitar, softly strummed a couple of chords, and adjusted the knobs of an amplifier. Then, turning to face the congregation, he struck a powerful blast on the guitar and let it ring and reverberate through the building as he beamed a great smile out upon the crowd. This was the opening call to worship.

I looked closely at the man. He appeared to be well into middle age—maybe late fifties or early sixties. He was dressed in work clothes—matching blue cotton pants and shirt—the kind of clothes worn by mechanics and shop workers all over the country. Above the pocket of his shirt was an oval white name tag, but from where I was seated I couldn't read the inscribed name.

In spite of his age he was a powerfully built man, with broad shoulders, long muscled arms, a narrow waist, and long legs. He had a thick head of white hair combed back in an elaborate 1950s-style pompadour.

He looked out upon the crowd again and struck another powerful chord that sent vibrations resonating through the building. The buzz of voices died to a low hum. The people moved from the aisle and into the pews, but no one sat. The ones who had been sitting got to their feet, and everyone looked forward expectantly.

The man on stage looked out across the faces before him and let his eyes play across, and touch, every individual. Then, lifting his head and eyes to the ceiling, he tore into a scalding guitar riff that was so intense it seemed as though it would peel the very paint from the walls. The man's fingers flew across the strings of the instrument like they were possessed by a will of their own. The music that cascaded from the guitar pulled a collective sound of awe from the throats of the people. More than a sigh, it was a prolonged gasp of admiration. Or was it, perhaps, exaltation?

Striking the final note, his head lifted and eyes closed, he worked the neck of the guitar until he had milked every last fading decibel from the pulsating string.

The place went hush—utterly quiet. The man opened his eyes, and with a beatific smile on his rugged face he

addressed the crowd in a voice that was no less powerful
and rich than the sound that came from his guitar.

"The Bible tells us."

He struck a twanging chord, threw back his head, and
called out in a loud voice.

"To make a joyful noise—unto the Lord!"

Another chord . . .

"Can I get an amen here?"

The crowd, with hands raised and voices lifted, shouted,
"Amen! Yes, Lord! Praise Jesus!"

Another chord, louder and more intense.

"I said, the Bible tells us!"

Chord.

"To make a joyful noise—unto the Lord!"

*"Praise the Lord! Amen! Jesus love! Tell it, brother!
Praise him, praise him."*

Short riff . . .

*"For where two or more are gathered together in my
name . . ."*

He assailed the guitar, hurling himself into a driving
instrumental that would have caused even Jeff Beck and
Eric Clapton to hang their heads in shame. The people
lifted their arms and hands and called out in many voices.
Excitement electrified the room. It went on and on as the
excitement built.

Then the man suddenly slapped a hand over the strings
and killed the music. The crowd went mute and stood frozen in place. The only sound in the building was the soft
hum of the amplifier.

The man leaned forward and called in a loud whisper, "I
am there amongst them."

He strummed softly.

"He is here amongst us. Do you feel him, people? Do
you feel the presence of your Lord? He is here—he is here."

The crowd rose up on their toes. Arms lifted higher, while some of the worshipers stood with upturned faces and tightly closed eyes.

The congregation moaned their plea, "Yes. Oh, yes. Come in, sweet Jesus. Come down, Holy Spirit."

I found myself straining forward, white-knuckled hands gripping the back of the pew in front of me, breath caught short in my throat.

Then the man on the stage leaped into the air, renewing his attack on the guitar. When he hit the floor again it appeared as if his legs had taken control of his body, and he danced across the stage as though compelled by a hidden force. He threw forth one shivering leg, the toe of the uplifted foot just skimming the surface of the floor, the pulses of his lower body propelling him across the stage as the music overwhelmed the house.

The voice of the crowd rose in intensity along with the power of the music. How a lone man could wrench such sound from a single instrument is something beyond explanation.

Then he made another tremendous leap into the air that carried him almost to the ceiling. When his feet hit the floor again he threw back his head and sang out in a compelling and powerful voice that positively electrified the room. And with his first words, I felt chills rushing down my spine.

I once *was lost in siiin*
But Jesus *took me in*
And then a little light from heaven filled my sooooul
It bathed *my heart in love*
And wrote *my name above*
And just a little talk with Jesus made me whoooole

He gestured with his guitar, and at his cue the congregation joined in at full-throated cry. As the guitarist worked his magic, the voices raised the roof, and the very walls of the building seemed to throb with the passion of the song.

> *Now let us*
> *Have a little talk with Jesus*
> *Let us*
> *Tell him all about our troubles*
> *He will*
> *Hear our faintest cry*
> *And he will answer by and by*
> *Now when you*
> *Feel a little prayer wheel turning*
> *And you*
> *Know a little light is burning*
> *You will*
> *Know a little talk with Jesus makes it riiiight!*
> *Makes it right*

People were literally dancing in the aisles. Jumping, singing, their bodies rocking and swaying with the music. One old man was down on his knees in a state of ecstasy, pounding the floor with an open palm. If there *is* such a thing as the Holy Spirit, it was here, and it was upon these people.

I had heard this old hymn a thousand times in my life, but never like this. It was done in a driving, pulsing, rockabilly rhythm, tinged with a taste of raw country blues, and garnished with the accents of the people. And I realized, this is where rock and roll came from, the backwoods and churches of the Deep South—from the uninhibited worship of the black and white outcasts, our own *untouchables*—the lowest of American society. The moves made by a young Elvis in performance were the same as the ones made by the man on the stage. And the sound that poured forth was pure Carl Perkins and Jerry Lee Lewis.

I was grabbed body and soul, pulled in by the emotional vortex of the music and the moment, and soon found myself giving voice with the others. I glanced over at Patricia and saw she had joined in, too.

I may have doubts and feeears
My eyes be filled with teeears
But Jesus is a friend who watches day and niiiight
I go to him in prayer
He knows my every care
And just a little talk with Jesus makes it riiiight

Now let us
Have a little talk with Jesus
Let us
Tell him all about our troubles
He will
Hear our faintest cry
And he will answer by and by
Now when you
Feel a little prayer wheel turning
And you
Know a little light is burning
You will
Know a little talk with Jesus makes it right
Makes it riiiight

Pastor Truman Rainwater—for that's who I now knew the man on stage to be—with the last few stanzas of the chorus brought the house back down to a bubbling roll. He strummed the guitar as he looked again upon the congregation and allowed a relative calm to descend upon the house.

"You know why we here tonight, dear ones—and so does the Lord above. It's the midweek tune-up. We halfway through the week now, between one Sunday and t'other— the midway point, when the Evil One has got you square in his sights and he's been whispering sweetly in your ear. You know it's so. You've heard him. He's been trying to deceive you 'bout what you should be doing with your life. How you would be better off . . . *happier*"—chord— "*healthier*"—chord—"*wealthier*—if you'd just . . ."

Chord: *"Tell that lie . . ."*

Chord: *"Steal that money . . ."*

Chord: *"Cheat, and blaspheme, and . . ."*

Chord: (In a lower voice) "Curse your God."

The crowd groaned with spiritual pain at the very thought, "Noooo! Help us, Lord Jesus."

Rainwater continued, "And that's why we here tonight, beloved sisters and brothers in the Lord."

Chord: "To fortify our spirits for the struggle of life!"

Chord: "To give us the strength we need for the never-ending battle with Satan!"

Chord: "To put on the full armor of the Lord, and gird our loins as warriors in God's holy army."

When Rainwater launched into another song, the congregation went wild with joy and spiritual ecstasy. The worship became a free-for-all. People danced, jumped pews, knelt in the aisles, and prayed. One woman lay flat on her face up near the altar, her arms moving in a swimming motion. Some people stood praying with uplifted hands and faces, tears streaming down their cheeks. Others lunged back and forth, arms held high, speaking in tongues. Here and there, a few, their heads bent to the back of the pew in front of them, sat silently in private prayer.

Rainwater looked upon the crowd with the face of a contented father. He gently touched the heads of several people who knelt at the altar. Then, he swung his guitar into place and began another song. This time with an achingly imploring tone but a power that seemed to come from the core of Earth itself.

> *Would you be free from your burden of sin*
> *There's* pow'r *in the blood*
> Pow'r *in the blood*
> *Would you o'er evil a victory win*
> *There's wonderful pow'r in the blooood*

Everyone, with stamping feet and clapping hands, joined him in the refrain, and I was among them. The building physically shook with the emotion of the song.

> *There is pow'r, pow'r*
> *Wonder-working pow'r*
> *In the blooood*
> *Of the laaaamb*
> *There is pow'r, pow'r*
> *Wonder-working pow'r*
> *In the precious*
> *Blood of the laaaamb*

> *Would you be free of your passion and pride*
> *There's pow'r in the blooood*
> *Pow'r in the blooood*
> *Come for a cleansing*
> *To Calvary's tide*
> *There's wonderful pow'r in the blooood*

There is pow'r, pow'r
Wonder-working pow'r
In the blooood
Of the laaaamb
There is pow'r, pow'r
Wonder-working pow'r
In the precious
Blooood of the laaaamb

There would be no sermon delivered in a bored drone to a bored congregation. This *was* the worship service. It was worship in its purest form. I looked about me and realized that here was to be found only the slightest veneer of Christianity. Sure, they quoted the Christian Bible, and they called upon Jesus Christ, but they could have used another name, one more ancient, and another sacred script, if only they knew it existed.

For as I watched and listened I knew that this was a gathering as old as our race. This was how our ancestors worshipped their deities when gathered in community among the sacred oak groves of Ireland and Britain, or along the jungle-shaded banks of an African river. This was the essence of a pure humanity, expressing itself with a collective consciousness to a God created in *their* own image—a tangible God, one who was close, personal, and accessible.

The singing, shouting, and praying went on for another hour, Brother Rainwater shepherding his flock through the hills and valleys, the swamps and deserts, of worshipful free-form expression. At last it began to wind down.

Rainwater unplugged the amp cord from the guitar and set the instrument aside. The room calmed and became still. Lifting his hands, a broad loving smile on his face, he addressed the congregation.

"Brothers and sisters in the Lord. I don't know about you, but I've been filled. I've had me a dose that cures all ills, a dose of that Holy Ghost medicine, a dose of the *Father's* medicine, that will get me through this coming week."

The crowd: "Amen, brother. Yes, Jesus. Praise his name."

"But there's others in our hearts—friends and loved ones, even enemies—others out there, lost and alone, who don't know the divine physician, who don't have the prescription for the life-giving medicine. So let's keep them always in our prayers. Let's pray that they, too, find God's loving touch, and let's conduct our lives that we might be a living example of the loving graciousness of our sweet savior, Lord Jesus Christ, who gave his life that all might live."

Crowd: "Amen. Amen, brother. Hear us, oh Lord."

Rainwater then stepped from the platform, and as he walked quickly down the aisle said, "Brother Alvin, will you lead us in a closing prayer?"

Rainwater stood by the door as the prayer was said, and then, as the people filed from the building, he shook hands, spoke with, and hugged each and every person.

Patricia and I waited quietly until the last, and when there were only a few people left she squeezed my hand and whispered, "I'll wait for you in the car."

"All right," I replied.

I handed her the keys. She slipped out the door as Rainwater was speaking with an elderly couple. And then, he and I were the only two left.

"Brother Rainwater," I said as I stepped forward and offered my hand. "My name's Kennesaw Tanner."

Rainwater shook my hand with a firm grip and fixed me with a warm yet penetrating eye.

"Truman," he said. "Call me Truman. It's good to have

you here with us tonight, son, and I hope to see you again. But I don't think you're a local boy, are you?"

"No, sir, I'm not. I'm here because I wanted to talk with you about one of your former members—Tonya Causey."

Rainwater's eyes softened, and he said in a gentle voice, "Ah, little Tonya. What are you looking for, brother? What do you want to know about Tonya?"

"At the request of Joree Causey, the girl's mother . . ."

He nodded that he knew who Joree was.

"I'm looking into the last year of Tonya's life, and the circumstances leading to her death. The official finding was that she committed suicide, but Joree doesn't believe that."

Rainwater looked at me silently for a second, his eyes flitting back and forth over my face.

"This is a personal matter for you, isn't it, son?"

It was a question I hadn't expected, and until now had not really considered. It was my turn to reflect silently.

"Yes, sir, it is," I admitted.

"Walk with me, son," he said.

He then turned out the lights in the church, and when we stepped onto the porch, he closed and locked the door. He then led the way across the churchyard, empty now except for my car and the commercial truck.

"I'm not trying to rush you—we'll talk as long as you want. But I've got a load to pick up at the port tonight, and my old truck needs to warm before we get on the road," he said as we walked across the yard to the truck.

"Just a second," he said as he climbed in the cab and started the engine. When the motor was running smoothly he climbed back down and led me away where we could speak undisturbed by the rumble of the diesel engine. We stopped and stood face-to-face.

"There are other girls from this area who are also missing. Did you know that, Brother Tanner?"

I felt as though I'd received a jolt from a cattle prod.

Others? I mouthed.

"Yes, sir," he said. "Four other young girls—four—that I'm aware of."

"But missing—not dead?" I responded.

Rainwater shook his head. "Not that anyone knows. But they *are* missing. Their families haven't heard from them in months and have no idea of their whereabouts."

"Do you know who they are? Do you know the families?" I asked, my mind awhirl with the thought.

"I do," he said. "One of them is my own granddaughter."

I was stunned at the revelation. I stood and thought a bit before I spoke again.

"Your granddaughter?"

"Yes, sir, my granddaughter. Run off and ain't been heard from since. Sixteen years old. Her name is Mary Beth, but she's such a tiny thing we always called her Chigger."

"Does the sheriff know this? Are your granddaughter and the other girls on a missing persons list?"

"I don't know what the sheriff is aware of, but no, I doubt they are on any list. Each one of the girls said they had found a job in Savannah, and just eventually fell out of contact with their family," he stated.

"Had they been sending money home after they left?" I asked.

"For a while," he replied.

"Your granddaughter, too?"

"Yes," he responded.

"And when did this all start?" I queried.

"About a year ago."

About a year ago, I thought. *Around the same time Tonya went away.*

"Truman, can you tell me what kind of a girl Tonya was—what she was like?"

Rainwater hesitated before speaking, as though searching his mind, or searching for the right words.

"She was a sweet girl," he said in a low voice. "Sweet, and trusting, and burdened with an inner pain. She never believed she had much worth as a human being. Her spirit was lonely, and she felt small."

She felt small, I thought, *small and alone in the world. And now she is gone. How many other vulnerable human beings does that describe on this planet? How many other troubled souls?*

"Truman, do you know if she had a boyfriend, or perhaps a special friend who might have known where she went?"

He shook his head. "Boys, I can't say—I don't know. She was good friends with Sandy Willis. But Sandy doesn't come here anymore, not since Tonya disappeared."

"And the other girls, were they members here?"

He shook his head again. "No, just girls from this county. Little country girls."

"Were they all about the same age?" I asked.

"Pretty close," he said. "Between fifteen and twenty, near as I can recall."

There has to be a connection here, I thought. *I don't know what it is, but something links those girls. Something ties them to a common fate. Find out about one and you find out about them all.*

I handed Rainwater a card. "Would you call me if, later, something else comes to mind? And could I get your phone number so I can call you if I have some other questions?"

"Certainly," he said as he gave me his number.

"Truman, I'm glad to have met you," I said as I took his hand. "And I'm sorry to hear about your granddaughter."

He held my forearm with his other hand and looked me in the eye as we shook.

"Thank you. I believe you're a good man, Kennesaw Tanner. And I think you're on the right side—on the Lord's side."

"I hope so. Good night, Brother Truman."

"Good night, Brother Kennesaw. God be with ye."

Truman Rainwater climbed into the cab of his truck. The air brakes released, and he pulled away, the sound of the engine rising and falling, quickly at first, and then in a lengthening cadence, as he went through the lower gears and picked up speed.

I walked to my car and slid in beside a dozing Patricia. She roused when the dome light came on. Stretching and yawning like a big feline, she looked at me with smiling eyes.

"That was quite a date, Tanner. I feel like I've run a marathon."

"It is kind of draining, isn't it?"

"I'll say," she said. "Like being wrung out and hung up to dry. Why don't you get us back to town and we find some food? I'm starving."

"On the way," I replied as I cranked the engine. Putting the car in gear, we pulled away from the churchyard and onto the rutted dirt road that ran somewhere between Hopelessness and Destitution.

CHAPTER 15

A FINE DRIZZLE FLOATED LAZILY ON the night air, leaving a mist just thick enough to shorten the range of the headlights and obscure the sides of the road. At the next intersection I turned right, toward the small crossroads town of Guyton, where we could pick up old U.S. Highway 17. I thought it would shave a few miles off our route back to Savannah.

It was as black as a night can be, the darkness punctured by our headlights, and shoved aside only here and there by the dim porch lights of the few houses we passed. We were on a long, straight portion of dirt road when, in my rear-view mirror, a set of headlights appeared. They held steady for half a minute or so, and then began to close rapidly.

Soon the lights were right behind us, right on my bumper. They were set high, the lights of a pickup. They held there for a few seconds before falling back a couple of car lengths. Then they charged up again—flashing repeatedly from high to low beam. I opened the console, took my pistol in hand, and stuck it under my right thigh.

"What's that all about back there?" Patricia asked as she turned and glanced out the back window.

"I don't know, but I don't like it. Get your pistol ready. I'm in no mood to play stupid redneck road games."

Patricia got her gun in hand just as the truck swung out to pass, flashing its lights and now honking the horn. I dropped my window, picked up my pistol, and let it rest just below the window frame.

I held my speed—you never try to run from a road confrontation—and then our pursuers accelerated sharply and pull up alongside. I laid the muzzle of the pistol on top of the window frame and angled it upward.

In a split second we were running side by side, then the passenger window of the truck went down and a teenage boy, his hair flying in the wind, stuck his head out. He had a big grin on his face.

"Hey, mister," he yelled. "Your left taillight is out."

"Yeah—z'at so?" I called in reply.

"Yeah," he called back. "And with them out-of-county tags on your car, if the sheriff gets ahold of you, it'll be a big ticket. Just thought you'd like to know. Might save you some trouble."

"Okay. Thanks, bubba," I shouted back.

"Aw'right. Y'all have a good un," he yelled.

The boy put up his window, the driver tromped down on the gas pedal, and leaping ahead of us, they quickly pulled away. As the truck's taillights faded to red dots in the distance, I put my pistol back in the console. I heard the click of the safety going back on as Patricia also put her gun away.

I glanced over at Patricia. "Thought for a few seconds

there we were about to have ourselves a *Deliverance* moment."

"Is that what you call it? I thought *Deliverance* happened up in the mountains."

"It's a metaphor, Detective, for unpleasant encounters with rustic natives," I deadpanned.

"Well. At least they were friendly natives," she responded. "But you did get that part about the sheriff and out-of-county tags, didn't you?"

"Yeah, but so what? It's a time-honored Southern tradition for the police to prey on outsiders."

"Really?" she retorted. "And just where did you get that idea?"

I glanced over again and saw that she really was piqued at my comment. "From every small community, rural county, and GI town I've ever been in," I replied. "And don't look so hurt about it. Savannah may cater to visitors—after all, tourism is a big money maker for the city. But out in the hinterlands, the stranger is often viewed as an unclaimed sheep, ready for the shearing."

I glanced back over again and saw a sly smile.

"Okay, Tanner. But now that the excitement is over, get us to town. I'm still hungry."

Forty minutes later we were sitting in a little Thai restaurant, sipping Japanese beer and working on a large plate of chicken larb. I spooned the larb onto a lettuce leaf, rolled it into the shape of a taquito, and took a bite.

"Delicious," I said with a sigh before taking another bite.

Patricia took a bite, then a sip of beer, and dabbed her lips with her napkin.

"The preacher have anything useful?" she asked as she rolled another lettuce leaf.

"Background, really. Nothing solid. But it does speak to Tonya's overall state of mind. He said she felt small."

Patricia sat silently a second before replying, "Small equals vulnerable."

"That's my thought exactly," I responded.

"Well, if that's the case, maybe you can . . ."

At that second I felt my phone begin to vibrate. I plucked it from my pocket, looked at the screen, and brought it to my ear.

"Yeah, it's Kennesaw," I said.

I listened a few seconds.

"Slow down, Danny Ray. And say that again."

I listened.

"Are either of you hurt?" I asked. "Okay. I'll be right there."

"Sorry, Patricia," I said as I stood and put some money on the table. "We've got to go—er, I have to go. But I think you'll want to come, too. You'll probably be called on this anyway."

"What is it?" she asked as she grabbed her jacket and purse.

"I think it was Leon Wren. And it seems this time, he finally killed my truck."

We ran out to my car, and I put the pedal down.

Patricia flashed her badge, and the cop at the barrier waved us through the police barricade. I parked just down the street from the nearest fire engine, and we walked to the smoldering ruins of what was once an auto shop and, out back, Danny Ray's home. It was now just so much charred concrete block and collapsed angle iron. I found Danny Ray and Parker standing on the sidewalk watching the firemen prowl through the rubble, hosing down the hot spots.

"Danny Ray—Parker, y'all remember Detective Latham, don't you?" I said as I put a reassuring hand on Danny Ray's thin shoulder.

"Miss Patricia," Parker said, taking his hat in one hand

and Patricia's in the other. "I'm glad to see you again but sorry for the circumstances."

"Hello, Mr. Wells—I mean, Parker," she said as he began to protest.

"Mr. Pledger," she said as she turned to Danny Ray.

Danny Ray nodded and then ducked his head. I looked closely at my friends. Both men were smudged with black soot and I could smell the stench of scorched hair.

"You sure you're both all right?" I asked. "Have you been checked out by the medics?"

"Yes, Kennesaw. The EMTs gave us a good going-over. We're okay," Parker replied.

"I'm going to check with the investigator. I'll see you in a little bit," Patricia said as she turned on her heel and strode to a nearby unmarked police car.

"What the hell happened?" I asked.

In what had once been the service bay of the shop, I finally identified the mangled carcass of my Bronco. *Ashes to ashes,* I thought.

"Danny, help me out if I leave anything amiss," said Parker.

Danny Ray looked up and, nodding his head, spoke for the first time. "'K-k-kay," he stammered.

"We worked at the boat until after dark and then stopped here so that Danny Ray could retrieve something from his trailer before we went to supper."

Danny Ray nodded his affirmation of Parker's words.

"We were just coming back up the alley when there was the sound of breaking glass and then a big flash of fire at the front of the building."

Danny Ray nodded again.

"We ran out to the edge of the street, and in the light of the flames, saw a huge man—he was bald-headed—just as he lit what can only be a Molotov cocktail—it was a rag fuse stuck in the neck of a bottle—and threw it through another window of the shop."

Leon Wren, I thought.

Parker reached up and wiped his forehead, leaving a white streak where the soot rubbed off.

"We yelled at him, but he just pulled out another bottle, lit the fuse, and threw it at us. It landed on the sidewalk, over there, just barely missing us. We ran back down the alley to avoid the flames, and when we came back to the street again we saw him climb into a truck and take off. We then ran to the store at the corner and got them to call the fire department. When we returned—it was only a couple of minutes later—the fire was already out of control. We went to Danny's trailer to try to salvage what we could, but it was too late. The fire had spread to the back of the building. It was all gone."

I reached out and gripped Danny's shoulder again.

"Your garden, too, Danny Ray?" I asked in a sympathetic voice.

Danny Ray looked at me from beneath the brim of his cap. His face was set and his lips pressed tightly together. "My garden, too," he said quite distinctly in a pained voice.

"Jesus," I muttered, involuntarily.

I turned again to Parker.

"Can you describe the truck they were in?"

"It was a new red Chevy. It had big tires and the frame sat high on a lift kit."

Junior Causey's truck!

"When the man got in the truck, was he the one who drove, or was it someone else?" I asked.

"No, he got in on the passenger side. The truck was already running and waiting for him. As soon as he climbed in, they took off."

"Anything else you can remember?" I asked.

Danny Ray looked at me. "Sh-sh-shots," he said.

"Oh yeah," Parker joined in. "When the fire bomber threw the Molotov at us, whoever was in the truck fired what sounded like a couple of pistol shots at us—a quick pow-pow."

"Y-y-yeah. Two," added Danny Ray with a vigorous nod.

I looked from my scorched friends to the collapsed and still-smoking building and thought about what had happened.

Junior had followed my truck to the auto shop, and then told Leon where to find it. That much was obvious. All they'd had to do was check with the tow company that had hauled it here. In a way I had brought this on Danny Ray and his brother-in-law.

No, that's nonsense, I thought. *It was those two sorry bastards who had done this—they and they alone. And by God, I was going to see that they paid a dear price for their act of arson and the attempted murder of these two gentle beings. Yes, a dear price indeed.*

"Danny Ray," I asked my friend. "Do you know Leon Wren? Have you ever seen him before?"

Danny's face screwed up, his eyes twitched, and his mouth worked. "W-w-w-once. L-l-l-long time ago."

"Was it him? Was he the one who did this?"

Danny Ray bobbed his head up and down. "Y-y-yeah. Was him."

"Let's talk to Detective Latham. She'll want to hear this."

I led us to where Patricia was talking to a uniformed sergeant. Patricia talked to Parker and Danny Ray, and then stayed until almost everyone had cleared out. Then she turned to me.

"If they knew where your truck was, they also know the car you're driving. You said you got it in Rincon, didn't you?" she posited.

"Yeah, I've had that thought, too," I replied.

"I won't tell an old dog how to suck eggs," she responded. "But if it were me, I believe I'd change vehicles."

"My thoughts exactly," I said.

"I'll ride back to headquarters with the sergeant," she said as we turned and walked toward the patrol car sitting just down the street.

"Call me tomorrow, when you get the chance. And I'll call if anything worthwhile pops up. Maybe Sheriff Zimmer can get his hands on those two. More than likely they're back in Effingham already. Mutts like those two seldom stray far from their own territory."

"Yeah, maybe," I replied. "But I'll call, no matter what."

"Okay, Tanner," she said as she held the open door of the cruiser. "Once again, you sure know how to show a girl a good time."

She must have seen the look on my face, because she quickly added, "Hey, that's a joke."

"I know," I said. "I was just thinking of what a cauldron of crap this is. Seems like when I stuck a stick in it and began to stir, some of it spilled over the sides and splattered on some innocent people."

"How very poetic," she retorted with arched eyebrows and a sardonic smile.

"Yeah, well, I do my best," I said as I squeezed her hand. "Good night, Patricia."

"Good night, Kennesaw."

She got in the car and pulled away, leaving Parker, Danny Ray, and me the sole inhabitants of the street.

"Guys," I said as I rejoined my friends on the sidewalk. Let's get some take-away Chinese and go back to the boat. Danny Ray, you stay with me and Parker for the time being. Once we get you two cleaned up and fed, we have some work to do before it gets daylight."

Fortunately, they had been able to save Danny Ray's truck. They headed directly back to the *Miss Rosalie*, while I stopped at Wang Cho's House of Delight and picked up a bounteous spread of food.

After the guys had showered, fed, and rested a bit, we loaded into Danny Ray's truck and my rental car and drove through the darkened streets of Savannah to Bob Martin's cabin on Dutch Island. I followed along as Danny Ray led us to the place without a single hesitation or wrong turn. When he pulled into, and stopped, in a narrow dirt drive that seemed to disappear into a blackened jungle, I got out and unlocked a sturdy gate made of two steel posts set on either side of the drive with the bar of the gate being made of a length of four-inch diameter steel pipe. We pulled both vehicles through the gate, which I then closed behind us.

We drove for almost a hundred meters through a tunnel of vegetation, arriving at last in a clearing of about a half an acre. Sitting just at the edge of the salt marsh, where the land dropped off with a ragged edge, was an old shack, its tin roof shining dully in the light reflected by the low clouds. The place had the feeling of utter desertion. Far away, across the marsh, where the salt creek made a sweeping bend back to the east, I could see the faint night-lights from a few of the Dutch Island mansions.

"Danny Ray, let's leave your truck here and we'll go back in my car. Okay?"

Both men silently nodded their heads, and I realized I had been speaking in a whisper.

"There's no need to go in the cabin yet," I continued. "We'll head back to the boat, get a few hours' sleep, and then set out before daylight. When the sun comes up, all I want anyone to know is that *Miss Rosalie* is gone."

"Right," whispered Parker.

"Ch-ch-ch-check the dock," Danny said in a low voice.

"Good idea. Lead the way," I said.

Danny Ray guided us by a narrow boardwalk that ran along the side of the cabin. A set of stairs led down the steep bank of the bluff to the dock below. I walked to the end and peered down at the water. As Bob had said, the dock was set in a cut in the bank. The cleft in the shore was maybe thirty feet wide at the mouth, tapering sharply as it plunged landward, and was perhaps seventy-five feet deep.

At the end of the dock I found a length of crab line coiled on top of a piling. I threaded one end of the line through the lanyard hole in my pocketknife and then lowered it into the water at the dock's edge. I measured the line in double arm's lengths as I pulled it back up, and found the water to be about sixteen feet deep.

The tide was in now, I reflected as I looked out across the silent marsh and down the creek to where it disappeared at the bend. Bob was right, there would still be ten or more feet of water here, even at low tide. We should have no trouble getting *Miss Rosalie* safely to the dock. We would come up the creek on the next rising tide.

"Ready to go back," I whispered to my comrades as I removed the line from my knife and clipped it back to my waistband.

"Let's go," murmured Parker. Danny Ray nodded his head and, turning silently, led us up the dock and back to the front of the cabin. We climbed into the car, and within a half hour we were back aboard *Miss Rosalie*.

CHAPTER 16

I LEANED MY HEAD OUT OF THE pilothouse door and called softly across the deck to Parker, who stood at the ready, "Cast off."

Parker let loose the line he had been holding and waved his hand to signal we were free of the dock. He then pulled in the line and coiled it before walking to the bow and taking station there. I felt the falling tide take hold of the boat and watched closely as, inch by inch, we began to drift slowly away.

I waited until I saw a gap of three or four feet between the wooden dock and the side of the boat before slipping the transmission into forward. The prop dug into the water with a firm bite, and our backward drift stopped. Then, as the boat began to creep forward, I gave the wheel a slight roll to starboard and executed a wide sweeping turn in the channel, one that brought our bows about in a one-eighty and pointed us downstream.

I looked out the pilothouse again, this time to our rear, and could just make out the silhouette of Danny Ray following along in the sea skiff. The thick fog that lay in the marsh obscured the rest of the world from view, and within a matter of seconds, we, too, were hidden within its veiled embrace.

I felt, through the soles of my feet, the slow throb of the diesel engine as it pulsed belowdecks, but the sound it made was little louder than the gurgle of water that slipped past the stern. The night face of the creek was as placid as a millpond in summer, and in our solemn predawn march, we left barely a ripple to mark the history of our passage.

This is the time of clandestine movement, I reflected. The dark hours, when the world is utterly quiet. Its denizens huddled deep within their burrows, and even though held in the protective grip of sleep, yet still, they anxiously await the safety of the daylight to come. For all creatures of Earth instinctively know this to be the time when the monsters of our collective unconsciousness prowl the world in search of the unwary and unprotected. It is the time of disappearance and of the unseen passage—for purposes of both good and evil. It is a time I have made use of on many occasions before.

When we reached the mouth of the creek, where it joined up with Bull River, Danny Ray circled *Miss Rosalie* to gain Parker's attention. Parker left his post at the bow and came aft where he caught the line Danny tossed and quickly tied the skiff to the stern. Danny Ray clambered aboard and both men came to join me in the pilothouse where we stood in the eerie red glow of the binnacle light.

"How far downriver?" Parker asked in a whisper.

I reached up, adjusted the radar screen, and studied it for a few seconds. The channel ahead was clear of any other boats and the banks were plainly visible on the instrument. We were alone and in the middle of the channel. I gave the GPS a quick glance and noted our position.

"We'll make our way to the center of Wassaw Sound and then, just as the tide turns, head up the Wilmington River. All goes well, we'll arrive at Bob's dock just before daylight. If we hit any bumps on the way up, we'll just let the rising tide float us over. Total time should be four to five hours," I answered, also in a whisper.

Parker nodded his head in reply, while Danny Ray stared forward, peering intently into the fog and darkness, watching for unseen obstacles. Just then, he lifted his left hand and waved it slightly to the side.

"Th-th-th-that way. T-t-ten degrees," he said, in a quiet voice. "L-l-low spot."

I gave the wheel a slight turn and watched the bow of *Miss Rosalie* come smoothly to port. Just as the turn began, I glanced at the face of the depth finder and saw the bottom of the river rise sharply to within two feet of *Miss Rosalie*'s keel, but then drop away again to more than thirty feet of water as the turn was completed.

A few seconds later Danny Ray lifted his right hand and pointed straight forward. I brought the wheel back to its previous position and checked our location on the GPS and the radar. Danny Ray nodded his head in satisfaction and dropped his hand back to his side.

How could he possibly have known exactly where we were, much less that an unknown hump was before us? I wondered.

I've never known another man with Danny Ray's uncanny piloting abilities. It's as though he can find his way by sense of smell, or like some sort of seagoing homing pigeon with the imprint of the Earth's magnetic field upon his brain. Whether it was by the elapsed time of movement, or a subtle change he detected in the flow of the water, I could not tell. But Danny instinctively knew there had been a shift in the cut of the channel, and he knew which way led to deeper water.

And that's the inexplicable part of all this. It is one thing to learn and memorize a fixed route, that's something even we dullards can do. But the channels of these tidal waters never stand still and are forever changing. Filling here and cutting there—shifting with every tide, storm, and river flood—they are never at rest. But by some virtue that can only be explained as genius or magic, Danny Ray Pledger is utterly attuned to the brackish rhythms and salty pulses of these waters and is completely at one with them. They speak to him, and he knows them in their secret ways.

The river soon widened, so that we lost contact with either bank and were utterly lost within a universe of white upon white and gray upon gray. But our progress was swift as we fell downstream with the rapidly falling tide.

"Parker," I said, turning to our silent companion. "Think you could rustle us up a pot of coffee?"

"You must be a mind reader, Kennesaw. That was my own thought just this second. Coffee for all hands, coming up directly," he said as he left the pilothouse and headed for the galley.

I should get a pot to keep here in the pilothouse, I realized, *for times such as this. I wonder why I've never thought of that before.*

It wasn't long before Parker returned with a pot of coffee and three cups. I took the proffered cup and thanked him. Danny took a cup, but his eyes never strayed from their hold on the route ahead.

In the distance, diffused and softened by the fog, I saw a

blinking red light. I watched and counted. It blinked every two and a half seconds. I checked the GPS and the radar and determined this to be the buoy marking the center of Wassaw Sound. I started to give the wheel a turn to starboard, but Danny Ray arrested me with a touch of the hand.

"W-w-wait. F-f-fetch th-th-the b-b-buoy to p-p-port. Th-then turn d-d-due west," he instructed.

I did as he said. Holding our course, I waited until the flashing buoy was fifty feet off the port beam before making the turn to a heading that pointed us directly west. Within five minutes I made out the faint red glow of another buoy. This one flashed its light every four seconds. I turned up the resolution on the GPS to determine which buoy this was just as Danny Ray announced in a whisper, "W-W-W-Wilmington River."

A check of the screen and a glance down at the paper chart told me that he was correct; we were in the deepest part of the mouth of the Wilmington River and about to begin our ascent upstream.

Danny Ray leaned out the door of the pilothouse, turning his head from side to side as though trying to gauge the direction of the faint breeze.

Coming back inside, he said, "T-t-tide is changing."

That, too, was correct. The rising tide would assist our passage upriver.

It was a long stretch as we made our silent way through the darkness. The lights of Wilmington Island rose to starboard and then disappeared behind. Then, as we met the Intracoastal Waterway, we immediately made a hard looping turn to port that pointed us almost due south, bringing us into the waters of Skidaway River. We followed the deep waters of the Skidaway until we reached a point where Danny Ray plucked me by the sleeve.

"O-o-okay. Y-y-you follow now," he said.

"I'll stay back just far enough to keep you in sight," I replied.

"Y-y-yeah," Danny Ray responded as he turned to leave. Parker went with him.

I pulled the throttle to idle, leaving *Miss Rosalie* making just enough headway to give the rudder control. I heard the outboard motor of the sea skiff as it coughed to life and then Parker's low call of, "Clear," as he cast off the towline.

As Danny Ray pulled alongside *Miss Rosalie* he looked in at me and pointed his arm forward in the *follow me* signal. I flashed the navigation lights off and back on in response. As Danny Ray motored ahead and took his position out front as scout, Parker went and stood in the bow to serve as intermediary and interpreter. From the pilothouse I could just make out the faint white glow of the skiff's stern light as it led us upstream by an unseen watery path.

We held the same course and speed for another half mile or so until Danny Ray slowed down and made a sharp turn to starboard into the mouth of a wide creek. We were beginning the approach to Dutch Island.

The creek narrowed and then split. Danny Ray guided us to the left of the split and then slowed again. He then began to make a series of S-turns back and forth across the channel. Always searching for the deepest water, and always keeping us in the deepest cut. I flicked my eyes from Danny Ray to the depth finder and saw that though the depth of the water had shallowed greatly, there was always just enough to allow *Miss Rosalie* safe passage.

After a bit, Danny Ray struck and held to a more or less straight course, slowing only occasionally to make extra sure of a particular stretch of water. The creek continued to steadily narrow until, rounding a bend in the channel, I saw something on the bluff above and realized it was the roof of the shack peeking above the obscuring fog.

Danny Ray stopped near the end of the dock while I held off in midchannel. When he made a hand signal that I should back into the cut and tie up bows facing out, I waved a hand out the pilothouse door that I understood his meaning and called to Parker in a voice just loud enough to be heard the length of the deck.

"I'm gonna turn us around, come aft, and toss Danny Ray the lines as we pull up to the dock."

Parker walked to the stern and stood at the ready. The tide was still rising, so I had a bit of a dance turning *Miss Rosalie* in the narrow channel and then backing her up perpendicular to the flow of the water. But Danny Ray had foreseen the problem. Using the skiff as a tugboat, he dashed fore and aft, and from side to side—like a herding dog maneuvering a flock of sheep—pushing with the bow of the skiff here and there, wherever his effort had the most effect, and within minutes, we were tied safely and securely at our new dock.

I gave the instruments one last scan, turned off the electronics, and switched off the engine. All was quiet. As I stepped out of the pilothouse I looked to the east, and there on the indistinct horizon was a faint smear of color giving herald of a new day.

Danny Ray and Parker had just finished with the lines. As they turned to face me I could see the condensation of their breath in the chill morning air.

"Dang, if it ain't cold this morning," I said, a plume of fog accompanying my words. "What say we go below where it's warm and get a few hours' shut-eye. Then we can check out the cabin and see what we need to do next."

"I'm in agreement there," said Parker as he rubbed his hands together vigorously and then blew into them.

Danny Ray bobbed his head up and down. "Y-y-yeah," he stammered, as much from the cold as anything else.

"Last one in, close the door," I said as I led the way below, my companions close on my heels.

I had a great two hours of especially deep sleep that left me rested and ready for a new day. I let my comrades sleep a little longer as I went to the galley and busied myself with fixing a large breakfast. I was sure the guys were as hungry as I was. The passage we had made during the night, though not hazardous, was mentally taxing and hence quite tiring. That few hours' sleep, followed by a hearty meal, was just the thing to put us all back in top form.

While I cooked, I also thought. And I came to the conclusion that perhaps it was best that I find Parker and Danny Ray another place to stay—at least for a while.

Leon's firebombing of the auto shop was an attack directed against me, but these two men had taken the brunt of it. Until Leon was run to ground, or I had a face-to-face confrontation with him, anyone close to me was in possible danger.

Just as I was pouring the eggs into the skillet, my two friends made their daylight appearance.

"Is that the aroma of biscuits I detect emanating from the oven?" asked Parker as he came into the galley.

"That's a keen nose you have there," I said as I sprinkled cheese into the eggs and gave it all a stir.

"Should be, it's large enough," he replied, reaching up and touching the organ so obviously in question.

Danny Ray went to the counter and poured a couple of cups of coffee. Passing one of the cups to Parker, he then proceeded to set three places at the galley table.

"Morning, Danny," I said as he went about his task.

Danny looked up and gave me a grin, which I returned with a nod and a smile of my own. Speech is always a difficult matter for Danny Ray, but especially so in the morning.

"Eggs are ready," I said, setting the skillet on a cold eye of the stove before taking an oven mitt and removing the pan of biscuits from the oven.

"Eggs, biscuits, bacon, and grits—grab it and growl," I announced as I picked up a plate and began to fill it.

We ate in contented silence, and then, when we had finished the meal, I told Danny Ray and Parker the thoughts I'd had about their safety. Danny Ray looked not at me but at Parker, who, taking a sip of coffee, finally spoke in response.

"Last night, right after the fire and before you arrived, Danny Ray told me you would feel that way—that you would want us to remove ourselves to another location."

Danny looked over and gave me a short nod.

"And we determined right then that we were going nowhere."

I started to interrupt, "But I need to tell—"

Parker cut me off and continued, "Danny told me all about the girl, and her mother, and about this Leon Wren. So it's not like we have no idea of what may be going on here. But there's more to it than just that, Kennesaw."

Parker fixed me with his eye. "Miss Cyriah told me I must stay with you until your task is completed. She said I was to live where you live. Me, and your friend, 'the one whose speech is fragile, but whose spirit is a citadel,' in her very words.

"We were to stay with you under the same roof, no matter where that may be, no matter what happens. And that is what Danny Ray and I intend to do, Kennesaw Tanner. You have no more choice in the matter than we do. And the decision is no longer in your hands."

I looked to each of the men and saw the resolution in

their faces. The very thought of such friendship, and what it meant, brought a tightness to my throat that caused a momentary struggle for breath.

"Thanks, men," was my reply.

There was nothing further I needed to add to those words. But once again I found myself wondering how Cyriah could be so attuned to this. I also knew that neither she nor Danny Ray had ever laid eyes on one other. Her knowing of Danny Ray's existence was much the same as Danny's knowledge of the waters—it was just something that *was* and could not be explained.

Putting aside the esoteric, we then got down to the practical business of the day. Parker would begin work on the boat while Danny and I would depart to run a few errands. Or in actuality, Danny would chauffeur me until I could get a new set of wheels. First thing I did was to call the agency for the car I had rented and tell them where they could pick it up.

Parker gave Danny Ray a short list of a few items he needed and then we were off. First stop was my bank where I wrote a check for cash. The next stop was Mad Marvin's Wonderful World of Wheels and Deals.

Marvin MacAllistair was an old comrade. Years ago we had both served in the First Ranger Battalion, here in Savannah, on Hunter Army Airfield, which meant we were both full-blooded members of what's known in the army as "the Ranger Mafia."

Marvin's passion had always been old cars. While on active duty he had saved his money with miserly diligence, then, risking every penny he owned during one Homeric night in Las Vegas, he increased his cash twentyfold—and walked away with it all. With his Vegas winnings he had opened a used-car lot dealing exclusively in old cars. Or as Marvin liked to refer to them: *motor vehicles with class and style*. I tended to agree with him in that assessment. In fact, I had bought my late lamented Bronco from Marvin.

I had Danny Ray drop me at the corner of the lot and continue on. As I strolled through the field of gleaming cars an old Chevy caught my eye. I was just walking over to take a closer look when a huge hand clapped me on the shoulder.

"Ranger Tanner! Hooah, brother! Ain't seen you in a coon's age! How you been, man?"

Marvin had put on even more weight since I had seen him last, but unlike most heavy men he was elegant in his dress and his carriage. His bearing was that of a man of distinction. He was dressed in cream-colored slacks, an open-neck white shirt with gold cuff links, and a wool blazer that must have cost more than my entire wardrobe. The Italian loafers he wore would have paid for *Miss Rosalie*'s next paint job. Who knows what he paid for a haircut.

"Marvin, you're looking prosperous," I said as we shook hands. "How are you doing? How's business?"

Marvin gave me a flash of his perfect teeth. "Business is down, brother. Down as low as I've ever seen it. But how am I doing? I'm great, that's how I am. I do what I love. I have a wife and two daughters I adore—and who don't think I'm all that bad, either. We live in a wonderful home that is filled with laughter and love. So without trying to sound like I'm bragging, I can't think of a more fortunate man than me. But how 'bout yourself? How's life these days?"

"Fine as frog's hair, Marvin."

"Ha-ha-ha. 'Fine as frog's hair.' That's a good one, Kennesaw. You always did know how to turn a phrase. 'Fine as frog's hair,' I'll have to remember that."

"Feel free to use it as your own, Marvin. But I'm here looking for a car. Think a veteran can get some service in this place?"

Marvin swung an expansive arm that took in the whole lot at one sweep.

"The pick of the litter is yours for the asking. Let's walk and talk while you look. Find what you want, and I'll make you a deal that will knock your socks off—the old *Ranger* discount," he said as he tugged the corner of his eye in a sly gesture. "But what happened to that sweet little Bronco? Somebody offer you too much money for it—more than you could turn down?"

"No, it burned up last night, Marvin."

"Oh," he said as he placed a placating hand on my arm. "I'm sorry to hear that. That was one fine little truck, and those are becoming more and more rare. Your loss is a loss for us all."

I had to smile inside. Marvin's words made it sound as though I had lost a family member, and one who he himself had known and admired. It was pretty obvious that Marvin loved not just his business but also the cars themselves. We arrived at the Chevy.

"This one, Marvin," I said as I touched the trunk lid. "What year is this one—a '73?"

"You have a good eye, and you're pretty close. This one's a '74."

Marvin walked to the front and opened the hood. No sooner had we had stopped at the Chevy than a young man came hustling over and handed Marvin the keys to the car. He was dressed in an almost exact imitation of Marvin, right down to the loafers. He even carried himself like Marvin. The only difference, other than age, was waist size and skin color. Whereas Marvin wears the ruddy tones of northern European ancestry, the young man's forbearers were African. And East African, I thought, from the shape of the man's head and face and the reddish hue of his skin.

"Thank you, Taylor," Marvin said as he accepted the keys. "I want you to meet an old friend. This is Kennesaw Tanner. We spent some time together in our misbegotten youth."

"Pleased to meet you, Taylor," I said as I shook the young man's hand.

"The pleasure is mine, sir," he responded, with a firm grasp, before returning to the office across the lot.

"Good-looking young fellow," I said to Marvin as Taylor retreated. "Been with you long?"

Marvin watched the young man depart with a look of pride on his face. "Yeah, a little more than a year. He'll soon be my son-in-law. He's engaged to my oldest. I'm hoping to keep him here with me and take over the business some day. He has a degree from Emory and some great ideas about expanding this operation."

"I'm happy for you, Marvin."

"Yeah, thanks. And now about this car," he said as he handed me the keys.

Marvin went over the car in great detail. The old Chevy was one of the last of its breed: the large, powerful American car. It had a four-hundred-cubic-inch engine with a four-barrel carburetor. The car was long, low, and heavy. It had such a potent power-steering pump that you could turn the wheel effortlessly with just the tip of a finger. The body, the engine, transmission, and interior were better than new. The previous owner—a middle-aged man—had spent five years putting the car into perfect condition. It was better now than the day it had rolled out of Detroit.

"What happened to the owner?" I inquired.

"He got to drive it for a year. Then—cancer. He died four weeks after the diagnosis. I bought the car from the estate. He was a friend of mine."

Marvin gave me a sad eye. "Tells you to eat your cake first, doesn't it."

I nodded. "Yeah. I think it does," I responded. "So let's write the papers on her."

"I haven't even told you the price, Kennesaw. You're depriving me the pleasure of seeing your face when I tell you what an astounding deal I'm going to make you."

"Let's go inside, Marvin. You can tell me in your office."

"You are a strange man, Kennesaw," he said, shaking his head as we crossed the lot. "A very strange man indeed."

Now this is a *car*, I said to myself as I cruised away from the lot. She handled with authority and aplomb. I could feel the power under the hood ready for instant use, and she braked with a confident firmness. The body was tight, with nary a squeak nor a groan. The handcrafted interior was a study in the upholsterer's art. It was obvious the previous owner had loved this car.

My first stop was at the pet store to buy a cat carrier. Then it was off to the vet's to pick up Tybee. The veterinarian came out to speak with me about the little fellow. She told me that, as I had suspected, Tybee was indeed a he. And that he had been close to starvation when I had found him. He had been covered with fleas and full of internal parasites, but had no injuries or infections and was coming along nicely now—all he needed was proper nutrition. She told me he was probably five or six months old, and that when his condition improved a little more—say, in a month or so—that I could bring him in for neutering.

My last stop was the auto shop where I hoped to find Danny Ray's brother-in-law. He was there, poking through the ruins of the shop and shaking his head at the tragedy that had befallen them.

"Thank God," he said, "I still had insurance. At least I

can rebuild, and you and the others with cars here will be repaid."

We exchanged insurance information, and I departed.

As I drove back to Dutch Island I tried to make sense of what had happened last night. Why attack a car? Why burn down a building and endanger lives just to destroy a vehicle? It was an act of sheer madness.

But the larger question was why had Junior Causey bailed Leon Wren out of jail in the first place, and why was he driving him around as he executed his mania? And then, why had Junior shot at my friends? Maybe it was something Joree could enlighten me on. I wished to hell someone could.

I was back at the fish camp just in time to join the boys for lunch. We took our sandwiches up to the picnic table just above the dock and enjoyed the meal in the thin sunlight that trickled through the broken clouds. Tybee had a dish of cat food and then curled up on the end of the table for a nap.

Parker wiped his lips with his paper napkin and spoke.

"Kennesaw, we should take a look at the cabin this afternoon and see what it needs for us to move in. Danny Ray and I have concluded that, before anything else, we need to rewire the living quarters of the boat and run some new hydraulic lines, which means we'll have to pull apart a great deal of the interior of the boat."

"No time like the present," I replied. "Let's give her a gander."

We walked around to the front of the cabin. I inserted the key in the lock, and we went inside. The cabin was one large room, maybe sixteen feet wide and twice as long. There was a window on each side of the front door, and there were two additional windows on the right side of the room as you looked toward the back.

At the far end of the room was a small kitchen with a propane stove, a sink and counter with shelves above, and an ancient refrigerator that looked like it had been new when Eisenhower was president. In the corner opposite the kitchen a doorway led into a pantry, and from the pantry another door led into a tiny bathroom with a sink, toilet, and shower stall.

A second door in the bathroom took you out into the shed, which was open to the back of the house and gave direct communication with the dock. I assumed this was so if the wives or other women were visiting the camp they had ready access from the dock to the bathroom. It had the look of an afterthought. In fact the door was almost blocked by stuff stacked up in the shed.

We went back inside and looked around. Parker opened the fridge and saw that it was clean inside but not running. He looked behind and, finding the cord, plugged it in. It began to hum.

The center of the room was given over to two old sofas and a couple of chairs. A cast-iron, flat-topped woodstove sat in the center of the windowless wall. Against each of the long walls of the room were arranged two sets of army bunk beds made up with army-issue blankets. The place was a little musty but other than that, it was clean and snug.

"Pretty nice, eh?" I remarked.

"Palatial," replied Parker. "As comfortable an abode as could possibly be imagined."

"Y-yeah," affirmed Danny Ray.

"Well, what say we grab what we need from *Miss Rosalie* to set up housekeeping, and then we can get on with the day's activities. I know you two want to get started on the boat, and I still have a chore or two to accomplish today," I declared.

In less than a half hour we had the cabin arranged to our

satisfaction. When we each had selected our bunks, Danny Ray took the blankets and bedding outside to air out, while Parker and I knocked cobwebs out of the corners of the ceiling, put out fresh roach bait, and gave the place a good sweeping. We opened the front and back doors to let some fresh air flow through the place, and then I brought in a double handful of firewood to check the draw of the stove, which as it turned out, worked just beautifully.

When we finished, Parker stepped to the refrigerator and put his hand inside.

"Cold as the arctic," he announced as he closed the door. "There's nothing like American domestic appliances. They are still the gold standard by which all others are judged. Why, that fridge is nearly sixty years old and still works like a champ."

Parker shook his head in wonder and gave the refrigerator a fond pat on the head.

"Back to work!" he shouted, gesturing upward with his index finger. "We have much to accomplish, and time tarries not. Come, Danny Ray. We must obey the call. Let us plunge headlong to our task and put to right that which cries out for the application of our wondrous powers."

"O-okay," Danny said with an amused grin at Parker's theatrical exhibition.

"Don't let me slow you down," I said. "I'll see y'all later this evening."

When the guys headed for the boat, I picked Tybee up from his napping spot on the end of the bench and carried him inside the cabin. I put his new bed on the floor over near the woodstove, on the side of the cabin I had selected for my bunk. Then I poured him a container of dry food and a bowl of water, and placed these for him in the kitchen. His litter box went in the pantry. With that, he, like the rest of us, was fixed with all the comforts of home.

He had sniffed around the cabin while I was taking care of his housekeeping but now, as I prepared to depart, I found him curled up asleep on one of the sofas.

"Sleep on, little dude," I said as I looked down upon the small creature. "Eat and rest. You are among friends."

I retrieved the keys to my new-old Chevy. It was time to go meet Sandy Willis.

CHAPTER 17

I MADE MY WAY TO ABERCORN AND from there over to Oglethorpe.

The bus station sits in an area that looks pretty much like where you would expect to find a bus station anywhere in the country. Only a few blocks to the north, the high arch and gleaming piers and wires of the Talmadge Bridge soared into the sky, dominating the view from all directions. How ironic, I thought, as I pulled into the parking lot and switched off the engine, that Sandy should select this as the place of our meeting, in the very shadow of where her friend had died.

As I climbed out of the car, I looked downriver and noted that the clouds were beginning to thicken into a solid mass once again. It would rain again by sundown. I walked across the lot toward the front of the station and threaded my way through a small crowd milling around the front doors.

Once or twice a year, I take myself on a long bus trip. I do it because of the people I meet. I've often thought that were I ever to take up writing and become a novelist, I would people my books with the characters I've met on the bus. The two most poignant and tragic figures I've ever encountered on my trips were an old woman and her mentally deficient adult son, on their way to Texas to witness the execution of another of her sons.

I sat and talked with the woman all the way across Georgia, Alabama, Mississippi, and Louisiana. Every hour or so she would excuse herself and run to the lavatory, where she would wail out her grief, terror, and frustration for the son she was soon to lose. While the woman shrieked and screamed in the toilet, the son would sit quietly, playing with his fingers and humming a rhythmless tune. I still consider it a monstrous act of cowardice on my part that I jumped bus in New Orleans. But I could not force myself to cross the border into Texas with that heartbroken woman and her son. I could not muster the courage for the final part of that horrible journey. I only wish the man who had signed the death warrant—the man who *prided* himself on signing more death warrants than any governor in Texas history—I wish he could have made that trip. Instead, he became president.

I walked inside and looked around. The place was busier than I had expected, but I guess the difficulties of the times have a lot of people on the move. I started to circle the interior and saw Sandy at the same moment she noticed me. As I walked over, she stood and hugged her purse to her body.

"Hello, Sandy. Why don't we go outside and talk? My car is in the parking lot and we can go anywhere you want."

She merely nodded her head and marched to the door. As we exited I pointed down the sidewalk.

"This way," I said.

At the car, I held the door for Sandy and then got in on my side.

Sandy was turned sideways in the seat, looking at me, her purse held to her breast with both arms as though it were a source of protection.

"Do you really want to help, Mr. Tanner?" she asked, launching right in. "Or are you just up to something else?"

I held her face with my eyes. It was tight with suspicion and maybe a bit of fear. But her eyes were clear and questioning. She was trying to determine her next step and didn't know how to go about it.

"Sandy? What is everyone so afraid of? What are *you* afraid of? It seems to me that everyone who knew Tonya Causey lives in a stew of utter fear. When I went up to see Joree the other day, at the mention of Tonya's name, her own brother ran from the house screaming.

"When I stopped to see you and was attacked by Leon Wren, I told myself that it was merely a coincidence—a chance encounter with a lunatic. But I've since found out that it was Junior Causey who bailed Wren from jail and then drove him last night where the two of them firebombed a building and took shots at two of my friends.

"So if you think I'm in this just for grins and giggles, why don't you get your narrow little fanny out of my car and carry it back to Effingham where it belongs."

I leaned across the car and threw open the passenger door. "'Sides, your boss wants to know when you'll be back to work. They need your help, Sandy—apparently there's been a run on lottery tickets, Beanee Weenees, and chewing tobacco," I concluded.

Sandy compressed her lips into an almost invisible line, her face turned a dark color, and her look hardened even more. Then a grin suddenly split her face, a hand flew to her mouth, and throwing back her head, she let loose with a guffaw.

"Oh hell!" she exclaimed. "I don't know what I was expecting, but it sure wasn't that. *Beanee Weenees?* And *chewing tobacco?* Lord, Mr. Tanner, that's just crazy."

"The name is Kennesaw," I reminded her.

"Yes. Kennesaw. I remember," she said, a more open look now on her face.

"But my question remains, Sandy. What is everyone so frightened of? Even Joree talked in circles the other day. And no one seems to know where Tonya was during that last year."

Sandy became serious again.

"There *is* someone who knows about Tonya. Her name is Amber, and that's where we're going now. I told her about you, and she's willing to meet with you. But you've got to promise me you'll go easy with her. She can't take a lot, and if it gets to be too much on her, you'll have to leave."

I lifted my right hand. "Agreed."

"I don't know this girl real well myself, but Tonya thought a lot of her, and she told me if anything was to ever happen I was to get ahold of her."

Sandy looked me closely in the eye. "But I didn't. I didn't have the courage to until I saw you the other day. That's when I called and came down to see her."

Sandy nodded her head toward the street. "Pull out and turn right. It ain't but a few blocks from here."

"Put your seat belt on, Sandy," I directed as I switched on the engine.

We maneuvered a few blocks south and then west until we arrived in an older neighborhood. Not an "old" neighborhood as in "colonial" or "antebellum," but older, as in the Depression. The houses were only one step up from shotgun shacks and looked to have been built during the thirties to house railroad workers. At least that was my suspicion, as the main rail lines into town and a large freight yard were within sight. As we parked in the muddy yard of the house Sandy indicated, I realized that here was a neighborhood where the Depression had never really gone away.

Kids idled on the broken sidewalks and played in the muddy yards. Skinny dogs prowled and nosed through the heaps of trash in the gutters. Broken-down cars sat in the street and in the drives. A sense of despair painted the community with the colors of dejection and defeat. And I wondered again, how does a child possibly escape from this?

Sandy led the way up the cracked and broken walk to the porch. At the door she stopped and looked up at me with what I took to be hesitation, or perhaps uncertainty. I reached across her shoulder and rapped my knuckles on the door frame.

A faint voice from within said, "Y'all come on in."

I turned the doorknob, and we went inside. As the door swung open a wave of hot, stale air gushed outward and washed over us. We had entered into the living room. In the right corner of the room a hallway led to the back of the house. In the middle of the right wall a door led into the kitchen. And in the far left corner of the room, under the pale light of a small lamp, a human face was turned in our direction. Sandy hesitated in front of the door, as if reluctant to cross the room. I stepped past her.

As I approached I realized that the face belonged to a young woman. She was lying on a daybed with a stack of quilts and an old-fashioned chenille bedspread pulled up to her chin. Only her face and arms were exposed above the bedcovers. She smiled as I came near and nodded to a nearby chair.

"Pull up and sit down," she said in a voice only slightly louder than a raspy whisper.

I brought the chair close to her side and sat. Leaning over I took both her hands in mine. They were cold and no larger than the hands of a child. Her arms were like skin-covered sticks, and her face had the emaciated and skeletal look of a concentration camp victim. The whites of her eyes were a sickly thick yellow and her dark brown skin had a yellowish cast also. The girl was dying, and her end was not far away.

"Hello, Amber. My name is Kennesaw," I said in a soft voice. "I really thank you for allowing me to call on you. It appears you haven't been feeling too well lately."

Her face and eyes burned with an inner heat, one that seemed to be consuming her from within. Her small hands moved within mine as she entwined several fingers between my own.

"Kenny-saw? That's a funny name—Kenny-saw. But I like that name, it different—and you handsome, too. You got a wife, Kenny-saw? You got a woman? I bet you got plenty a women."

I shook my head and smiled. "No, Amber. No wife, no woman. It's just me."

Amber made a face to indicate her disgust, "Phewww," she exclaimed through pursed lips. "The womens 'round here'bouts must be blind *and* crazy, ain't one of them grabbed hold of you yet. I tell you, if I was my old self, I'd make a run for you, yes, I would."

"That's sweet of you, Amber, and very flattering."

Just then, Sandy stepped closer and announced, "I'll wait outside so you two can talk. I'll be out on the porch having a cigarette if you need me."

I looked over my shoulder. "Okay, Sandy."

Amber watched the retreating Sandy wordlessly. When the door closed she looked up at me again.

"She scared," the dying girl said matter-of-factly. "She scared to be close to me—to be close to somebody that's dying. It like they think they gonna catch it theyself—like death gonna jump off a me and grab them, too.

"My sister, Naomi—she who live here with me—her and her husband, Willamon—she scared, too, but not fo' herself, she scared fo' me. But them church ladies? You know who they is, them big hat ladies? Them *do-gooders*? They come one time, on account of Naomi go to they church, but soon as they laid eyes on me they trot they big asses right out that front do', 'cause they scared. They scared I got AIDS, and they say that God give that disease to vile sinners as punishment fo' they perversions. Naomi tried to tell 'em it ain't AIDS, that I got pancreatic cancer. But I tell her it don't make no difference to me. I don't want them self-righteous bitches up in here no way and no how."

Amber then shifted her hands and took mine in hers.

"But you ain't," she whispered as she looked deeply into my eyes. "You ain't scared, are you? You ain't scared of me at all."

I held her look and behind those burning and luminescent eyes I felt that I could catch just the faintest glimpse of the timeless and beautifully animated being that resided behind those windows on the soul.

"No, I'm not. But how about you, Amber? Are you frightened?"

She held me with her eyes and gently rubbed my hands between hers.

"No," she said with a slight shake of her head. "I ain't scared. Not no mo'. I was at first—and then I was mad— mad as all hell, but then that went away, too, that *and* bein' scared. And after that, I was just sad. Real sad and real lonely."

"Amber, is there anything I can do to help?"

She squeezed my hands and smiled.

"You already done have," she said. "With this." She lifted our hands and shook them gently. "With this—with this right here. You touched me—and you ain't pulled away. Nobody touches me no mo', Kenny-saw. The hospice lady do, but that just a professional touch—it ain't got no real meaning to it. Naomi do, but that like she cleanin' up a table, or the flo' when it dirty. But this." She lifted our hands again before laying them back on her thin breast. "This here is a human touch, and Kenny-saw, I cain't tell you what it mean to me. They ain't nothin' else like it in the world—the touch of a human hand."

My throat tightened and my eyes filled. I struggled to contain myself. When I thought I could speak again I asked, "Do you have a minister, Amber? Somebody you like to talk with? Somebody you trust?"

"Naw." She shook her head. "The one from the church where them ladies come from ain't no mo' inclined to me than they was."

"I know a man, Amber, a good man. A *real* man of God. A man who loves people the way we're supposed to love others. If I asked him to call on you, would you like to see him?"

"If *you* say he a good man, yeah, I'd like to have him come by. I'd like to talk to somebody can tell me what come next, tell me what gonna happen when I leave outta this place."

"I'll call him right now if you like."

"Yeah, go ahead," she replied.

I reluctantly removed my hands from hers and stood.

On the nightstand nearby was a tall fast-food plastic cup with a straw sticking out of the lid.

"Can I get you anything, Amber? Do you need something to drink?"

"I sho' could use some ice water," she said, her tongue flicking involuntarily over feverish lips.

"I'll be right back," I said, picking up the cup and heading to the kitchen.

I filled the cup with ice and water, then pulled out my phone and punched up a number. Truman Rainwater answered on the second ring. I told him who I was with and gave him the situation. He asked where we were, and when I told him, he said he was just then dropping off a trailer at the port authority and could be there in fifteen minutes. More than that, he knew the neighborhood.

I handed Amber the cup and helped hold it, and put a hand behind her neck, while she took a drink. A few drops trickled down her chin. I dabbed them away with a tissue from the box on the nightstand.

Amber took a sigh and then looked up.

"Now then," she began. "You want to know about Tonya, ain't that right?"

"Yes, I do, Amber. Anything you can tell me, I want to hear it."

"Well, all right," she breathed. "But it ain't pretty. I'll be tellin' you things 'bout myself, too, and I hope you don't think too badly about me, or about Tonya, neither."

"Amber," I said. "The only people I judge harshly are those who intentionally hurt other people. Not the ones who get hurt or hurt themselves."

Amber reached out and took my hands again.

"Well, this is the way it was. . . ."

The dying girl took me through a morass of corruption

and depravity. A tale of young girls—the poorest of the poor—lured into the lowest and most defiling level of the underground sex trade—a trade that flourishes under our very noses. Girls held in near slavery. Held by threat, abuse, violence, and drug addiction. Girls made to prowl the nocturnal parking lots of the large commercial truck stops, providing sexual services for the drivers.

Amber told of how the girls are recruited with promises of fancy clothes, jewelry, big money, and great living in swanky hotels. The reality is anything but that. They live in cheap dives and are treated as virtual slaves. Talk back to a pimp, and get a fist in the mouth. Complain, and take a beating. Try to run away, and it's really bad—that's when a girl just might disappear for good.

After a while the girls descend into despair and drug use. The pimps supply the drugs, and the cost is taken out of her meager earnings. In fact, *everything* is deducted from their supposed pay: food, clothes, housing, and doctor's visits. And once the drugs kick in, the girl comes to find she now owes more money than she's making. That's about the time she hits bottom.

"It has to be organized to operate on the scale you've told me about. Who runs all this, Amber?"

"Used to be that man, Big Smoke Wren, until he got his'self burnt up in that fire. Since then, I don't know. Some of the girls say it was that nephew of his, that Leon. But that cain't be. Leon, he so stupid, he cain't scratch his ass wif both hands. No, they use Leon when they really want to scare somebody—or to git rid of 'em fo' good. That Leon, he crazy, and I mean *evil* crazy."

"So you don't have any idea who runs things now?" I asked.

"No," she replied, shaking her head. "Weren't long after Big Smoke burnt up that I got sick, and they chunked me out. Since then, I ain't heard nothing."

"But why doesn't anyone go to the police?"

"The *po-leece*? The po-leece, hell! They know all about what go on at them truck stops, Kenny-saw! It cain't happen wi'out they *lettin'* it happen. An' they all get they cut of it, don't you think they ain't. Why, a po-leece car pull up in one a them lots at night, and a girl is sent straight to his car. He put her in the backseat like they goin' to jail. But he drive to some dirt road where they do they little bidness and then come on back. That how it work, Kenny-saw. An' that why when a girl disappear, ain't nobody care what happened to her at all."

Of course, I thought. *How could it be otherwise? The real question is just how deeply it goes and how widespread is the extent.*

"Tell me about Tonya, Amber. What was she like?"

"She were a sweet girl, Kenny-saw. She weren't cut out fo' that kinda life. She tried to run onct, and when they caught her, that Leon, he mess her up bad. The really terrible thing was that her own brother was one of the drivers, and sometimes, he would haul her to the truck stops his'self." Amber stopped and shook her head at the thought of such depravity.

I was thunderstruck. *Junior was on the inside and, for all intents and purposes, was pimping his own sister. No wonder he didn't want questions into Tonya's life and disappearance—he was a part of it.*

"Amber, who might know about Tonya at the end? Who might be willing to talk to me about her?"

"They's a girl called Sweet Thang. You get ahold of her, and she'll talk to you. You just tell her you talked to Amber, and she say it all right. She ain't afraid of 'em—she make 'em too much money, and she kinda crazy herself. But she loved Tonya. You find Sweet Thang, and she'll tell you what she know."

Amber then gave me a list of the truck stops where Sweet Thang worked. Apparently she was quite popular and well-known among the drivers, and only worked a few places. Amber also told me of the other lots that were controlled by the former Wren Gang. From what I could gather there were several other cartels that owned the rights to trafficking in other areas, with each gang jealously guarding its turf.

The effort to talk was wearing on Amber. She had to lie back and rest and breathe deeply before she could speak again. I waited until she nodded that she was okay and asked my last question.

"Amber, what happened to Tonya? Did she try to run again, and if so, did they catch her and kill her? Or do you think she came to the point she could stand it no longer and took her own life?"

Amber's eyes were huge in her emaciated face. She took several breaths and replied after a moment. "Kenny-saw, *whichever* way it mighta happened—no matter what—in the end, *they* was the ones killed her, don't you reckon?"

I took a breath. "Yes," I sadly agreed. "Ultimately, they are the ones responsible for her death."

Then another thought came to mind.

"Amber, did you ever hear of a girl called Chigger? A really small girl—small and young—sixteen or seventeen."

Amber took a deep breath and exhaled. "I know her. She was *always* gettin' into trouble and got treated real bad, 'til they just sorta broke her spirit. I felt real sorry fo' that girl."

"The preacher who's coming to see you—Brother Truman Rainwater—will you tell him about Chigger? It'd be mighty important to him."

"Is it important to you, Kenny-saw?" she asked with a squeeze of my hands.

"Yes, it is, Amber. It's important to me, too."

"Then I tell him," she replied. "But now, I want you to do somethin' fo' me, Kenny-saw."

"What's that, darling? What can I do for you?"

"I want you to bust 'em all up. I want you to bring down they filthy house—bring it down right 'round they ears. I want you to tear 'em all to pieces. You a strong man, Kenny-saw, and you can do that. Will you? Will you get them po' girls loose?"

I lifted Amber's hands and kissed her fingers.

"I'll do everything I possibly can, Amber—everything I can."

"Good," she said. "I know you will. It funny, ain't it, Kenny-saw? You just have walked in here, an' I ain't laid eyes on you befo' in my life. But I feel like I knowed you since I was a little girl. I wisht I had a knowed you befo', Kenny-saw. Befo' I got sick. I wisht I'd a had a friend like you. Things mighta turnt out different than they did."

"Well, we know each other now, don't we, darling girl? And I'm glad I met you when I did."

Just then came the rumble of a truck pulling up on the street out front.

"That sounds like Brother Truman arriving. I'm gonna go now and leave y'all alone." Amber started to protest, but I gently shushed her. "You're gonna like him, Amber, and I know he's going to love you. And what you and he have to say to each other is private and personal. But I want to come back and see you again—often. Can I do that?"

"I sho' would like it if you would, Kenny-saw."

"All right then, I'll be back—soon."

I leaned over and kissed her on the cheek. Amber put a hand on my neck and held her face tightly—fiercely—against mine. I felt the wet trickle of tears on my face.

"Thank you," she whispered as she turned her head

slightly and kissed the corner of my mouth. "Thank you for coming to see me."

Footsteps sounded on the porch, followed closely by a knock on the door. Amber released her hand from my neck, and I stood.

"Soon, Amber. I'll see you soon," I said, lifting my hand in departure.

I turned to cross the room and, opening the door, found Rainwater standing there. He quickly shook my hand, but even as we spoke he was squinting past me with a look of concern on his face.

"Brother Kennesaw," he said as he peered over my shoulder.

I took him by the elbow and led him to the side of the bed.

"Truman, I want you to meet Miss Amber. She's a mighty special lady, and she has some things she'd like to speak with you about.

"Amber, this is Truman Rainwater; he's the man I told you about. I know you two are going to get along fine," I said as Truman and I stood at the bedside. "And now, I'm gonna leave."

Amber glanced from Truman to me and nodded her head.

Truman reached down and touched her hand. "Hello, sweet child. I shore am glad to meet you. Brother Kennesaw called and told me what a doll you were—and I'll tell you the truth—he didn't exaggerate, not nary a bit."

A giggle escaped Amber's lips. She gave me a glance. I waved my fingers and blew a kiss.

See you, I mouthed and turned for the door.

Behind me I heard Truman ask, "Do you mind if I say a little prayer, Amber? Just a little one—a prayer for you and me."

I closed the door as quietly as I could and stepped softly across the porch. Sandy was sitting on the hood of my car, smoking a cigarette and bouncing a crossed leg with impatience. Behind her, dominating the background, soared the Talmadge Bridge.

CHAPTER 18

"YOU CAN DROP ME AT THE BUS STA-tion," Sandy said as we got in the car.

"I can take you anywhere you'd like to go, Sandy."

"That *is* where I'd like to go," she replied. "I got a ticket for a bus that leaves in . . ." She consulted her watch. "Forty minutes."

"Back up to Rincon?" I inquired. "I can drive you back home and save you the time and the bus fare."

She looked at me silently for a few seconds.

"I ain't going home," she responded. "I'm going to Seattle. I got an aunt up there who has her own little coffee shop. Her husband died last year, and she's been running the place by herself since then. Said if I get myself up there I can have a job in the shop and live with her in her house. And I figure Seattle is about as far away from Effingham County as you can get and still be in the United States."

"I wish you well, Sandy. I hope it works out and you find what you're looking for."

I understood her motivation. In my case, I had fled Dade County, Georgia, just as soon as *I* was able. I was seventeen years old at the time. Fortunately for me, it was the United States Army that gave me a needed refuge and a chance at life.

"Sandy, unsolicited advice is just about worth its weight in air, but if I had any words of recommendation for you it would be this: As soon as you get to Seattle and settle in, find the local community college and start taking courses. Find something that gives you joy and fulfillment and get a degree in it. It will give you the means of becoming truly independent, of never having to depend on another person to take care of you, and you'll never regret it."

"Funny you should say so—I was already thinking of that," she replied.

As I pulled to the curb in front of the station, Sandy put her hand on the door but hesitated a second.

"Tonya never did have no luck," she said. "Nothing ever went her way, no matter what she tried to do. But she didn't deserve to end up the way she did."

"Sandy, nobody does," I responded. "But did you know the kind of life Tonya had slipped into?"

Sandy looked downward and nodded her head.

"I did—but then, I didn't—I didn't want to know, I guess. 'Cause if I ever stopped and told myself I knew—and didn't do anything to help—then I was sort of a part of it all, too. And I couldn't admit that to myself. I couldn't face it—it was just too ugly."

Sandy lifted her eyes to mine.

"I ain't proud of myself, Mr. Tanner—not at all. But if this helps—and you're able to find out what happened—

well, I know it will mean a lot to Joree. And she deserves better than what she's had so far."

"Sandy, I think you've had to learn a lot more about life than someone should at your age. I hope you find contentment in Seattle. I wish you happiness."

"Thank you," she said.

She held my eyes a second longer, then stepped out of the car and walked into the bus station. She did not look back.

I cranked up and, pulling into the late afternoon traffic, made my way back to Dutch Island.

I ARRIVED BACK AT THE FISH CAMP JUST as the partially hidden sun was touching the tops of the trees on Dutch Island. I walked down to the dock and found Parker and Danny Ray up to their shoulders in dismantling *Miss Rosalie*'s interior.

"Good God a'mighty, boys," I exclaimed in a state of mild shock when I saw the level of destruction they had wrought. "It looks like a bomb went off in here."

Parker looked up with an apologetic grin. "Looks worse than it really is, Kennesaw. Believe me, there's a method at work here. It may be difficult to discern, but it exists. We just have to remove most of the paneling and the floors to get at the wiring and the hydraulic lines. After that, everything will go back together nicely."

"Y-yeah," Danny Ray contributed with a sly grin of his own. It was obvious he was enjoying my reaction.

I looked around again, and to tell the truth, I could detect no pattern to any of it whatsoever.

"Well, Parker, it looks like I'm just going to have to take your word for that. And by the way, have y'all had anything to eat?"

"What time is it?" Parker asked.

"'Bout half past five," I replied, consulting my watch.

"Did you know it was that late, Danny Ray?" Parker asked.

Danny Ray shook his head to indicate that he didn't.

"I guess we sort of lost track of time, Kennesaw," Parker replied sheepishly. "We must have gotten caught up in our work."

"Well, why don't y'all cease operations for the time being and come up to the cabin and get cleaned up? I've picked up some grub for us. It's time you took a break."

"Okay, we'll be right up," Parker said. Danny Ray nodded in the affirmative.

By the time the guys came in I had the table set with some of Kentucky's finest fried poultry, along with all the fixings. I opened a tin of food for Tybee and put it in his dish in the corner of the kitchen. He pounced on the cat food like it was live prey. The men did the same with the chicken.

"I'm going to be out for the evening," I announced. "Don't wait up, and . . ." I shot Parker a pointed look, "don't you two work too late, either. I figure a man is incompetent if he can't get his work done in an eight-hour day. Besides, there's a lot to accomplish, and you can't do it all at once. So pace yourselves."

Parker wiped his lips with a paper napkin and leaned back in his chair.

"Oh, that was good," he said.

"I'll send the colonel your compliments," I responded.

"We only have a bit left to do—and I want to have that done by the time we finish today. It shouldn't take more than—what do you think, Danny Ray, an hour or so?"

"'B-b-bout that," Danny replied with a bob of the head.

"Okay," I said. "But no more than that, and then knock

off. I'll bring in some firewood before I leave, but keep an eye on that stove. I won't trust it completely until we see where the hot spots are and know it's not going to crack and spill out hot coals. You never know about the condition of these old cast-iron stoves—they can fool you."

"I have a scrap sheet of quarter-inch steel I can slip underneath. That ought to give a good measure of safety," Parker said.

"Perfect. That will make me feel a lot better," I replied as I stood to clear off the table. What I didn't say was that I'm terrified at the thought of a house fire.

The meal over, Parker and Danny Ray returned to their work. Tybee curled up on one of the beds, and I prepared to leave. But first, I went to my bed and, opening the foot-locker I had brought from the boat, retrieved and put on my shoulder holster. I then charged a round into the chamber of my CZ 75, slipped on the safety, and inserted the pistol snugly into the holster. An additional two magazines of ammo went into the pouch hanging beneath the other shoulder. I checked the fit of the familiar rig and then slipped on my jacket.

I now felt ready for any firebombers I might encounter in the great unknown. If I met Leon Wren again—and I was pretty certain he would give me cause to take action—I would be fully ready from now on. I considered taking one of the shotguns with me but decided to leave it where it was stowed, on the floor beneath my bed.

I topped up Tybee's water bowl and filled his dry-food plate before bringing in several armloads of wood. The last item I took from the locker was a handheld CB radio. I turned on the switch and checked the battery level. All okay there, I clipped the radio to my belt. Satisfied that everything was in shape here in the cabin, I picked up my car keys and headed out into the gathering darkness.

Amber had informed me of the places I was most likely to find Sweet Thang. One was south of town about forty miles, at a place just off the I-95 corridor called Sally's. In fact most of the stops Amber had named were along I-95, from just over into South Carolina, down to the Florida border, along with a few headed west along I-16 in the direction of Macon.

I made my way in heavy traffic over to the 204, and from there, south to U.S. 17. I stayed on 17, crossing the Ogeechee River at Kings Bridge, and continuing on until I came to Richmond Hill, where I jumped onto I-95.

The trees flanking the interstate presented a tall and forbiddingly dark wall on either side of the highway corridor that seemed to exclude the rest of the world. It began to rain again, a light floating rain, little more than a dreary mist, that was just enough to cause me to hit the intermittent wipers now and then but not enough to keep them on. I watched closely for deer and wild hogs—the sides of the interstate were littered with their dead carcasses. And at interstate speed, a collision with either one could total a car.

The old Chevy rode and handled like a dream. *When this is all over, I think I'll take a long road trip—maybe out west and down into Mexico. It's just the right time of year for that,* I told myself. After a while I saw a sign that announced in brightly reflective letters:

EXIT 67
ONE MILE
FOOD—FUEL

I lifted my foot from the accelerator and slowed to make the turn. A tractor-trailer in front of me did the same. I held back to stay out of the spume thrown up by his tires and coasted off the ramp to the yield sign below. The truck turned to the right, and after giving him a few seconds to move ahead, I did the same.

Surprisingly, it was almost ten miles to Sally's Truck Stop. The place was situated in a huge clearing on the side of the road and gave the appearance of having grown piecemeal over the decades of its existence. The fuel pumps were located to the left side of the main store. It was a large operation, able to refuel a dozen trucks at a time. Behind the fueling area was a massive garage and workshop complex. The main building held the store and a restaurant.

To the right rear was the overnight parking. The parking lot was graveled rather than paved, and the farther I proceeded to the rear, the less good the lighting until I arrived at the very back of the lot, which was in utter darkness. Only a few trucks, their diesel engines idling to keep the heaters on, were parked back here.

I found a place, where the darkness was deepest, at the far corner of the lot, backed in, and turned off the engine. Picking up the CB from the passenger seat, I turned on the volume, dialed up the appropriate channel, and adjusted the squelch until the hissing went quiet. Now the waiting began.

There was a lot of chatter on the radio, but most of it was from drivers out on the interstate. Now and again, someone would hail a trucker as he pulled into Sally's, but so far, nothing more than that.

I turned on the engine now and then to defog the windshield and throw a little heat into the interior of the car. After a while the rain increased, and then began to come down with a steady intensity. Water began to pool here and there across the parking lot. Then the rain ceased altogether and a feeble moon began to shine through the thinning clouds.

I sat listening quietly, lost in thoughts of other times I had waited patiently for something to happen—or not happen. A couple of hours passed in this fashion, and I was giving serious consideration to pulling the plug when suddenly, the radio squawked.

A girl's teasing voice came over the air. "Hey, y'all. Any a you boys at Sally's looking for a little company this evening? Come back."

I picked up the radio and held it near my chest. A man's voice answered, a voice with a flat Midwestern accent.

"Hey there, darling, you got the Missouri Rambler here—who am I talking to? Come back."

"Where you at, Rambler?" the girl responded.

"I'm in the red flatbed rig with the load of iron, sitting here in the middle of the lot. Where are you?"

"You look out toward the front of the lot—I'm in the white van headed your way," the girl answered. "Me and a bunch of my friends."

"You and your friends—are y'all the friendly type?" the man asked in a teasing voice.

"Oh, we mighty friendly!"

"Well, girl, come on over here and we'll see just how friendly you are!"

At that second a white van rolled to the center of the lot and came to a stop. Nearby a truck flashed his exterior cab lights on and off several times. A man got out of the driver's side of the van and opened the side door. Three girls in skimpy outfits hopped out. One girl went straight to the truck that had flashed its lights. The door of the truck opened and she climbed in. The other two girls disappeared among the trucks in the lot. The van driver returned to his seat.

I picked up the CB and pressed the Push to Talk button,

and spoke into the mike, "Hey out there, this is Cracker Daddy callin' for Sweet Thang. You out there, Sweet Thang? Come back."

I released the button and listened. The only reply was the electronic sizzle of the radio. I tried again.

"Sweet Thang, this is the original Cracker Daddy. You here tonight? Now don't play games with me, darlin', I only stopped here to see you. Come back."

The radio hissed for several seconds and then a man's voice replied, "Sweet Thang ain't here tonight, Cracker Daddy, she had another engagement somewhere else. But if it's some fine commercial company you lookin' for this evening, we got a nice selection for you to check out."

I waited several seconds before keying the mike again.

"Thank you, buddy, but no, thanks. I'll have to pass and get on down the road. Sweet Thang is a favorite of mine, and I only stopped here on account of her. Maybe I'll catch you the next time through."

"Ten-four, good buddy. You don't forget us now," came the response.

I turned off the radio, put it in the glove box, and cranked the engine. I was debating whether to call it a night or go to one of the other places on the list Amber had given me, when a bobtail rig pulled into the parking lot. It cruised along slowly, its headlight out, illuminated only by the cab lights. Finding its place at last, the truck parked a few spaces over from the hooker van. *Something gives here,* I thought. Switching off the engine, I decided to watch and see what happened.

Ten minutes or so later, one of the girls reappeared and hopped back in the van. A short time after that, the first girl I had seen, the one on the radio, climbed down from the truck cab she had entered. A few minutes later, the last girl came walking slowly across the lot. As she walked past the bobtail rig, the door of the cab opened and a man hopped to the ground.

The girl had her head down and gave the man no notice as she continued toward the van. The man watched her for a second and then called out. I couldn't hear what he said, but at his words the girl froze in her tracks and then slowly turned to face him. The man took several steps forward and stopped, silhouetted by a distant light. It was Truman Rainwater!

I stepped out of my car and quietly closed the door. Was this Rainwater's granddaughter? Had he found the girl so quickly? Staying back in the shadows, I eased forward so that I could hear. Rainwater held out his arms and took another step. I was within thirty feet now.

"Mary Beth? Darling? It's me. Your grandpa."

"Paw-paw?" I heard the girl say in a tiny and incredulous voice.

"Yes, honey, it's Paw-paw. I've come to take you with me, sweetheart. I've come to take you home."

"Paw-paw!" she squealed as she ran to Rainwater's open arms and buried her face in his chest.

"Paw-paw, oh, Paw-paw," I heard her muffled sobs.

Rainwater enfolded the girl in his arms and bent his face to her head. He had one arm around her and a hand on her head. He caressed her hair and muttered softly, over and over again, "Mary Beth, oh, my baby, oh, my sweet child."

"Come," he said at last. "Let's go home."

He kept an arm around the girl, and she had both of hers around him, as they turned and walked to his truck. They had taken no more than a few paces when the man in the van ran over, waving his arms and shouting.

"Hey, hey, hey there, old-timer. Chigger's gotta check in

with me first, and then we gotta make a deal. You know how it is, Dad—no money, no honey; no finance, no romance."

Rainwater stopped and, turning his head, looked over his shoulder. He stared at the man for a second. When he spoke it was in a deadly tone of voice.

"Brother, this girl is going with me, and if you make the least effort to interfere with our departure, I swear before the living God I will put you in the hospital. Now git!"

Rainwater turned his back and resumed the march to his truck. The pimp stood gaping a second as though stunned and then launched himself across the lot.

"Like hell she is," the man yelled. "And if there's anybody's goin' to the hospital, it's you, old man. You turn loose a that girl right now!"

In a flash, Truman Rainwater scooped his granddaughter up in his arms, bounded to his truck, and, opening the door, pitched the girl inside.

"Lock the door," he called just before turning again.

The pimp closed with Rainwater, yelling and cursing as he came. When he was within arm's distance, Truman let fly with a long, stiff punch that set the boy on his ass.

Truman turned again and stepped to the running board of the truck. He had just inserted a key in the door when the pimp got to his feet and reached inside his jacket; I saw the pistol at the same instant that Truman Rainwater heard the click of the safety going off.

"You son of a bitch! I don't know who you think you're foolin' with, but you get that girl out here this second, or I'll blow your head off!" the man spluttered in rage and anger.

With his free hand he reached up and wiped the blood from his mouth but kept the gun trained on Rainwater.

Rainwater turned his head and gazed down on the man with a look of dismissal.

"Son, if you use that thing, you better hope to kill me quick, 'cause if not, I'll send you to meet your maker."

Rainwater opened the door of the truck. The pimp ran closer. I drew my pistol and, holding it at the low ready, began to close with them.

"You asked for it, old man. Now here it is," he shouted, raising his gun and pointing it at Rainwater's back.

I stepped close, stuck the muzzle of my pistol under the man's ear, and clicked off the safety. He froze like he had been splashed with liquid nitrogen.

"Hold real still for a second," I whispered. "This thing's got a hair trigger, and I don't like it to go off until I mean it to. Now, you lower that gun hand to your side and let your grip go slack."

He did as instructed. A girl from behind us shouted, "Dewayne, what's goin' on out there?"

"Just act like she's your girlfriend and ignore her, Dewayne. That'll be the healthiest thing you can do," I said as I reached down and took the pistol from his unresisting hand.

"'Cause I gotta tell you something, bubba, it would give me a great deal of pleasure to scatter the top of your skull all across this parking lot," I hissed.

Rainwater cranked his truck and looked down upon us. Our eyes met, and he gave me a nod. The air brakes shooshed as they were released, and then, putting the truck in gear, Truman Rainwater and his prodigal granddaughter pulled away.

"Wave to them, Dewayne. Let them know you're happy to see them go," I cajoled.

"Man, this is some . . ." he started to protest. But I cut it off with a knee slammed into his tailbone and a rap on the head with the pistol.

"Wave, boy," I said.

Dewayne lifted a hand and waved, but I must say, it was lacking in what I considered to be sincere enthusiasm.

When Rainwater was out of sight I turned us back in the direction of the van.

"Let's march, Dewayne. You and me aren't finished yet." I lowered the pistol so that the muzzle was on his spine, just above the belt line.

"Walk easy, Dewayne," I said in a pleasant voice. "Gun went off now, you'd be paralyzed for life. And somehow or other, I just don't believe you know anybody that would change your colostomy bag for you."

"My what?" he asked.

"The bag you'd have to shit in for the rest of your life," I replied.

"Oh."

We arrived at the van. The two girls were watching us with wide eyes.

"Dewayne is finished for the evening, ladies. He and I have declared a holiday. Would either or both of you like to take off? You're free to go if you like, and Dewayne's not going to do a thing about it. Are you, Dewayne?" I said, giving him a jab in the spine.

One girl put a hand to her mouth to stifle a giggle. The other looked on with wide eyes.

"Mister, you don't know what you're getting yourself into," Dewayne said through anger-clenched teeth.

The giggling girl spoke up.

"No, mister, I think we gonna stay. We ain't got nothing else to do."

"Okay, ladies. It's your choice, but I wish you'd reconsider. I can give you a ride to wherever you'd like to go, and old Dewayne here isn't going to interfere—are you, Dewayne?"

I jabbed him with the pistol again, but Dewayne did not feel inclined to make a reply.

"Okay then, it's your choice. Now, watch this.

"Dewayne, let's me and you step to the front of the truck. Okay, now take three steps to the right. Now, down on your knees with your fingers laced together on the back of your head. That's good, that's real good, Dewayne. Now, cross your ankles behind you, and sit back on your heels."

One of the girls called out, "Oh my God! He's going to kill him!"

Dewayne's body began to tremble in expectation of the shot.

I walked to the rear of the van, always keeping my gun on the kneeling Dewayne. The girls looked at me in fear and puzzlement as I passed the open door of the van. When I came to the rear of the vehicle, I took out my knife, flipped open the blade, and stabbed it deeply into the sidewall of the tire. The air whooshed out in an explosive burst. I stepped to the front of the van and did the same thing to the front tire. The van dropped low on its side. Both girls giggled aloud this time.

"Dewayne, much as it grieves me to lose your company, I've got to go now. But if you like breathing air and feeling that old heart beating in your chest, you'll stay just where you are until you're damn certain I'm long gone. 'Cause the next time I have to deal with you I'll put something on your ass that Mr. Clean won't be able to take off. Also, tell Leon we met. He'll know who I am."

I turned and backed away, walking sideways with my pistol at the ready. *I really would like to shoot that boy,* I admitted to myself.

I got in my car and pulled away. I drove in a wide arc around and behind the van so that I could keep an eye on

Dewayne as I made my departure. As I hit the pavement at the front of the lot, I cast a glance in the mirror and saw him still kneeling in the gravel with his hands behind his head. Then he got up and ran to the van.

Good luck with those tires, Dewayne. That should keep you occupied for a half hour or so, even here, where, as the sign out front says, We Fix Flats 24 Hours a Day.

I pulled onto the road and motored away. The sky had cleared a bit more and the moon threw a thin illumination across the land. I rounded a slight curve in the highway and saw before me a long straightaway cleaving through the forest and swamps. I reflected on how things had worked out this evening. I hadn't made contact with Sweet Thang, but Truman had found his granddaughter, and I'd had a great time. I only wish it had been Leon and Junior there at the lot. But there would be other nights. As the saying goes: Hope springs eternal.

I was pretty sure Rainwater had enough sense to know that his granddaughter would have to go into hiding. He was going to have to watch his back trail, too. But somehow or other, I had the feeling Brother Rainwater knew how to handle himself. As for me, I'd check those other places in my search for Sweet Thang. And if I had to, I'd change cars. In fact, it was a good idea that I rent another car for my next foray.

I don't think Dewayne had gotten a look at what I was driving, but it was a good bet the girls had. And I was pretty certain they were going to be as helpful as possible to Dewayne and his superiors. I came to a stop at a crossroads and then continued on.

In the far distance, a set of headlights appeared in my rearview mirror—they were closing fast. I held my speed at five miles an hour above the limit. If it were a cop he wouldn't pull me over for speeding—and this time, all the lights on the car were in working order.

The car came on rapidly until it was a couple of car lengths behind. It held there for half a minute with its lights, irritatingly, on high beam. Then, he swung out to pass. I drew my pistol from the holster and held it on my lap.

The car—it was one of those four-door Dodges favored by would-be thugs—flashed by with a burst of speed. As it pulled back in front of me, the driver hit the accelerator and rapidly pulled away. I thought I saw two people in the front seat but the windows of the car were so darkly tinted I couldn't be sure. I continued on at the same speed but kept the pistol held in my lap.

A few seconds later, and more headlights came into the rearview. These, too, were closing rapidly, and there were lots of them. The lights set high—like on a truck—there were fog lights below the bumper and off-road lights up on top of the cab. The effect in the rearview was blinding. I turned the mirror so that the gleam of the lights was thrown back at its source.

I held speed as before and within seconds the truck was on my bumper. I glanced in my side mirror and caught the faintest glimpse of *something* as it came out of the passenger window.

At the sight of the movement, I immediately dropped low in my seat. Just as I did, *bloooom*, the back window of the Chevy exploded inward from the blast of a shotgun.

I tromped down on the accelerator, simultaneously pointed the pistol up over my left shoulder, over the top of the seat, and slapped the trigger—*pop-pop—pop-pop—pop-pop.*

The old Chevy was fast, but the truck on my ass was even faster. Instantly, and with a tremendous burst of speed, he swung up alongside. I saw the shotgun barrel sticking out of the window, swinging down on me for the kill. I swung the pistol and fired two more rounds into the door of the truck, while at the same time, I tapped the brakes of the Chevy.

The truck leaped forward in a surge of power. The shooter fired. The red tongue of the muzzle blast slashed the night just in front of my windshield. Then, as the rear wheel of the truck came in line with my front bumper, I nudged the Chevy over and gave the truck a tap in the wheel well. The effect was instantaneous and dramatic.

The rear wheels of the truck lost their grip on the road and began to swerve away, trying to overtake the front wheels. The truck, its wheels skidding like he'd hit a patch of ice, slid broadside across the front of my car. I hit the accelerator to give an additional shove, and the truck went completely out of control.

The shooter fired again, wildly, the shot going straight up in the air. Then the truck slammed into the low abutment of a bridge. I saw his undercarriage as the truck lifted up on its side, and going airborne, disappeared from my view. As I powered past, I heard a mangle of crunching metal and breaking glass, and then a huge splash. I hit the brakes hard, making the tires squall, then let off just enough to stop the skid. The big Chevy slowed as though we'd hit a pond of molasses.

At the far side of the bridge I turned around and raced back to the other end. Pulling to the shoulder of the road, I punched on the emergency flashers, grabbed a flashlight from the glove box, jumped out of the car, and ran out on to the bridge. I cast the light out across the black water of the swampy creek. The glare of the light found the truck lying on its left side, the water almost to the level of the passenger door. I shined the light on the water around the truck and saw a head bob up. The face turned toward me, the eyes wild and scared. At least one of my attackers was alive.

"Where's the other one?" I called. Fully expecting an "I don't know" or "He's dead."

Before the man in the water could answer, another voice called from the darkness, "I'm over here—behind the truck."

I played the light on the truck again and saw another head on the far side of the cab. He had his hands on the edge of the cab and was just lifting himself above the surface of the water.

"Can you boys swim?" I called.

"Yeah," came one reply. The other said, "This water's cold."

"Well, come to the light. But if I see that shotgun again, it's me will do the shooting this time. And at this very minute, I ain't feeling so pleasantly disposed with you two."

I shined the light on my pistol so they could see it pointed in their direction.

"Don't shoot, mister—I think I'm hurt pretty bad," said the man at the truck.

"We comin' out, mister. Just don't shoot. 'Sides, we was only foolin' around. We didn't mean no real harm," lied the other one as he floundered in the water.

"Yeah? Well, I was only playing, too, but not anymore. Give me the slightest reason, and I'll shoot you both where you are and leave you for the crawfish. Now, you—the one out there in the water—come help your buddy. I ain't about to get my feet wet for the sorry likes of you two dumb-asses."

I walked to the end of the bridge and stepped carefully down the low embankment to the water's edge. Placing the flashlight on the ground, I let the beam shine across the surface of the water to show them the way to safety. Then I dialed 911 and gave the dispatcher the gist of the situation and an approximate location. After that, I called Patricia to let her know she could find me at the Liberty County jail. About the time the two swimmers made it to the bank, sirens were howling in the distance and coming on fast.

CHAPTER 19

"BOY, TANNER, YOU SURE HAVE A knack for losing car windows, don't you?" Patricia chuckled when she saw my Chevy.

"At least it's only the one window this time, and I can drive it home. If they'd have made good with that second shot, it would have been all over but the shoutin' for yours truly," I replied.

I peered into the back window of the Chevy and surveyed the damage. Amazingly, the back glass had absorbed the full impact of the shotgun blast, and though shattered glass was scattered all over the interior of the car, there was no further damage.

If he had fired an immediate second shot, things would have turned out differently, I thought. It had been close. I reached up, touched the pendant that hung from my neck, and said a silent prayer of thanks.

"It was good of you to come down, Patricia. I thought

things were about to get a little iffy with that investigator. You were just the sort of personal reference I really needed."

"You want to tell me what this was all about?" she asked in a concerned voice.

"Tonya Causey, Leon Wren, and a lot more stuff besides that. But let's get out of here, and I'll fill you in completely. What say we get back to town and find a place where we can talk. For some reason or other, I don't feel all that welcome here."

"I know an all-night joint on Abercorn, near the mall," she said.

"Okay, I'll follow you," I replied.

It was after four in the morning as we left the town of Hinesville fading in the rearview mirror. The air blowing in through the open back of my car was very cold on my neck. But at least it wasn't raining. Less than an hour later we were sitting in a booth at the Waffle House.

The waitress set two cups of coffee on the table and walked away. As I reached for a packet of sweetener to put in my coffee I looked at my hand—it was trembling.

I poured the contents of the packet into the cup, and as I stirred I took a survey of myself. The muscles of my chest and abdomen were rigid, my shoulders were knotted with tension, and my jaw was clenched.

Breathe, Tanner. Take a deep breath, and now take another one. Relax, relax. Let your muscles sag. Let them go limp and rest. Let it go—let it all go.

My body was reacting to the stress. I had come close to being killed and had also come close to taking two lives— maybe even a third, counting Dewayne. It's not like in the movies, where someone commits all sorts of mayhem and walks away as if nothing happened. You can*not* come away from such an experience unaffected. The only person who *could* do so is a psychopath. When I lifted the cup to my lips my hand was steady again.

Patricia listened quietly, but with a professional intensity, as I told her everything that had happened since we were last together. When I told her what Amber had said about the police knowing what went on at the truck stops but looking the other way, if not taking favors to allow it to continue, her brows knit and I saw her bristle a little.

We all have our tribes that we protect, and when one of our own is disparaged, we circle the wagons to fend off criticism—and cops, as much, or more so, than anyone.

"There's no proof of that happening," Patricia interjected with some heat.

I was silent a second and held her gaze before speaking again.

"Patricia, from what little I saw at that one place, it could not go on—it could not exist—without official knowledge and official protection. And from the information Amber gave me, these truck stops where this takes place are all located in small rural counties. There is a tradition to this sort of thing along the highways of the South. I'm sure you've heard the stories of Ludowici."

Ludowici, in Long County, Georgia, less than twenty miles south of Sally's, had been notorious for its speed traps, tourist clip joints, and the crooked political machine that ran it all. The little town sat on the main East Coast highway to Florida and thrived on scamming the passing tourists. In spite of the efforts of three successive governors, the only thing that had brought an end to the depredations was when I-95 was built and the place was relegated to backwater status.

"Yes, I know about Ludowici," Patricia replied. "And

I'm sorry, Kennesaw. That was a knee-jerk reaction on my part. I'm more interested than anybody in stopping corrupt cops—they make it hard on all the rest of us."

"Had you not shown up when you did, I think *I* was the one who was going to be charged with assault, not those other two boys. Even though I never said so, it was apparent the investigator knew I had been in some sort of altercation at Sally's. But whatever he *thought* he knew couldn't be twisted sufficiently—or admitted—to allow him to charge me. But he was close. However, as it was, he did keep my pistol for evidence."

"What if this *is* true? What do you want to do, Kennesaw?"

"Do you have a good contact in the GBI, the Georgia Bureau of Investigation?" I asked.

The GBI are the straight shooters in the state of Georgia. They have an unsullied reputation for rectitude and moral courage. When official wrongdoing is uncovered they are the only ones in the state with the standing and the clout to get to the bottom of the situation.

Patricia nodded. "Yes. I have a very good contact at GBI headquarters in Atlanta."

"Amber will testify," I said. "She has nothing to lose. And I'll bet the Rainwater girl will also—and if she's not willing, she can always be subpoenaed. These are two witnesses right there who can name names and give dates and locations. That would make a heyday for a sharp district attorney and grand jury."

I stopped a second and then went on. "Patricia, there are girls out there being treated in a way no human being should have to endure. Yeah, I know—some of them are there willingly—but even if they are, it's still wrong. And there are others—the Tonyas and the Chiggers—who are nothing more than slaves. And how many of those girls—when their useful days are over, or if they become a liability—how many of them, like Tonya, just disappear? Who makes it right for those girls? If you and I won't do it, Patricia, then please tell me who will."

Patricia held my eyes with hers. "I'll call," she said at last. "I want to meet Amber first, but yes, I'll call."

"I'll take you to her this afternoon. But you have to assure me that she, and the identity of her family, will be protected—even from your own department. People connected with this have died already. And don't forget, I was almost one of them."

"Kennesaw, sometimes you just chap my rear end! Do you think I just started this job? Of *course* her identity will be protected! My God, what's the matter with you!?"

I lowered my head and feigned an appearance of contrition. Then looking up again, I reached across the table and took Patricia's hands in both of mine.

"And I mean that for you, too, Patricia. You need to stay low until a clean sweep is made of this outfit. I don't want you becoming a target also."

"You just look out for yourself, Tanner, and I'll do the same for me. But if you ever feel you're in need of police protection—well, you can put yourself in my hands," she said in a teasing voice.

"For a second there, Patricia, I thought you might be serious."

"Who says I'm not?" she replied with a gentle smile.

"Ah," was the only reply that came to mind. Then, "What say we order breakfast?"

The sun was lifting over the horizon as we stepped outside.

"I'll call you later with the time to see Amber. Let's meet at the bus station and go from there," I said as we came to Patricia's car.

"You've got to do something about that car, Kennesaw," she said, looking at the shot-out rear window. "Every cop who sees you is going to pull you over. It looks exactly like what it is—a car that's been involved in a shoot-out."

"Think you could maybe write me a note—sort of an official excuse or pass?"

Patricia laughed as she got into her car. "You're on your own with that one, Tanner. Make your own excuses."

"Well, if that's the way it's got to be, I'll just make the best of it," I said. "See you later this afternoon, yes?"

"Yes," she replied. "This afternoon. See if you can stay out of trouble until then."

"I'll give it a try," I said.

Patricia waved and wheeled away.

Damn, I thought as I watched her go. *I'm glad to have her for a friend. And is that all she is to you, Tanner, just a friend? Because if the answer is "I don't know" or "I'm not sure," then that's an answer in itself.*

That's too much to think about right now. Let's have this conversation later.

Okay, but it's not going to go away just because you're uncomfortable. You can delay it, but you can't act like the question doesn't exist.

Yeah, but later. When I can give it the attention it deserves.

I climbed into the old Chevy and pointed her toward Dutch Island. "You're a good car," I said as I gave her a pat on the dash. "I think you saved my life."

Fifteen minutes later, I pulled into the yard in front of the cabin.

The morning was clear and the day was bright as I switched off the engine, parked in front of the cabin, and got out. I heard work noises coming from the dock. Danny Ray and Parker were at it already. I really needed to lie down and catch a few hours' sleep, but I'd feel like a real slouch if I did that while the guys were working on my boat. So, I went down to the dock to lend a hand.

Parker and Danny Ray greeted me perfunctorily and then stuck their heads back into their work. It was obvious they were consumed by what they were doing and had little time for social pleasantries. I acted as an additional set of hands and did what I was told. Then, checking my watch, I saw it was time to leave again. The guys barely looked up when I announced I was departing again.

"Sure, Kennesaw," and, "S-s-see you," they said.

I retrieved a change of clothes and my other CZ 75 from the bunkroom. Yeah, I have two of them. When I find something I really like, I always buy a backup. Then I went up to the cabin to shower and head out on my next errand. After that, I was determined to come back and take a long nap before meeting Patricia and taking her to see Amber.

Shaved and showered, I phoned Marvin MacAllistair and told him what I needed. When I arrived at his lot, he was waiting for me.

"Oh, Ranger," he exclaimed when he saw the back windshield of the Chevy. "Who did that? An irate husband?"

"A couple of country boys I ran into, Mac. They thought they were being cute," I replied.

"Well, you're lucky it was only glass. When you called, I sent my man straight to the supply house. We can have you fixed up and on your way in nothing flat."

"You didn't have to send to Atlanta? That's amazing. I thought *everything* had to come from Atlanta," I said.

"I keep my sources close, Kennesaw," Marvin responded with a wink and a nod. "Only way to operate in this business. *Vintage* does not mean *slow*."

Marvin was true to his words. Forty minutes later, I drove out with a new back windshield *and* a fresh wax job.

I was just turning south on Waters Street when the phone rang.

"Kennesaw, oh honey. The ambulance just picked up Bob and took him to the hospital," Fran Martin said in a breathless rush.

"What happened, Fran? Where are they taking him?"

"I found him collapsed on the floor of his shop and called nine-one-one. The paramedics said they're taking him to Candler. I'm so upset I don't know what to do," she said in a voice wrought with emotion.

"Where are you, Fran; are you still at home? Is anyone with you?" I asked as I pulled into a parking lot and turned around.

"I'm at home. Linda, my next-door neighbor, is here with me."

"Well, wait right there. I don't want you driving. You go pack yourself an overnight bag and put together a toilet kit for Bob. I'm on the way and will be at your place as fast as I can. Okay, Fran?"

I heard her breathing on the other end as though she was having a hard time catching her breath.

"Okay, Kennesaw. But hurry."

"I'm on the way, Fran. Just hang in there."

I may have set a record for getting to Tybee. Fortunately traffic was light and I saw no cops—or more correctly—no cops saw me. When I arrived, Fran was doing better than I expected. She was composed and in control of herself. *She's a tough gal,* I reflected as we headed back to town.

At the hospital we found that Bob had already been moved from the emergency room to the ICU. A young doctor came out to speak with Fran.

"Mrs. Martin, Bob has suffered a partially collapsed lung, and since that's his *only* lung, it gives us a lot of concern," he reported.

"Is he—?" she began before the doctor cut her off.

"We have the lung reinflated, and he has some assistance breathing. But I want to run some tests and see what brought this on. But first we've got to get his oxygen count up and see an improvement in his overall condition. After that, I think Mr. Martin will begin to feel a lot better."

"Can I see him, Doctor?" Fran asked.

"Sure, but let's keep it short for the time being. We don't want to fatigue him," the doctor replied.

"Fran, I'll wait out here for you," I said.

"Don't leave me, Kennesaw," Fran said in a pleading voice.

"I won't, sweetheart. I'll be right out here." I gave her hand a squeeze.

"'Kay," she said, her eyes large with concern. "I won't be long."

Fran went in to see her husband. I went to the ICU waiting area and took a chair.

Bob will be mad as hell when he wakes up, I thought.

The last thing he would have wanted was to be carried to the hospital. I imagine, when he collapsed, he fully intended to die right there on the floor. It was only a fluke that Fran had found him when she did and called for an ambulance in time. I didn't know who I felt most sorry for—Bob, because he couldn't die the way he wanted to—or Fran, because he might.

Fran came out a few minutes later and sat next to me. She was quiet for a few minutes, and that is very uncharacteristic of Fran.

"He looks like hell, Kennesaw. I've never seen him look so bad," she said in a hollow voice.

I put an arm around her shoulder and pulled her over to me. She buried her face in my chest and began to weep silently—her chest and shoulders heaving with muffled sobs.

"It ain't fair, it ain't fair," she said over and over again. "It just *ain't* fair."

After a while, she sat up and wiped her face.

"Damn that man!" she said with vehemence. "You just shouldn't love somebody as much as I love him. I don't know what I would do if I lost him. I think I'd just lose my mind."

There was nothing I could say, and I don't think she wanted me to. I sat and held her hand and listened. After a while I went to the cafeteria and brought us back some lunch. While out, I called Amber to set up a time to see her and then called Patricia. After that, Fran and I sat and waited. Periodically a nurse would stick her head in and give us an update. The television set on the wall in the corner contributed its inanities as the afternoon dragged on. Then, looking at my watch, I realized I had to leave if I were to meet Patricia on time.

"Fran, I've got somewhere else I have to go. Will you be all right here for a while?"

"Kennesaw, you get on and do what you have to do. My daughter will be here soon, and you've done more than enough already," she said.

"All right," I replied as I stood. "Call me immediately if there's any change."

I leaned over, and we exchanged a kiss.

"I will, honey. And thank you for everything. You've been a lifesaver."

"All right, Fran. Bye."

"Bye, darling."

I would have to step on it if I was to meet Patricia at the bus station by four o'clock.

"You shouldn't have," Patricia remarked when we got out of the car and she saw the flowers in my hand.

"I didn't, Patricia."

She gave me a playful face as we mounted the steps. At the porch, I knocked on the door.

"Come in," spoke a faint voice.

We entered the darkened room. I took Patricia by the elbow and guided her to the corner where Amber lay on her bed.

"Amber," I said as I leaned over and gave her a kiss on the cheek. "This is my friend Patricia Latham. She's the police lady I told you about. She'd like to hear the story you told me.

"And these," I said as I placed the bouquet of flowers in her hands, "are for you."

Amber held the flowers on her breast and stared at them with wonder. With the tips of her fingers she gently touched the petals of each blossom, then brought the spray to her nose and drew in a breath.

"I never had no flowers—never in my life. *Nobody* has ever brought me flowers before, Kenny-saw. Never," she exhaled in a raspy voice. "This is just too . . ."

She began to weep, the tears puddling in the corner of her eyes and rolling down her cheeks.

Patricia lifted a hand to her throat and stifled a sob.

"Well, I thought you deserved them," I said. "And I think you make the flowers look pretty."

"*I* make the flowers look pretty—you funny, Kenny-saw."

"Can I put them in some water for you, Amber?" I asked.

"Not right now," she replied in a small voice. "I'd like to hold on to them for a little while."

"Whatever you like, Amber. Whatever makes you happy. Is your sister home this afternoon?" I asked.

"No, she workin' the second shift at the port—she and

her husband, Willamon. But you ain't got to worry 'bout them. *I* own this house, not them. I have who I want to here, and they ain't got no say about it."

"Okay, Amber. Do you feel up to speaking with Patricia?"

"Yes, I do. Sit down, pretty lady," she said to Patricia as she continued to finger the flowers. "Sit down and ask yo' questions. I tell you anything you want to know."

Patricia pulled a nearby chair close to the side of the bed and sat. She took a small voice recorder from her purse and, holding it up to view, asked, "Do you mind if I record our conversation, Amber? I'd hate to miss something important."

"That's fine with me. You record all you like. But I got a question for you first, Miss Patricia. Is Kenny-saw yo' man? 'Cause I know if I was you, he'd sho' be mine."

Amber looked up at me with a mischievous smile on her face. I grinned in reply.

Patricia stuttered, "Well, I—I mean that—well . . ."

Amber looked again at Patricia.

"I always thought it funny how white people blushes red when they embarrassed. That one thing don't happen if you black—leastways, nobody can tell it if you do."

Amber giggled at Patricia's discomfort, and then Patricia, realizing Amber was being playful, laughed aloud.

"I claim my right to remain silent about that, Amber," Patricia replied.

"Okay," said Amber. "But I might just ask you again sometime."

"I'll be ready the next time you do," Patricia said as she reached over and patted Amber's hand.

"I'm going to step out for a minute, but I'll be right back. Is that okay with you, Amber?" I announced.

"Yes," she said. "Me and Miss Patricia will be fine."

I went back out to my car and drove to a nearby Mexican restaurant. I doubted that Amber had eaten much and I thought some *caldo de pollo*—Mexican chicken soup—would give her strength and maybe lift her spirits some. I knew that the simple act of talking was very fatiguing for her. When I returned, she and Patricia were deep in conversation. I went to the kitchen, filled a bowl with the soup, opened the saltine crackers, and brought it to the bed on a tray. Amber protested at first that she wasn't hungry, but I insisted that she at least try a little bit. She managed to finish half the bowl.

"That was good, Kenny-saw," she said as she pushed the tray aside. "That was good, but I cain't eat no mo'."

"You did good, Amber. And I'm glad you enjoyed it," I responded as I picked up the tray to carry it to the kitchen.

"Let's keep on, Patricia," Amber said. "'Cause I don't know how much longer I can talk befo' I give out. When I get tired, it hit me all of a sudden-like, an' then, that's it."

"Okay, Amber," Patricia said, clicking on the recorder. "You were telling me about the houses where the girls are held. You want to pick it up from there?"

"Yeah, I remember. Well, as I was sayin' . . ."

The food seemed to have given Amber new energy. Sometimes she would become short of breath and have to rest for a few minutes before continuing, but she kept at it with surprising tenacity. I hovered in the background, staying as quiet as possible, and replenishing the drinks as they ran low. Patricia, periodically, would ask a question for clarification, but by and large, she let Amber talk. I stayed as long as I could but finally had to announce my departure.

"Ladies, I hate to leave you, but I have to go. Amber, is there anything you need before I take off?"

Amber reached a hand to the flowers that now sat in a vase on her nightstand and shook her head.

"No, Kenny-saw. But I hope you come back soon," she said.

I leaned over to give her a kiss.

"I will, Amber. Very soon."

"Okay," she replied.

"I won't be much longer, either," Patricia declared. "Call me later?"

"I'll call," I said.

"And be careful," Patricia rejoined. "I don't want to have to come bail you out of trouble again."

"I can't promise anything there, but I'll do my best," I replied with a smile. "Bye, ladies."

"Bye," they replied as I headed for the door.

It was after seven in the evening as I got in my car, and the night was fully dark. My destination was a truck stop in South Carolina, about an hour away on U.S. 17, between the small towns of Pocotaligo and Yemassee. I debated taking the Talmadge Bridge over the river and following 17 all the way but decided to go up to I-95. It was a little bit farther, but I would certainly save time on the interstate. First I checked my phone for messages. I had felt it buzzing in my pocket while inside with Amber. I hit the Speak button and ran the message.

"Mr. Tanner—Kennesaw—this is Joree Causey. Could you call me back as soon as you get this message? I'm real worried about Junior. I ain't seen him since you was here, and he won't answer his phone. I've asked around, and ain't nobody else seen him, neither. I'm scared somethin' mighta happened to him. Call me back when you can, please. Bye."

Junior is out ferrying around his partner in crime,

Leon. That's why you haven't seen him, I thought. *And if I see him first, well, he may not look so good afterward.*

I hit the button to call Joree but got her answering service. I left a message for her to return the call. Then, cranking the engine and listening for a few seconds to the satisfying rumble of those eight Detroit cylinders, I set out for South Carolina.

Thirty minutes later, the Savannah River was well to the rear. I was past the Hardeeville exit and almost to the turnoff for Pocotaligo, when the phone rang. I answered; it was Joree.

"Oh, I'm so glad I finally got ahold of you," she said. "I've been worried sick about Junior. I ain't seen him since the other day. He ain't called, and I can't find nobody that knows where he is," she blurted. "I think something mighta happened to him; something bad."

I was just forming an answer when Joree continued, "Well, Lordy, speak of the devil. Here comes a truck up into the yard. That might be him now."

I heard her open the door, and then she said, "Why yes, it's his truck all right. He's pullin' up to the door right now.

"Junior, is that you out there, honey? I been so . . ."

Blamm! A gunshot rang out.

I heard a thump as a body hit the floor and then, *Blamm!* Another shot fired.

"Joree! Joree! Are you there? Joree! Answer me!" I yelled into the phone.

A car door slammed and then, over the phone, came the sound of breaking glass, followed by a whoosh.

"Joree! Talk to me. Answer the phone, Joree!" I called.

Over the open phone connection came the crackle and roar of fire. Then a car door slammed again, followed by the loud, deep sound of a powerful engine as a vehicle drove away.

"Joree! Joree!"

The crackle grew louder, and then the connection went dead. There was an exit off the interstate about a mile ahead. I pounced on the accelerator, and as the Chevy leaped forward, I punched up the number for Sheriff Anson Zimmer.

CHAPTER 20

BY THE TIME I ARRIVED AT PANTHER Creek, the trailer was little more than a sodden, steaming mass of charcoal and twisted metal. The coroner stood with Sheriff Zimmer as three firemen carefully probed the wreckage.

"I think this is it," one of the firemen announced. "Yep, I'm sure. Here's a body."

Another fireman stepped closer and shone his light where the first man had indicated with his pole. In the harsh beam of the spotlight I saw what at first appeared to be a blackened log. A closer look showed the log to have the remnants of arms and legs pulled tightly into a fetal position. The coroner stepped in and took a look.

"It's a human body, all right. Let's get a bag over here and get it picked up, boys," he said in a sad voice.

The coroner turned to the sheriff and nodded in my direction.

"Anson, you say this man was on the phone with her when it happened? He was *sure* it was Joree Causey he was speaking with?"

"I can state that it *was* Joree on the phone," I announced.

The coroner looked over as though he was surprised I could answer for myself.

"Yes, Rayford, that's correct," Sheriff Zimmer replied. "Mr. Tanner called in that he was on the phone with her when he heard shots fired. He called me, and by the time Deputy Travis arrived on the scene, the walls were already falling in. You know how fast these old trailers burn. By the time the fire department got here all they had left to do was spray down the ashes."

"Since the possibility exists that a criminal act was committed, the body will have to be sent to the crime lab in Atlanta. It will be a couple of weeks before we have a full report back again."

"I understand, Rayford," the sheriff said.

"Well, in that case, I'll go. The body will be at the hospital morgue, and I'll see that it's transported to the lab tomorrow."

"All right, Rayford. I'll touch bases with you in the morning. Good night."

As the coroner departed with his grisly find, Sheriff Zimmer and I walked away from the others.

"You say that just before you heard the shots, Joree said it was Junior pulling up in the yard?" Zimmer asked.

"She didn't *say* it was Junior—she said it was Junior's *truck*. She called his name, but it wasn't as though she recognized him. It sounded to me as though she were asking if that was him, and she wasn't sure."

"Hmm," was his reply.

"Sheriff, there's something I don't understand. Maybe you can tell me why Junior Causey was the one who bailed Leon Wren out of jail and then was driving him around. It was Junior's truck that was seen in Savannah when Leon firebombed that auto shop. And it was probably Junior who fired those two shots at my friends."

Zimmer studied the toes of his boots. "I wish I knew myself. The judge set the bail pretty high. Then, Junior came in out of the blue and posted a cash bond. Since then, the only time those two have surfaced was the other night in Savannah and now possibly here."

"Why kill his mother?" I asked. "Is he as crazy as Wren?"

Zimmer looked up. "I don't think we'll know anything for certain until we grab them. But we've got a call out for both of them in Georgia and Carolina. I believe we'll have our hands on them pretty soon. Boys like these two always stay close to home. They just don't know where else to hide."

There was a lot I could have said, but for once, I kept it to myself. For some reason I did not feel compelled to contribute more than was apparent here. And if *I* saw Leon Wren *or* Junior Causey—well, let's just say we were *all* in for an exciting time.

"Sheriff, if you don't need me, I'd like to leave. This place gives me a bad taste in the mouth."

"No, you can go on, Mr. Tanner—Kennesaw. I have your statement, and if anything else comes up, I'll give you a call."

"Good night, Sheriff."

"Good night. Drive carefully."

It seemed an especially long drive from Panther Creek back to Dutch Island. I hadn't slept in more than a day and a half and I was groggy with fatigue. My head ached, and my eyes felt like scorched cinders rattling loosely in their orbs. The smell of burned human flesh hung in my nostrils like a bad cold, and I could not rid my mind's eye of that charred and blackened stump that had once been a living human being—Joree Causey—a woman I had known.

Was there no end to the misery associated with that

family? Tonya dead; Joree murdered; the son, Junior, possibly the killer of his own mother, and in all likelihood, complicit, in one fashion or the other, with the demise of his sister.

What the hell is it with these people? They don't just invite catastrophe, it's as though they continually invent it, nourish it, and grow it as a crop. As though tragedy is contained within the very marrow of their bones.

I wanted to assign blame—to blame *someone,* anyone— for the failings of these people, this family I had come to know and to recognize as fellow beings. I wanted to blame them for their predicament. And blame they certainly bore. But was that all there was to it? Were they the only guilty ones? And perhaps that was the source of my anger and frustration: the realization, as the saying goes, that "There, but for the grace of God, go I."

And then, from his masterwork *The Prophet,* the recollected words of Kahlil Gibran came to my mind, as they often do when I am confused and unsure and groping for answers to a particularly human predicament.

> *Oftentimes have I heard you speak of one*
> *who commits a wrong as though he were*
> *not one of you, but a stranger unto you and*
> *an intruder upon your world.*
> *But I say that even as the holy and the righteous*
> *   cannot rise*
> *beyond the highest which is in each one of you,*
> *So the wicked and the weak cannot fall lower than the*
> *   lowest*
> *which is in you also.*
> *And as a single leaf turns not yellow but*
> *with the silent knowledge of the whole tree,*
> *So the wrong-doer cannot do wrong*
> *without the hidden will of you all.*

Like a procession you walk together
towards your god-self.
You are the way and the wayfarers.
And when one of you falls down he falls
for those behind him, a caution against the stumbling
    stone.
Ay, and he falls for those ahead of him,
who though faster and surer of foot,
yet removed not the stumbling stone.

Had those of us *faster and surer of foot* done what we could to remove the stumbling stone from the path of the Causeys and others like them? Or had we, from our position of advantage and safety, stood complacently on the sidelines—a hidden sneer on our lips and the secret joy of condemnation in our hearts—as we watched their fatal descent?

Is that why we cheer and celebrate our heroes? Because we know that we too partake in part of their greatness? And is that also why we despise and detest the failures among us—for the same reason—because we know that we, too, contain that lesser part of the human ingredient?

I honestly don't know the answer to those questions. Though it sometimes seems that, as a people, we Americans greatly prefer condemnation and retribution way more than making the effort to help a weak and struggling soul. It was a question I would have to pose to both Cyriah and Truman Rainwater.

I was so drowsy that I found myself sitting at traffic lights after the light turned green—it taking a while for the information to flow from my eye, to my mind, and then to my foot. I turned on the vents and pointed them toward my face. Maybe the chilly night air would help keep me alert until I arrived home.

Finally, I pulled into the drive. I left the door of the

car open as I got out and unlocked the gate to the drive. I pulled through and, getting out again, swung the bar back into place. In the darkness, it was too much work to fasten the lock and chain again, and besides, there were only a few hours until daylight.

I parked near the side of the cabin and got out quietly. I hoped the door wasn't locked. I gave the knob a turn and, quietly as I could, went inside.

The room was comfortably warm, with a faint red glow coming from the woodstove. A dim light in the kitchen gave just enough illumination to keep me from stumbling and bumping into things. Parker was snoring softly and contentedly in his bunk. Quiet as I was, Danny Ray stirred and lifted his head. When he saw it was me he turned over and settled again.

Tybee was asleep on the foot of my bed. He awoke as I undressed and, after yawning, arched his back and stretched first one leg and then the other before lying down again in a curl and going back to sleep. I draped my clothes on the top bunk, but put my shoulder holster and pistol on the floor at a place just below the pillow. At last, I climbed into the bunk and stretched out.

My God, it feels good to be here. I'll bet I could sleep 'til noon. And tomorrow, when I am fresh again, and my mind is better able to function, I will determine where things stand, and what I should do next. Yeah, tomorrow . . .

Sleep claimed me as its own and took me far away.

CRASH! I STRUGGLED UPWARD FROM A deep and dark place.

What was that? What time is it? Is it morning already? Why is it so light?

My sleep-drugged and unfocused eyes came open to

find the interior of the cabin illuminated by a dancing, flickering light. I sat up and looked around. *What the hell is it?* Then I knew—*fire! Had the old woodstove burst? Who cares now—the only thing is to get out!* A glance told me the front of the cabin was burning furiously. I leaped out of the bunk, yelling as my feet hit the floor.

"Danny Ray! Parker! Get up! Get up! We're on fire! Get out of here! Get out!"

Both men rolled out of their beds and looked about wildly. At that very instant a fusillade of gunfire erupted outside, the shots tearing through the door and the front windows, bullets gouging long furrows in the floor and knocking chunks of wood out of the back walls.

We were under attack! Leon had found us here!

"Down! Hit the floor!" I yelled as my friends stood gaping in confusion. "On the floor!"

A blazing bottle hit the edge of the window and exploded in a shower of flame as gunshots continued to pound the cabin. I grabbed the shotgun from beneath my bunk and fired back out through the shattered window.

Bloooom! Bloooom!

The shotgun roared and echoed horrifically within the confined space of the cabin, but it did its job—the shots stopped for a second.

I glanced across at my friends, who were both huddled on the floor near their bunk. I knew what I had to do.

"Parker!" I called as I slid the shotgun across the floor. "When I hit the door, empty the shotgun out the window. Then both of you haul ass out the back door. Get to the boat and call for help!"

Parker looked at the gun that had come to rest near his hand. He shook his head.

"I can't," he said in a tortured voice. "I've never fired a gun in my life."

Danny Ray didn't hesitate. He scrabbled across the floor and tucked the butt of the shotgun in his shoulder.

"R-r-ready!" he said as he gave me a steady look.

I retrieved my pistol, grabbed two magazines from the shoulder holster, and looked back at Danny Ray.

"When I get to the door, open fire. When you've emptied the magazine, get out. There are five more rounds in the butt pouch on the gun—reload as you go. And there's more ammo in the boat.

"Parker," I said, "as soon as Danny opens fire, you scoot. Cut the lines on the boat and pull away. Everybody got it?"

Both men nodded and said, "Yes."

"Okay. Here goes."

I slithered across the floor as more rounds poured into the cabin and another Molotov cocktail hit the front of the building. The fire was growing by the second.

I came to a halt near the door, looked back at Danny Ray, and nodded. Danny Ray came to his knees and opened fire. Behind him, Parker scooped Tybee up in his arms and dashed for the back of the building.

Blooom! Blooom! Blooom!

I jumped to my feet and crashed through the door as the shotgun continued to give voice behind me.

Blooom! Blooom!

The only answer to an attack is a counterattack. I launched myself outside and hit the ground running. Directly in front of me, not twenty feet away, stood Leon Wren, lighting the fuse to another firebomb. Behind him, in the darkness, a gun barked repeatedly. Off to the right and farther still, another gun coughed and flashed, but it was Leon I zeroed in on.

My arms extended straight forward, my pistol leading, I charged at the huge man. Leon lifted the cocktail. I could see the bottle, the wick burning, in perfect clarity. Just as his arm swept forward to throw, I fired.

Pop! Pop!

The bottled exploded in Leon's hand, the flaming liquid cascading down his right arm, across his chest, and down his legs. For a fraction of a second, Leon stared down on his burning body, a look of confusion and horror on his face. Then he ran. And as he ran a high-pitched scream of tortured anguish, like the wail of a wounded animal, spewed forth from his drawn-back lips.

He flashed past me, a flaming human torch, leaving goblets of flame spattering across the ground as he ran.

"Eeee!" Leon shrieked.

Without stopping my movement, I hurled myself toward the nearest shooter, the one in the darkness, just off the edge of the clearing. In front of me, more shots punctured the night. In the glare of the burning cabin, I caught a shimmer of movement behind the muzzle flashes. I fired as I ran.

Pop-pop, pop-pop, pop-pop!

I saw a figure drop. And then I must have tripped over something, because I hit the ground hard—face-first and really hard. So hard in fact that sparks flew under my eyelids, and the breath was knocked from my body. Somehow I kept my grip on the pistol and got my lungs working again. I knew I had hit the man to my front; the absence of shots from that direction merely confirmed it.

From my spot on the ground I rapidly low-crawled to the edge of the brush and into the cover of darkness. I turned now to the other attacker.

A muzzle flash pulsed from a spot down the drive. I came to my knees and returned fire, emptying the pistol as I did. Then I changed magazines and leaped once again to my feet. I ran as hard as I could, firing at the last place I had seen the muzzle flashes.

Pop-pop, pop-pop, pop-pop, pop-pop!

As I raced in beneath the canopy of the trees I heard a car engine crank up. I jumped to the side of the trail in anticipation of being charged by the car. Halfway down the drive, a vehicle slashed out from the bushes and, slewing wildly, turned instead toward the gate.

Silhouetted by the glare of the headlights, I saw the figure of a man behind the wheel. His foot was too heavy on the accelerator, the wheels spinning and slinging sand rather than gaining full traction. It gave me a chance at him. I lifted the pistol to just above the level of the tail-lights and charged after the car, firing rapidly as I went.

Pop-pop, pop-pop, pop-pop, pop—

The pistol went empty. At my final shot the car made it to the pavement and, tires squalling, bounded out of sight. Within seconds, he was out of hearing.

I slipped the last magazine into the pistol and, standing alone in the drive, wondered what to do next.

It came to me at last. *Parker and Danny Ray—had they made it out of the cabin and safely to the boat?* With apprehension and a sense of dread beginning to fill my chest, I turned back down the drive to see about my friends.

The leaping, howling flames of the burning cabin filled the clearing with a vicious—a satanic—luminosity. Slowly, I walked to where the man I had shot lay sprawled in the weeds. He was prone, face turned away, with his hands and arms drawn beneath his body and his legs pulled up to his side.

I stepped closer to see his face. *I know this man,* I thought. *But from where?* My mind was foggy, and I had difficulty remembering. *Come on, Tanner, who is this? What was his name?*

And then, realization struck me. *Yes, that's it—Travis. Deputy Sheriff Travis. Damn, that's who it is, all right! Zimmer's man, Travis.*

I turned and stumbled toward the cabin. My feet were heavy and it was a great effort to walk. The pistol was too much to carry any longer, and I let it fall from my hand.

There's no one else left here anyway. I can't use it anymore.

I continued on and saw that my car was part of the burning cabin.

How about that. I had parked too close to the cabin, and now look what's happened. Ha-ha!—Owww! It hurts to laugh. I must have pulled a rib when I fell back there. Damn, that really hurts!

I put my hand to the side of my chest.

My hand is all wet and sticky. I must have fallen in the mud. Ha-ha! That's funny. Went to a shoot-out and fell in a mud hole. Wallowing around like an old pig. Ha-ha! Ha-ha-ha!

I looked down at my side.

Yep, all dark and gooey. Ha-ha! I should be more careful about where I step.

I looked up again and out past the burning cabin, into the darkness beyond.

Hey, there's Miss Rosalie *out there in the creek. The boys must have gotten her away after all. That's good, 'cause it looks like the dock's burned up, too.*

She really looks pretty out there in the firelight; so clean and white and glistening. But who's that out there on the decks? Oh yeah—Parker and Danny Ray.

What are y'all waving at? What's that you're calling? I can't hear you.

It's all right, boys. It's okay. My car is burned up along with the cabin. But Travis is dead, and last time I saw

Leon, he was on fire. The other one got away, but I don't think he'll be back. He ran off like a scalded dog. Ha-ha! Ha-ha-ha!

What am I doing sitting here on the ground? I don't remember sitting down. But it does feel good to sit and rest. I'm so tired—yeah, I'm really tired.

Hey, look! Here come Parker and Danny Ray. Oh, that's so funny! Do y'all know you're in your underwear? Ha-ha! Oh yeah, that's right, me, too. We're all out here in our skivvies. I hope nobody else sees us like this! They'll wonder what we've been doing. Ha-ha!

Parker, you have such skinny legs—and both of you are so very white—you look like mullet bellies. Ha-ha-ha.

Danny Ray, it's hard to catch my breath, and my side hurts. I think I'll just lie down awhile. Yeah, I'll just lie down on my other side. Oh, that feels good. It's so hot here by the fire and the cool sand feels really good against my face.

Man, am I sleepy. I think I'll just close my eyes for a minute.

No, no, don't bother me, Danny Ray. Parker, you leave me alone, too. I don't want to get up. Just let me rest here for a little bit—for just a minute. I won't be here long, and then I'll . . .

CHAPTER 21

THIS IS SO GOOD—FLOATING OUT here on a gentle sea. The surface of the water barely moving, lifting and falling with a long, slow pulse—just enough to keep you from going completely to sleep and sliding under. I'll keep my eyes closed and float as quietly as I can. The water is so buoyant and silky feeling, so perfect—this must be off the beach at Isla Mujeres. Nowhere else in the world is the water this perfect or the sun so warm and gentle.

What's that? Somebody on the beach calling my name? I'll just float here and maybe they'll go away. What can be so urgent that I need to go in now? No, I'll ignore them. They can come back later.

"Kennesaw." Someone shook me by the arm. "Time for lunch and your noon meds. Wake up, you scoundrel!"

I opened my eyes. Nope, I wasn't at Isla, I was still

here in the hospital. I looked to the side and there stood Madilyn, the day nurse.

"Maddy, you just interrupted a trip to one of my favorite places. I was floating on a pellucid sea, a lovely island girl by my side, her bathing suit nothing more than two strands of dental floss, and then you come in here, howling orders like a drill sergeant," I scolded.

"That's what you get for not taking me with you," she fired back as she swung the lunch tray across the bed. She then handed me a tiny cup with some pills and pointed to the drink on the tray.

I swallowed the pills at one gulp and washed them down with a shot of juice.

"I sure hope you've brought Jell-O today, Maddy," I said as I sat up and reached for the cover to a dish. "You know I'm just wild about Jell-O. In fact, the only reason I even agreed to stay in this place is that I was promised I could have all the Jell-O I wanted to eat, and no questions asked. And now I come to find it seldom served more than three times a day. Madilyn, my love, I have been sadly misled."

Madilyn ignored me and reached across the bed to check the IV, her monumental bosom hovering over my face and blocking out the light.

"Maddy! Careful there! What are you trying to do, suffocate me? You know my breathing is impaired! My God, woman, point those things in another direction. You know I can't take that kind of excitement. What with me being in such a delicate condition and all, you're liable to send me back to the ICU."

Madilyn straightened again and gave me a stern look.

"I think the doctor should have sent you home yesterday, is what I think. You have the energy to be such a smart-ass, you have the energy to go home," she said in an admonishing tone of voice, but with a smile at the corner of her mouth.

"If I clean my plate, will you be happy with me again?" I asked with a lowered brow and a fake pout of contrition.

"Who said I was happy with you to begin with?" she fired back as she turned for the door.

"Madilyn, you sure know how to torture a man."

"Ha!" she barked as she left the room. Then, over her shoulder she said, "Bob Martin went home this morning. He's doing okay."

I smiled as I listened to her footsteps retreating down the hall. Madilyn had been an angel. I could not have had a more efficient nurse and a better companion for the last several days. And that was great news about Bob.

I lifted the cover of a plate. Hooray! *Meatloaf, mashed potatoes, and turnip greens.* I dove in with a real appetite. And I hadn't been kidding about the Jell-O—I really do enjoy it, it's right up there with Spam.

I was just pushing away the tray when there was a knock on the door and Patricia leaned in.

"Come in," I called and waved her to the chair. "You're too late for lunch, but maybe I can call room service and have them send up some ice water."

"How are you feeling today, Kennesaw? Did you rest well last night?" she asked as she lowered herself to the chair.

"Seems the infection's finally subsided. Second night in a row with no night sweats. Word is—unofficial, of course, until the doc swings by—that I may just get out of here today."

"Where will you stay when they let you out?" Patricia asked. "You know you're welcome at my place. You can have the guest room, and your buddies can come and go as they please."

"I know, and thanks for the offer, Patricia. But Parker

and Danny Ray have *Miss Rosalie* put back together again. And I can rest there better than any other place I know."

"Well, the offer is always there if you change your mind."

I reached over and touched her hand. "Thanks. Now, tell me about what's going on. What's the latest news out in the world of crime?"

Patricia was a fount of information today. Leon Wren was in the burn center in Atlanta, and it looked like he was going to live. When he ran past me he had plunged off the bank and into the creek. Parker and Danny Ray had hauled him out of the water and onto *Miss Rosalie*, and he had gone to the hospital in the ambulance with me.

Oh yeah—me. I had taken a round in the right side that had broken a couple of ribs going in and punched a hole in the lower part of my lung. Looking back on it, I realize that's what that fall I took was all about.

Deputy Travis was indeed dead. I had also hit the driver of the fleeing car. It was found by the responding cops less than two blocks away—crashed into a tree, with the driver—Sheriff Anson Zimmer—unconscious at the wheel with a gunshot wound, also in the right lung. In the trunk of the car they had found Junior Causey—alive and kicking—full of information and just itching to tell it all.

At some point, about the time I first showed up at Joree's, it seems, Junior had decided he wanted out—and that's when he became a liability to Zimmer. They had held him locked away in a safe house while Travis and Leon had been the ones who had firebombed the auto shop and then killed Joree. Junior was being set up to take the fall.

Seems the plan was to kill me, pop Junior in the head, and make it look like we had both died in the shoot-out. Of course I would have been burned to a crisp. The fact that Parker and Danny Ray had been at the cabin appears to have been a surprise.

Zimmer was singing also. As soon as he regained consciousness and realized the predicament he was in, he began to rat out every dirty cop and politician that he had on the books. According to Junior, it was Zimmer who had killed Big Smoke Wren and taken over the prostitution ring—or to put it exactly—he had induced Leon to do the actual killing.

The GBI was doing double duty, rolling up the net, hitting the safe houses where the girls were held, and questioning cops and county commissioners. One local politician had been apprehended trying to flee the country. And as soon as the word got out, several others had voluntarily come in to try and cut their own deals. Since the whole crime syndicate went across state lines the FBI had waded in, and they, too, were having a field day.

I had a standing invitation from the state and the federal district attorneys for interviews as soon as I was up to it. I imagined I would also be having a word or two with the grand jury.

"Patricia, you think they'll eventually get to the bottom of it all?" I asked.

"Yes, I think so. A few may slip by, but most of the players are going down," she answered.

"How high do you think it goes?"

Patricia hesitated a second. "There is some word—very quiet, of course—that it may go all the way to the State House in Atlanta. It appears there were several other similar rings operating around the state, with a lot of political types taking a cut of the action. From all appearances, Kennesaw, you've unleashed a tidal wave of legal action."

I reached to the pendant that hung from my neck and held it with the tips of my fingers. As soon as I was out of the emergency room, a kind nurse named Tryla, a Geechee girl from Pin Point, had recognized it for what it was and brought it to me. "I know you'll want this," she had said.

"I did little more than act as unintentional bait, Patricia. It was Joree, and Amber, and ultimately Tonya, who made it all happen. As soon as I started asking questions, Zimmer knew his house of cards was going to crash. If it wasn't me, it would have been someone else."

Patricia was looking at me with a solemn expression on her face.

"There's something else, Kennesaw. Something else I have to tell you."

"And what's that, Patricia? Why the long face?"

"I spoke with Naomi a couple of hours ago. Amber passed away during the night."

I felt something flutter in my chest and then depart—to be replaced by a sense of cold emptiness. I leaned back against the pillows and held Patricia's look.

That poor girl. That poor sweet girl. She was gone and out of harm's way. She was beyond suffering now, and for that, I was thankful.

"Did she give you the answer to the question I had you ask?"

Patricia nodded. "Yes. It turned out to be pretty close to what you thought. Tonya came to Amber's place before she jumped. She said if it was this way, someone would eventually find her body and ask questions. But if Leon killed her—as he had threatened to do—they would drop her body down an abandoned well at some old farmhouse, and no one would ever know what had happened to her.

"Amber waited thirty minutes after Tonya left the house before she made the nine-one-one call. A few minutes later, she had a neighborhood boy, who sometimes ran errands for her, make the second call from the same phone. Next day, she pitched the phone in the trash."

I took a few deep breaths and felt a stabbing pain in

my side. There was also a lump in my throat, and my eyes blurred.

What a hopeless predicament for that poor girl—for Tonya. No one to turn to. No one to help. The very institutions that were supposed to protect and defend her were the very ones that preyed upon her and threatened her existence. How wretchedly tragic. How terribly sad.

"Did Naomi give you any information about the funeral arrangements?" I asked when I could speak again.

"It's the day after tomorrow. A graveside service at Bonaventure. While she was still lucid, Amber asked Truman Rainwater to conduct the service. According to Naomi, Amber and Rainwater had become very close."

"Good," I remarked. "Will you be there, too?" I asked.

"Yes," Patricia replied. "I'll be there."

We were quiet for a minute or two. Then another thought occurred.

"How about Zimmer? What's next with him?" I asked.

"Turns out the bullet they took out of you was fired from the gun they found in his car," she answered.

"Lucky shot," I replied with a sniff.

"Yeah, well, that's one pretty good charge in itself—it ties him to the assault at the cabin—that, and the bullets from your gun they dug out of him," she responded.

"An Olympian feat, a Homeric display of shooting, if I do say so myself."

"Whatever," Patricia replied in dismissal. "I'm told his arraignment is next week. The state judge wants to bring charges first and not wait on the feds."

"I'd like to be there when it happens, Patricia. Think that can be arranged?"

"I don't see why not. And I'd like to be there to see it myself," she said.

"Well then, Detective. Can we call it a date?"

"It's a date," she replied.

"You'll have to drive, though," I said. "My car was destroyed in an accident."

"I was wondering what your insurance company has to say about that," she quipped.

"They are less than pleased, my agent tells me. And intend to pursue, with great vigor, the other parties involved."

"They better get in line," Patricia commented with a laugh.

"Oh no," I replied. "Those boys are in for some real trouble now. They don't know what they're in for; you don't fool around with the insurance industry."

"Whatever, Tanner. Whatever."

CHAPTER 22

I STOOD IN THE PARKING LOT AT THE back of the courthouse and waited. *It had been a good funeral,* I reflected. There weren't many of us there: Naomi and her husband, Willamon; a couple of their neighbors; and even a few of the big-hat ladies, which I'm sure would have pissed Amber off to no end. Parker and Danny Ray were there also, each looking good in their new suits. And of course, Patricia and I.

We all stood at the grave, looking upon the casket as Brother Truman spoke of love and redemption, of the gift of life, and the joy we find, even among the sorrow and suffering we all experience.

And then he sang, just he, in a fine, clear voice, and that was the real funeral, the one that touched all of us who had gathered in that beautiful cemetery to mourn the passing of the girl we knew as Amber.

It was an old mountain song from Appalachia, one

that immediately took me back to my childhood. Truman looked across our faces, from one to another, and then, lifting his eyes heavenward, he began to sing in a haunting tenor, his voice rising and falling in a quavering and mournful cadence.

> Troubles and trials often betray those
> causing the weary body to stray.
> But we shall walk beside the still water
> with the good shepherd leading the way.
>
> Going up home to live in green pastures
> where we shall live and die never more.
> Even the Lord will be in that number
> when we have reached that heavenly shore.
>
> Those who have strayed were sought by the master
> He who once gave his life for the sheep.
> Out on the mountain still He is searching
> bringing them in forever to keep . . .
>
> We will not heed the voice of the stranger
> for he would lead us home to despair.
> Following home with Jesus our savior
> we shall all reach that country so fair . . .

The song finished, Truman said a final prayer, and then the casket was lowered into the patiently waiting earth. Each person filed silently by and dropped a handful of soil into the open grave, the clods falling with a hollow ringing sound onto the top of the metal casket. And it was done.

Out on the mountain still He is searching; I heard those words again in my mind. At least some of the lost ones had been found again. Truman had his granddaughter back.

Other girls, too, had been recovered. But how many had disappeared for good, never to be seen aboveground again? Perhaps, God alone knows the answer to that.

The door to the back of the courthouse opened and a deputy stepped outside. He motioned to a pair of federal marshals, who stepped to a prisoner van and opened the side door.

"They're coming out now," announced Patricia, who stood at my side.

We had taken a vantage point at the corner of the parking lot, where we could watch and stay out of the way. I had not the least interest in the proceedings that had taken place inside. That was mere formality. This was what I had come for—to see Anson Zimmer, dressed in a prisoner jumpsuit and led away in disgrace. I wanted to see the fallen man. I wanted to see his degradation. I wanted to see the former sheriff as he was taken away, to be held in close confinement until the time of his trial.

A marshal emerged from the door and gave the area a quick glance. Then, from the darkened doorway, Zimmer appeared. His wrists were held together in front of his midsection, cuffed to a chain around his waist. He shuffled slowly and awkwardly, his head bowed with the effort of walking with shackled ankles.

As he stepped on to the sidewalk, he paused and, lifting his head, looked around the parking lot. His face turned in my direction and our eyes met. We held a gaze for a second, and then he looked away, as though he could not recognize me. The marshals on each elbow gave him a slight push, and he resumed his shuffle in the direction of the waiting van.

They swung off the sidewalk and out into the lot to walk around the back of the van to the other side, where the open door beckoned. At that instant came the harsh sound of squealing tires and the deep growl of a powerful engine. I looked over my shoulder just as a red pickup truck smashed through the steel gate of the lot and came roaring in with a crash. The truck sat high on massive tires, and it was gathering speed as it flashed across the lot. *It was Junior Causey at the wheel!*

I glanced back at Zimmer and his escorts. The marshals at his side saw the truck hurtling down upon them and dove away, leaving Zimmer transfixed where he stood. Several guns opened fire on the truck, but its momentum now could not be stopped. The irresistible force was about to meet the immovable object.

Zimmer ducked his head into his chest as though that would protect him. Men yelled incoherently while a half dozen pistols added to the cacophony. The front bumper of the truck plowed into Zimmer with a meaty smack, slamming him into the rear of the van and pinning him there. There was a loud crash of buckled and tortured metal and a small, short scream. And then everything went quiet and still, all except the hiss of a broken radiator.

Patricia and I ran forward as two marshals sprinted to the side of the truck, one covering with his pistol as the other jerked the door open. I looked inside. Junior Causey's body lay slumped across the steering wheel. A third marshal ran forward. While two of them provided cover, the other officer pulled Junior from the truck and lay him on the ground. A quick glance was all I needed to tell me that Junior Causey had been shot dead.

I moved to the front of the truck. Zimmer's shoulders and head were visible above the high bumper of the truck. As I approached, he turned his head in my direction and looked at me with vacant and uncomprehending eyes. His lips moved but no sound emerged.

And then a voice from somewhere nearby called out,

"Oh my God! He's been cut in two! His legs are lying on the ground!"

I saw recognition come into Zimmer's eyes. He bent his head slightly forward in a futile attempt to see what had happened to his lower body. Then, he turned his face toward me again, his mouth wide with terror at the realization of his fate. I smiled at him. I watched and smiled as the light in his eyes dimmed and finally went out. When I was sure that Anson Zimmer was dead, I turned and walked away. Satisfied that for once, justice had been done.

CHAPTER 23

IT IS A TOTAL OF TWO THOUSAND eighty-six paces from the foot of the Talmadge Bridge to its apex at midriver. I stood, my lower body braced against the railing, and looked eastward. Behind, I could hear the industrial sounds of the ports, but they were muffled and subdued, as if they had no wish to intrude their noise of activity upon the sleeping city.

To my right front the old city of Savannah lay quietly at rest, its night-lights sparkling in the chill of midnight. On the other side of the river rose those two monstrous towers that by day dominated the riverfront view. At night, their lights threw a belt of shimmering color reflecting and sparkling across the broad waist of the river.

Farther than the eye could penetrate through the intense darkness spread the great marsh, silently brooding in its green vastness and patiently counting the tides that rose and fell in their unfailing turn.

At the mouth of the Savannah, like guardian sentinels flanking their charge, lay the barrier islands of Tybee and Daufuskie. And beyond those two, the boundless immensity of the Atlantic Ocean.

The breeze that blew here, high above the river, was cold and insistent. It washed my exposed skin and sought to steal beneath my clothing. My breath blew in short clouds of vapor, and my lips and nose were cold.

I looked at my watch, its old-fashioned luminescent dial giving the hour and the minute.

It was just about this time of night that Tonya Causey had climbed over the railing, I thought. I put my hand to the cold metal pipe and measured its height from the ground. *Tonya was only five feet four. She would have had to jump up to catch the top of the rail with her waist and then roll over the top. Did she then sit there and take a last look at the world before dropping over the edge? Or had she slipped and tumbled wildly as she went over? Her last glimpses of life a terrifying blur of revolving black and gray, until her fall was suddenly and irredeemably broken by the hard surface of the river—harder even than concrete when hit from this height.*

It was a question I could not answer, and a vision I wished to shake. But I had not come here for answers. I had come, rather, to remember. To remember a girl I had not known and a mother and brother but briefly. To remember a young woman on her deathbed and an old woman in her wisdom. For Bob and Fran. For Parker, Danny Ray, Dolores, and Tyrone. For Patricia. I had come here to remember us all.

My arm lifted and my hand stretched forth. I held the flowers extended and poised over the abyss—then, slowly, one by one, my fingers opened and the bouquet fell away. I put both hands to the railing and leaned over to watch. The whiteness of the roses slowly fading, first to gray, and then to nothing, as they fell to the cold waters below—the river receiving my offering in secrecy and with grace.

I stood several moments longer, held rapt in silent contemplation. Then, turning my face toward the land below, I began the long descent.

M14G0610